RAVEN'S WING

OTHER FICTION BY JOYCE CAROL OATES

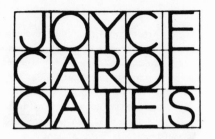

JOYCE CAROL OATES

RAVEN'S WING

A William Abrahams Book

E. P. DUTTON | NEW YORK

The stories in this volume were originally published, in slightly different forms, in the following magazines: "Raven's Wing" appeared in *Esquire* and was reprinted in *The Best American Short Stories 1985;* "The Seasons" appeared in *Ploughshares* and was reprinted in *Prize Stories 1985: The O. Henry Awards;* "Nairobi" appeared in *The Paris Review* and was reprinted in *The Best American Short Stories 1984;* "Golden Gloves" appeared in *The Washington Post Sunday Magazine;* "Harrow Street at Linden" appeared in *The Massachusetts Review;* "Happy" appeared in *Vanity Fair;* "Ancient Airs, Voices" appeared in *The Antioch Review;* "Double Solitaire" appeared in *Michigan Quarterly Review;* "Manslaughter" appeared in *The Malahat Review;* "Little Wife" appeared in *The Kenyon Review;* "The Jesuit" appeared in *The Missouri Review;* "The Mother" appeared in *Shenandoah;* "Testimony" appeared in *The Southern Review;* "Nuclear Holocaust" and "Little Blood-Button" appeared in *New Directions Fiftieth Anniversary Anthology;* "Surf City" appeared in *Partisan Review;* "Baby" appeared in *The Ontario Review.*

Published in the United States by
E. P. Dutton, a division of New American Library,
2 Park Avenue, New York, N.Y. 10016.

Library of Congress Cataloging-in-Publication Data
Oates, Joyce Carol, 1938–
Raven's wing.
"A William Abrahams book."
I. Title.
PS3565.A8R3 1986 813'.54 86-6256
ISBN: 0-525-24446-8

Published simultaneously in Canada
by Fitzhenry & Whiteside Limited, Toronto

COBE

Designed by Nancy Etheredge

10 9 8 7 6 5 4 3 2 1

First Edition

for Renée and Ted Weiss

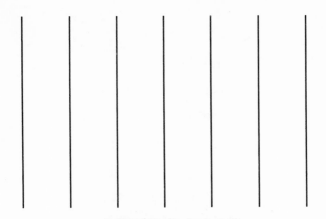

CONTENTS

| | | | |

RAVEN'S WING

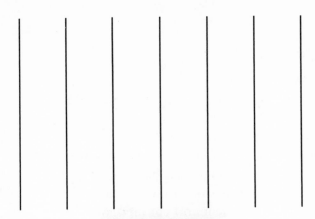

RAVEN'S WING

Billy was at the Meadowlands track one Saturday when the accident happened to Raven's Wing—a three-year-old silky black colt who was the favorite in the first race, and one of the crowd favorites generally this season. (Though Billy hadn't placed his bet on Raven's Wing. Betting on the 1.06 favorite held no excitement and, in any case, things were going too well for Raven's Wing, his owner's luck would be running out soon.) Telling his wife about the accident the next morning Billy was surprised at how important it came to seem, how intense his voice sounded, as if he were high, or on edge, which he was not; it was just the *telling* that worked him up, and the way Linda looked at him.

"So there he was in the backstretch, looping around one, two, three, four horses to take the lead—he's a hard driver, Raven's Wing, doesn't let himself off easy—a little skittish at the starting gate, but then he got serious—in fact he was maybe running a little faster than he needed to run, once he got out front—then something happened, it looked like he stumbled, his hindquarters went down just a little—but he was going so fast, maybe forty miles an hour, the momentum kept him going—Jesus, it must have been three hundred feet!—the poor bastard, on three legs. Then the jockey jumped off, the other horses ran by, Raven's Wing was just sort of standing there by the rail, his head bobbing up and down. What had happened was he'd broken his left rear leg—came down too hard on it, maybe, or the hoof sunk in the dirt wrong. Just like that," Billy said. He snapped his fingers. "One minute we're looking at a two-million-dollar colt, the next minute—nothing."

"Wait. What do you mean, nothing?" Linda said.

"They put them down if they aren't going to race any more."

" 'Put them down'—you mean they kill them?"

"Sure. Most of the time."

"How do they kill them? Do they shoot them?"

"I doubt it, probably some kind of needle, you know, injection, poison in their bloodstream."

Linda was leaning toward him, her forehead creased. "Okay, then what happened?" she said.

"Well, an ambulance came out to the track and picked him up, there was an announcement about him breaking his leg, everybody in the stands was real quiet when they heard. Not because there was a lot of money on him either but because, you know, here's this first-class colt, a real beauty, a two-million-dollar horse, finished. Just like that."

Linda's eyelids were twitching, her mouth, she might have been going to cry, or maybe, suddenly, laugh, you couldn't predict these days; near as Billy figured she hadn't washed her hair in more than a week and it looked like hell, she hadn't washed herself in all that time either, wore the same plaid shirt and jeans day after day, not that he'd lower himself to bring the subject up. She was staring at him, squinting. Finally she said, "How much did you lose?—you can tell me," in a breathy little voice.

"How much did *I* lose?" Billy asked. He was surprised as hell: they'd covered all this ground, hadn't they, there were certain private matters in his life, things that were none of her business, he'd explained it—her brother had explained it too—things she didn't need to know. And good reasons for her not to know. "How much did *I* lose—?"

He pushed her aside, lightly, just with the tips of his fingers, and went to the refrigerator to get a beer. It was only ten in the morning but he was thirsty and his head and back teeth ached. "Who says I lost? We were out there for five races. In fact I did pretty well, we all did, what the fuck do you know about it," Billy said. He opened the beer, took his time drinking. He knew that the longer he took the calmer he'd get and it was one of those mornings—Sunday, bells ringing, everybody's schedule off—when he didn't want to get angry. But his hand was trembling when he drew a wad of bills out of his inside coat pocket and let it fall onto the kitchen counter. "Three hundred, go ahead and count it, sweetheart," he said, "you think you're so smart."

Linda stood with her knees slightly apart, her big belly straining at the flannel shirt she wore, her mouth still twitching. Even with her skin grainy and sallow, and pimples across her forehead, she looked good, she was a good-looking girl; hell, thought Billy, it was a shame, a bad deal. She said, so soft he almost couldn't hear, "I don't think I'm so smart."

"Yeah? What?"

"I don't think I'm anything."

She was looking at the money but for some reason, maybe she was afraid, she didn't touch it. Actually Billy had won almost $1,000 but that was his business.

Linda was eight years younger than Billy, just twenty-four though she looked younger, blond, high-strung, skinny except for her belly (she was five, six months pregnant, Billy couldn't remember), with hollowed-out eyes, that sullen mouth. They had been married almost a year and Billy thought privately it was probably a mistake though in fact he loved her, he *liked* her, if only she didn't do so many things to spite him. If she wasn't letting herself go, letting herself get sick, strung-out, weird, just to spite him.

He'd met her through her older brother, a friend of Billy's, more or less, from high school, a guy he'd done business with and could trust. But they had had a misunderstanding the year before and no longer worked together.

Once, in bed, Linda said, "If the man had to have

it, boy, then things would be different. Things would be a lot different."

"What? A baby? How do you mean?" Billy asked. He'd been halfway asleep, he wanted to humor her, he didn't want a fight at two in the morning. "Are we talking about a baby?"

"They *wouldn't* have it, that's all."

"What?"

"The baby. Any baby."

"Jesus—that's crazy."

"Yeah? Who? Would you?" Linda said angrily. "What about your own?"

Billy had two children, both boys, from his first marriage; but as things worked out he never saw them and rarely thought about them—his wife had remarried, moved to Tampa. At one time Billy used to say that he and his ex-wife got along all right, they weren't out to slit each other's throat like some people he knew, but in fact when Billy's salary at G-M Radiator had been garnisheed a few years ago he wasn't very happy; he'd gone through a bad time. So he'd quit the job, a good-paying job too, and later, when he tried to get hired back, they were already laying off men, it was rotten luck, his luck had run against him for a long time. One of the things that drove him wild was the fact that his wife, that is his ex-wife, was said to be pregnant again, and he'd maybe be helping to support another man's kid; when he thought of it he wanted to kill somebody, anybody, but then she got married after all and it worked out and now he didn't have to see her or even think of her very much: that was the advantage of distance. But now he said, "Sure," trying to keep it all light, "what the hell, sure, it beats the Army."

"*You'd* have a baby?" Linda said. Now she was sitting up, leaning over him, her hair in her face, her eyes showing a rim of white above the iris. "Oh, don't hand me that. Oh, please."

"Sure. If you wanted me to."

"I'm asking about *you*—would *you* want to?"

They had been out drinking much of the evening and Linda was groggy but skittish, on edge, her face pale and giving off a queer damp heat. The way she was grinning, Billy didn't want to pursue the subject.

"How about *you,* I said," she said, jabbing him with her elbow, "I'm talking about *you*."

"I don't know what the hell we are talking about."

"You do know."

"What?—I don't."

"You do. You do. Don't hand me such crap."

When he and Linda first started going together they'd made love all the time, like crazy, it was such a relief (so Billy told himself) to be out from under that other bitch; but now, married only a year, with Linda dragging around the apartment sick and angry and sometimes talking to herself, pretending she didn't know Billy could hear, now everything had changed, he couldn't predict whether she'd be up or down, high or low, very low, hitting bottom, scaring him with her talk about killing herself (her crazy mother had tried *that* a few times, it probably ran in the family) or getting an abortion (but wasn't it too late, her stomach that size, for an abortion?), he never knew when he opened the door what he'd be walking into. She didn't change her clothes, including her underwear, for a week at a time, she didn't wash her hair, she'd had a tight permanent that sprang out around her head but turned flat, matted, blowsy if it wasn't shampooed, he knew she was ruining her looks to spite him but she claimed (shouting, crying, punching her own thighs with her fists) that she just *forgot* about things like that, she had more important things to think about. (One day Billy caught sight of this great-looking girl out on the street, coat with a fox fur collar like the one he'd bought for Linda, high-heeled boots like Linda's, blond hair, wild springy curls like a model's, frizzed, airy, her head high and her walk fast, almost like strutting—she knew she was being watched, and not just by Billy—and then she turned and it *was* Linda, his own wife, she'd washed her hair and fixed herself up, red lipstick, even eye makeup—he'd just stood there staring, it took him by such surprise. But then the next week she was back to lying around the apartment feeling sorry for herself, sullen and heavy-hearted, sick to her stomach even if she hadn't eaten anything.)

The worst of the deal was, he and her brother had had their misunderstanding and didn't do business any longer. When Billy got drunk he had the vague idea that he was getting stuck again with another guy's baby.

The racing news was, Raven's Wing hadn't been killed after all. It *was* news, people were talking about it, Billy read about it in the newspaper, an operation on the colt's leg estimated to cost in the six-figure range, a famous veterinary surgeon the owner was flying in from Dallas, and there was a photograph (it somehow frightened Billy, that

| | | | |

photograph) of Raven's Wing lying on his side, anesthetized, strapped down, being operated on like a human being. The *size* of a horse—that always impressed Billy.

Other owners had their opinions, was it worth it or not, other trainers, veterinarians, but Raven's Wing's owner wanted to save his life, the colt wasn't just any horse (the owner said), he was the most beautiful horse they'd ever reared on their farm. He was insured for $2,200,000 and the insurance company had granted permission for the horse to be destroyed but still the owner wanted to save his life. "They wouldn't do that for a human being," Linda said when Billy told her.

"Well," Billy said, irritated at her response, "this isn't a human being, it's a first-class horse."

"Jesus, a *horse* operated on," Linda said, laughing, "and he isn't even going to run again, you said? How much is all this going to cost?"

"People like that, they don't care about money. They have it, they spend it on what matters," Billy said. "It's a frame of reference you don't know shit about."

"Then what?"

"What?"

"After the operation?"

"After the operation, if it works, then he's turned out to stud," Billy said. "You know what that is, huh?" he said, poking her in the breast.

"Just a minute. The horse is worth that much?"

"A first-class horse is worth a lot, I told you. Sometimes three, four million—these people take things *seriously.*"

"Millions of dollars for an animal?" Linda said

slowly. She sounded dazed, disoriented, as if the fact were only now sinking in; but what *was* the fact, what did it mean? "I think that's *sick*."

"I told you, Linda, it's a frame of reference you don't know shit about."

"That's right, I don't."

She was making such an ugly face at him, drawing her lips back from her teeth, Billy lost control and shoved her against the edge of the kitchen table, and she slapped him, hard, on the side of the nose, and it was all Billy could do to stop right there, just *stop*, not give it back to the bitch like she deserved. He knew, once he got started with this one, it might be the end. She might not be able to pick herself up from the floor when he was done.

Billy asked around, and there was this contact of his named Kellerman, and Kellerman was an old friend of Raven's Wing's trainer, and he fixed it up so that he and Billy could drive out to the owner's farm in Pennsylvania, so that Billy could see the horse; Billy just wanted to *see* the horse, it was always at the back of his mind these days.

The weather was cold, the sky a hard icy blue, the kind of day that made Billy feel shaky, things were so bright, so vivid, you could see something weird and beautiful anywhere you looked. His head ached, he was so edgy, his damn back teeth, he chewed on Bufferin, he and Kellerman drank beer out of cans, tossed the cans away on the road. Kellerman said horse people like these were the real thing, the real fucking thing, look at this layout, and not even counting Raven's Wing they had a stable worth millions, a Preakness winner, a second-place

| | 9 | |

Kentucky Derby winner, but was the money even in horses?—hell no, it was in some investments or something. That was how rich people worked.

In the stable, at Raven's Wing's stall, Billy hung over the partition and looked at him for a long time, just looked. Kellerman and the trainer were talking but Billy just looked.

The size of the horse, that was one of the things, and the head, the big rounded eyes, ears pricked forward, tail switching, here was Raven's Wing looking at last at him, did he maybe recognize Billy—no, did he maybe sense who Billy was?—extending a hand to him, whispering his name. Hey, Raven's Wing. Hey.

The size, and the silky sheen of the coat, the jet-black coat, that skittish air, head bobbing, teeth bared, Billy could feel his warm breath, Billy sucked in the strong *smell*—horse manure, horse piss, sweat, hay, mash, and what was he drinking?—apple juice, the trainer said. *Apple juice,* Christ! Gallons and gallons of it. Did he have his appetite back, Billy asked, but it was obvious the colt did, he was eating steadily, chomping hay, eyeing Billy as if Billy was—was what?—just the man he wanted to see. The man who'd driven a hundred miles to see him.

Both his rear legs were in casts, the veterinarian had taken a bone graft from the good leg, and his weight was down—1,130 pounds to 880—his ribs showing through the silky coat, but Jesus did he look good, Jesus this was the real thing wasn't it?—Billy's heart fast as if he'd been popping pills, he wished to hell Linda was here, yeah, the bitch should see *this,* it'd shut her up for a while.

Raven's Wing was getting his temper back, the

trainer said, which was a good thing, it showed he was mending, but he still wasn't 99 percent in the clear, maybe they didn't know how easy it was for horses to get sick—colic, pneumonia, all kinds of viruses, infections—even the good leg went bad for a while, paralyzed, they had to have two operations, a six-hour and a four-hour, the owner had to sign a release they'd put him down right on the operating table if things looked too bad. But he pulled through, his muscle tone was improving every day, there he was, fiery little bastard—watch out or he'll nip you—a steel plate, steel wire, a dozen screws in his leg, and him not knowing a thing. The way the bone was broken it wasn't *broken,* the trainer told them, it was smashed, like somebody had gone after it with a sledgehammer.

"So he's going to make it," Billy said, not quite listening. "Hey. Yeah. *You.* You're going to make it, huh."

He and Kellerman were at the stall maybe forty-five minutes, and the place was busy, busier than Billy would have thought, it rubbed him the wrong way that so many people were around when he'd had the idea he and Kellerman would be the only ones. But it turned out that Raven's Wing always had visitors. He even got mail. (This Billy snorted to hear—a horse gets *mail?*) People took away souvenirs if they could, good-luck things, hairs from his mane, his tail, that sort of thing, or else they wanted to feed him by hand: there was a lot of that, they had to be watched.

Before they left Billy leaned over as far as he could, just wanting to stroke Raven's Wing's side, and two things happened fast: the horse snorted, stamped, lunged at his hand; and the trainer pulled Billy back.

"Hey, I told you," he said. "This is a dangerous animal."

"He likes me," Billy said. "He wasn't going to bite hard."

"Yeah?—sometimes he does. They can bite damn hard."

"He wasn't going to bite actually *hard*," Billy said.

Three dozen blue snakeskin wallets (Venezuelan), almost two dozen upscale watches (Swiss, German—chronographs, water-resistant, self-winding, calendar, ultrathin, quartz, and gold tone), and a pair of pierced earrings, gold and pearl, delicate, Billy thought, as a snowflake. He gave the earrings to Linda to surprise her and watched her put them in; it amazed him how quickly she could take out earrings and slip in new ones, position the tiny wires exactly in place, he knew it was a trick he could never do if he was a woman. It made him shiver, it excited him, just to watch.

Linda never said, "Hey, where'd you get *these*," the way his first wife used to, giving him that slow wide wet smile she thought turned him on. (Actually it had turned him on, for a while. Two, three years.)

Linda never said much of anything except thank you in her little-girl breathy voice, if she happened to be in the mood for thanking.

One morning a few weeks later Linda, in her bathrobe, came slowly out of the bedroom into the kitchen, squinting at something she held in the air, at eye level. "This looks like somebody's hair, what is it, Indian hair?—it's all black and stiff," she said. Billy was on the telephone so he had an excuse not to give her his fullest attention at the moment. He might be getting ready to be angry, he might be embarrassed, his nerves were always bad this time of day. Linda leaned up against him, swaying a little in her preoccupation, exuding heat, her bare feet planted apart on the linoleum floor. She liked to poke at him with her belly, she had a new habit of standing close.

Billy kept on with his conversation, it was in fact an important conversation, and Linda wound the several black hairs around her forearm, making a little bracelet, so tight the flesh started to turn white—didn't it hurt?— her forehead creased in concentration, her breath warm and damp against his neck.

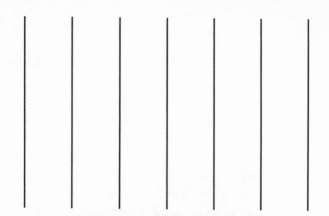

THE SEASONS

Joy, who is now twenty-six years old, is waiting to conceive *as if by accident* a child with the man she loves. This will be irrefutable proof, she reasons, that she loves him and that they must marry. Though she has not believed in God for perhaps thirteen years, she reasons too that conceiving a child in her special circumstances will be a sign of some kind, natural and healthy in effect but supernatural in origin. Her thoughts on the subject are kept secret from her lover, Christopher, but she suspects that he understands and concurs—he has developed such uncanny powers of intuition he sometimes knows what she is going to say before she says it. Frequently he reads her thoughts and announces them playfully, even in the presence of others. (Christopher is a playwright and his head is aswirl, he says, with dialogue. Stray floating dialogue. Aleatory sounds. So perhaps it is altogether natural that he can hear Joy's thoughts even when she doesn't intend to speak them aloud. Also, he loves her very much and certainly would marry her if she had his baby.) Only the accidental is truly significant in Joy's imagination because it is all that remains of grace, and all she remembers of "grace" is that an elderly Catholic novelist, a woman friend of her mother's, told her when she was twelve years old that grace is a direct visitation from God, *unwilled by man.* ("There is nothing we can do to deserve grace," the elderly woman told Joy, who was rather frightened at the time and anxious to escape. "It is a gift from God that not even the most impassioned prayer can guarantee.") Apart from the small circle of friends of Joy's parents in Minneapolis no one ever seemed to have heard of this particular Catholic novelist, so with the passage of years Joy stopped mentioning her. She has never brought up the name to Christopher, for instance, and isn't even certain at the present time that she remembers it correctly.

It is on a blowy and hazardous December evening, the day following the first snowfall of the season, that Christopher and Joy discover the starving kittens on a country road in northern New Jersey and bring them home to the Schankers' place in Millgate. (The Schankers are in Italy and Christopher and Joy are house-sitting for them. This is the third house in which they have lived since they met the previous January.) They are just returning from New York City, from a disappointing workshop production of

| | | | |

a play of Christopher's staged in an unheated studio near St. Mark's Place, and Christopher's head is so flooded with thoughts that he doesn't see the kittens by the roadside until Joy cries out excitedly for him to stop. By this time it is nearly one o'clock in the morning and Christopher has been driving nonstop for two hours and he couldn't have said whether he was exhausted by the strain of night driving or by the fresh wound of his play so crudely mangled—so *eerily* mangled it wasn't his any longer—or whether, in fact, he is on the brink of a bout of heart-thumping exhilaration and will be awake the rest of the night while Joy sleeps. (When Joy is exhausted she falls into bed and sleeps at once. This is a talent Christopher associates with his childhood, now long past, and tries not to resent in Joy.)

Christopher has become dazed and near mesmer-ized by the long drive, and when Joy seizes his arm and tells him to stop the car he hits the brakes at once, with-out question. Is it an animal? A deer? Has he hit some-thing? For most of his thirty-two years he has lived in cities and he hasn't entirely adapted to life in the country. As soon as dusk falls, in fact, he is besieged by ghostly figures of white-tailed deer running toward the road and preparing to leap into his windshield. ("By the time you see a deer," someone has warned him, "it's usually too late to avoid hitting it.") But though Christopher has seen a depressing number of dead deer along the roadsides—some of them so uncannily beautiful even in death it's difficult to believe they have been injured—he hasn't had an accident yet, or even a near accident.

Joy brings the kittens into the car, exclaiming over

them—Look at the poor things, the poor starving things, they've been abandoned, someone has dumped them here, someone has left them here to die—and Christopher's heart is won at once. The kittens are no more than a month old, mewing and squeaking, clearly ravenous with hunger, and far too immature to be frightened. White with gray markings, short-haired, with plaintive little faces and watery eyes and stubby tails: How could anyone do such a thing! How could anyone be so cruel! Joy is saying as the livelier of the two climbs up her arm, mewing loudly and evidently looking for milk. How can people be such monsters! Joy is saying passionately.

So they have no choice but to bring the kittens home with them and adopt them. The Schankers had had a cat, an obese Siamese, but the poor creature had died of old age a few weeks after Christopher and Joy moved in. The cat's death had upset Joy but the Schankers had told them they didn't really expect it to be living when they returned from Italy since it was twenty-one years old, a remarkable age for a cat, and quite old enough considering its irascible temper. "What should we do if it dies suddenly?" Christopher asked. He has never owned a pet and knows nothing about cats, only that Siamese are extraordinarily intelligent. "Bury it out somewhere in the woods," Mr. Schanker told him.

In the past ten or twelve years Christopher has been involved with a number of young women but he has never loved anyone as much as he loves Joy. She is nearly his height, slim-hipped, beautiful and melancholy and given to long brooding silences, with wild crimped chestnut-red hair and a very pale complexion. Even when her skin is slightly blemished or when a knife blade of a frown appears between her eyebrows she is remarkably attractive: Christopher thinks of her, with a tinge of resentment, as commandingly attractive. Her voice is soft and vague and sometimes trails off into silence, and her eyes have a queer ghostly-gray quality as if nothing is precisely *there* for her. "Do you love me?" Christopher asked when they first began living together and he'd follow her about the house, into the unfamiliar rooms, anxious that she might disappear. "Do you really love me?" he asked, and Joy would stare at him, baffled, as if she were frightened of giving the wrong answer. Sometimes she drew away from him, saying, "I wish you wouldn't look at me like that. I don't like it when people look at me, like that."

Christopher cannot now clearly remember several of the women with whom he was involved, but he knows that he imagined he was in love at the time, but was deluded. It angers him to realize he was deluded, but there you are. He has a romantic, easily excitable imagination.

When he sees Joy hugging the kittens, exclaiming over them, kneeling on the kitchen floor and feeding them milk in a saucer, tears streaming down her cheeks, he realizes suddenly that he doesn't know her at all. He has often worried that Joy is vague and unfocused and superficial in her emotions, that he is fated to love her more than she loves him—he couldn't have predicted the intensity of her concern for these pathetic little animals. And if they don't survive the night? If in fact they are already dying?

"Why are you crying, Joy?" Christopher asks

uneasily. When she doesn't look up he repeats his question in a louder voice; he is standing crouched over her and the kittens, still in his leather jacket and boots, wearing his gloves.

Joy has been susceptible to strange experiences for as long as she can remember. Once, as a child of nine, she was running in her grandmother's house, as she was forbidden to do, through an arched doorway and along a stretch of sun-spangled carpet—it seemed significant, that the carpet was sun-spangled at the time—when something happened, and the next thing she knew, she was being lifted from the floor. Both her parents were frightened that she had fainted but her grandmother said curtly, "Women in our family always faint." So it is that Joy does not mind fainting.

Shortly after Joy moved in with Christopher, in a small stone-and-stucco house overlooking the Raritan River—the Rutgers professor of Asian studies who owned it was traveling at the time—she was breaking eggs in the kitchen when a misshapen yolk streaked with blood slipped out of a shell: and she screamed for Christopher to come. "It's an embryo," she said, shielding her eyes like a child, "it's a living thing—I didn't mean to kill it—" Christopher was amazed that Joy could be so upset but he disposed of the offending egg—in fact, the entire bowl of eggs—and sat with Joy in the darkened living room for nearly an hour, hugging her, and comforting her, and telling her how much he loved her. Joy kept repeating that she hadn't meant to kill the embryo and Christopher kept repeating that she *hadn't* killed it, so far as he knew, so why didn't she simply forget about it? Joy buried her face in his neck and shivered. But she hadn't fainted.

Not long before they brought the kittens home she *had* fainted, at a rowdy informal party given by friends in Newark. Conversation had turned to open-heart surgery and to the implanting of artificial hearts, and Joy had gone dead white, and tried to get to her feet, but succeeded only in crashing heavily against a glass-topped table. Afterward, driving home, Christopher silently reached over to take her hand and squeeze it hard. Joy was a little drunk by this time and feeling unaccountably happy, as if she had narrowly avoided a terrible experience. She said, "You'd never want to marry a woman who breaks tables." Christopher said at once, "You'd never want to marry a man who breaks tables." It struck them both as hilarious at the time; they laughed, fairly snorting with laughter, for much of the drive home. The next morning Joy remembered the laughter but not its cause.

Must laughter have a cause, she wondered, when you are in love, and all the world is perfect?

Joy and Christopher sit in bed, playing with the kittens and thinking up names. It's remarkable how quickly, within a matter of hours, the kittens have been restored to life. Their stomachs are round and tight and full to bursting. Their tawny eyes, black slots at the centers, are bright and guileless. So far as Christopher can determine the smaller of the two is a female, the other a male, emboldened and really quite amazing in his fearlessness. Both are white with odd splotched gunmetal-gray markings on their heads and sides; their tails are gray with neat white

tips. There is something clownish about the markings—
the kittens have a fey, asymmetrical look—Christopher
even wonders if they might be slightly misshapen, their
tails so stubby, their heads so large for their bodies. Joy
says they are beautiful and not at all misshapen: they are
only a few weeks old.

Heloise and Abelard. Yin and Yang. Hamlet and
Ophelia. And what was Heathcliff's lover's name? Cathy?
Catherine? And there is John Thomas and Lady Jane.
When Christopher suggests Peppermint and Red Zinger,
Joy is offended, even angered. "You don't take anything
seriously," she says in a whisper. Poor Christopher is as-
tounded: hasn't he, of the two of them, always taken things
too seriously?

The kittens, taken to a vet in Millgate, are discovered to
be both male, so their names become Heathcliff and
Rochester. For a long while, until Rochester grows dis-
cernibly more husky than Heathcliff, it is difficult to tell
one from the other. By then Christopher and Joy have
moved from the Schankers' house and are occupying, for
a token rent of $100 a month, a studio apartment in a
converted carriage house a few miles north of Princeton.
Christopher's play, revised for the fifth time, is going to
be produced by the Houston Repertory in New York
City—or so he seems to have been promised.

Joy is studying macramé and pottery. And then modern
dance. And acting. And French conversation: she's a delightful mimic and languages have always been easy for
her initially. She begins a ten-week course in computer

programming but drops out after a few classes. She begins a six-week course in the techniques of real estate but soon drops out because her nature is violated by the idea of focusing so crudely and deliberately upon *selling,* and *making money,* and *competing with other persons.*

She takes most of her courses at Mercer Community College, where she has a job in the library. Then she gets a better-paying job at Western Electric as a receptionist, where she is much admired for her beauty, her clever clothes, her air of perfectly modulated calm. Even when she is nervous or anxious she gives no sign; her face is a cosmetic mask, her voice is controlled. She has learned to employ a "telephone voice" most of the time.

The years, Joy thinks. The seasons.

Sometimes it seems to her that she has been waiting to conceive a child with the man she loves for a very long time, that they have grown old together yet are still waiting for their lives to begin. Also, certain problems have arisen. Such as: Christopher is often too distracted with worry about his career to make love to her. Such as: she has lost so much weight without quite noticing it, her menstrual periods are erratic and widely spaced; does that mean she might be temporarily infertile?—"infertile" being a blunt neutral term that frequently assaults her when she isn't adequately busy.

Joy has only to close her eyes and (for instance) she is nine years old again running along her grandmother's hall, from the front foyer that smelled of floor wax to the old dining room, and then they are lifting her and staring into her face. But is the child's face really *hers?* And those faces—are they *theirs?* Do they (now) belong to anyone at all?

"Why do you think such disturbing things—can't you help yourself?" Christopher asks one day, watching her closely. Joy smooths the wrinkles from her forehead. She isn't certain she has spoken aloud. "If only you'd trust in me," Christopher says, burying his warm face in her hair, "if only you'd allow me to siphon off those poisonous thoughts."

He is embracing her so tightly she can scarcely breathe. She imagines her ribs are about to crack but of course they don't.

One overcast Saturday Heathcliff and Rochester are driven off to the vet's for their distemper shots and their "neutering" operations, which are evidently so painless (a local anesthetic is administered) they are running and tumbling about the house a few hours later and eating as hungrily as ever.

There is something so refreshingly comic about pets!—good-natured healthy nonpedigreed pets. Both Christopher and Joy speak amusingly of their twin cats to friends, Joy is always retrieving from one pocket or another coupons for cat food she has forgotten to redeem at the A&P, Christopher is always picking white cat hairs off his trousers. Within a year both cats have acquired distinctive habits and mannerisms and ways of calling attention to themselves. Rochester, for instance, is always hungry no matter how often he is fed. Whenever Christopher or Joy goes near the refrigerator Rochester is immediately underfoot, mewing plaintively and nudging with his head. Heathcliff prefers affection. In fact he has become oppressively affectionate—jumping onto Christopher's desk, purring loudly, making frantic kneading movements with his claws against Christopher's sleeves. Sometimes he is so grateful for Christopher's absent-minded attention he drools onto Christopher's papers. "For Christ's sake," Christopher shouts, "haven't you been weaned?"

When Joy is sick with a prolonged and debilitating case of the flu it is Rochester who lies with her in bed, sleeping contentedly for hours, and Heathcliff who cuddles up against her in the living room sofa. (At this time Joy and Christopher are renting a small house owned by a professor of American history at Princeton. Joy draws up an ambitious reading program for herself based on the professor's immense library and spends much of the winter dozing over books with titles like *Blacks of the Old South, Union Officer and the Reconstruction, American Slave and American Master.*)

Christopher's play opens to guardedly enthusiastic reviews and most nights the little theater is filled; unfortunately the play is booked for a three-week limited engagement only, and plans to produce it elsewhere never quite materialize. Christopher is gratified, however: he believes he has been baptized, he has proven himself— despite the strain and exhaustion of the past year he hasn't broken down. (The play is even nominated for a Drama Critics Award.)

He begins work immediately on a longer and more ambitious play set in 1950, "the legendary year of his birth." Joy is caught up in his excitement and speaks proudly of him to friends. He *is* a genius, she has known it all along, he isn't like other men. . . . Christopher and

Joy are photographed for an admiring article in a local
New Jersey paper: Playwright Christopher Flynn and his
companion Joy Stephens seated side by side on a sofa,
their hands tightly clasped, a white cat sprawled languidly
across their laps. Christopher Flynn holds himself rather
stiffly for the photograph, his deep-set eyes narrowed as
if in suspicion, or simple shyness; his close-cropped beard
appears to be a few shades lighter than his hair. He isn't
a handsome man but he exudes an unquestioning air of
authority. His companion Joy Stephens, however, is a
dreamily beautiful young woman with a sad, sweet, rather
haunting smile. Her name in the caption beneath the
photograph is "Joy Stehpns."

A feverish momentum carries Christopher through the
long quiet seemingly interminable workdays at home while
Joy is away, at Western Electric or at one of her classes.
(She has recently enrolled in a course in silk-screening at
the community college.) He writes from seven-thirty in
the morning until one o'clock in the afternoon, then from
approximately four o'clock until dinner. Often he writes
in the evenings as well, locked away in the room desig-
nated as his study. Sometimes the day's work has exhilarated or distressed him, or he has consumed too many
cups of coffee, or swallowed too many amphetamine tablets (*not* obtained illicitly—but given to him by a friend
of his who has a prescription), so that he ends up writing
during the night as well. Joy worries over his "pitiless
consuming of himself" but she provides most of his meals
and keeps herself and the cats out of his way. Perhaps
she will sleep with the middle-aged executive at Western

Electric who takes her to lunch frequently. Perhaps she will quit her job and see about establishing a permanent household. Or—since she is becoming quite absorbed in silk-screening—perhaps she will become an artist of sorts, after all. Her twenty-eighth birthday is drawing near.

Christopher is invited to have a drink with Mrs. Schanker in New York City, at one of the splendid new midtown hotels. He has not thought of her in a very long time and is mildly surprised to discover how youthful she is, for a woman in her late forties. Her hair is fashionably curly, her makeup is flawless. Why has she invited him for a drink? What is the purpose? So Christopher wonders while Mrs. Schanker talks and smiles and occasionally touches his arm. Evidently Mr. Schanker is seriously ill: but she is coy about actually naming the disease, or the organs it is ravaging. Christopher is at a loss for words. He says, "I'm sorry to hear that. . . . I'm sorry to hear that." (Lately it has come to Christopher's attention that a number of acquaintances of his and Joy's, and people he has known since college, have been taken seriously ill; or have actually died. But Joy insists that these events are accidental and not related to one another.)

Mrs. Schanker has several martinis and keeps muddling Joy's name. She embarrasses Christopher by asking if they plan to have a family someday, if they plan to get married. She asks about Christopher's new play and nods gravely when Christopher explains that he can't discuss his work—it makes him too tense. Twice, or is it three times, she asks about the kittens—"those darling white foundling kittens of yours"—and Christopher explains laughingly that they are hardly kittens any longer.

(Both are solid, husky, muscular cats, fully mature, with insatiable appetites for both food and affection. Rochester is so heavy that Joy staggers when she carries him; he has become a household joke, his nickname "Tank." Poor Heathcliff has developed a "fat pouch," a loose flaccid hunk of flesh that hangs down from his lower abdomen and swings when he trots, making him look pregnant. The vet says it's similar to a hernia in a human being, it isn't a health problem at all, both Heathcliff and Rochester are in superb physical condition. But, perhaps, slightly overweight.)

Mrs. Schanker reminisces about "Domino"—Christopher believes the name is Domino—and gradually it develops that she is speaking of the fat old cranky rheumy-eyed Siamese who died shortly after Christopher and Joy took responsibility for him. Christopher wants to joke that *that* had been a clever trick of the Schankers—to dump a dying cat on him because they hadn't the hardness of heart to have the poor thing put to sleep. But he senses this would be an inappropriate remark.

Some days afterward he realizes that Mrs. Schanker had (perhaps) wanted to initiate a love affair with him. Or the semblance of one. In fact, their meeting itself was a kind of love affair in embryo, a surrogate for the real thing, whatever the "real thing" is. He tells Joy about the meeting and the odd awkward conversation but he doesn't tell her about the miniature love affair. He muddles Mrs. Schanker's first name, which Joy insists is either "Lizzie" or "Bobbie."

Joy has become a vegetarian and has taken up membership in an Animal Rights organization in Philadelphia. For much of an elated week she is certain *though she does not hint of it to Christopher* that she is pregnant: but her condition turns out to be a false alarm. (She is furious with her gynecologist, who keeps insisting that water retention isn't unusual or particularly abnormal: hence Joy's swollen breasts and stomach and the sensitivity of her skin. "But I have never had this condition before!" Joy says angrily. Her voice rises to such a shrill pitch, the doctor's assisting nurse approaches Joy as if to comfort her, or restrain her. "It has never happened to me before, I don't even know what you're talking about!" Joy cries. "I think you're lying!")

One day while Christopher is in the city Joy does a forbidden thing, poking about in his study, scanning drafts and notes for his new play. It frightens her that she is living with a genius. Or with a man who believes himself a genius. It frightens her to discover that the play, though set three decades before, is clearly about Christopher and herself. Despite the fragmentary nature of the scenes and the messy scrawled writing Joy is able to piece together a narrative that relates to her own. She is "Lily," a somnambulist of "uncommon beauty" who has no center to her life, no focus, no identity. But it is said of her, admiringly, by her lover, "Alexander," that she is soulless and therefore cannot be injured. (Alexander defines himself as a "romantic cynic" who can be injured by virtually anyone and anything.) Lily is vague, superficial, charming in a childish manner; she has a habit of allowing her words to drift off into an inconclusive silence. . . .

By the end of the play Lily will have become catatonic, and committed to a mental asylum: and Alexander will spend the rest of his life mourning his loss.

"His loss . . . *his,*" Joy murmurs.

She has been absentmindedly scratching Heath-cliff's head and now the burly cat scrambles over Christopher's desk, knocking papers about, nudging and butting against Joy, near frantic with love.

One morning Christopher reappears in the kitchen just as Joy is about to leave for work and tells her, in a hoarse whisper, that he feels very strange. He doesn't feel like himself. He began work at seven-thirty but couldn't concentrate, his heart has been beating erratically, he has been thinking obsessively about. (And here he recites a now-familiar litany of anxieties. Past failures and humiliations; probable failures and humiliations to come. And his fear that his father, who has a serious heart condition, will die. And an old high school friend of his recently killed himself in San Francisco, leaving no note behind. . . .)

"When things speed up their meanings are lost," Christopher says.

The words are so precisely enunciated, Joy knows they are words from his play.

"When things speed up their meanings are lost," Christopher says, staring at her. "But we can't live if meanings are lost. We aren't human . . . if meanings are lost."

"Yes," Joy says carefully.

Across a space of several yards she can feel the trembling in her lover's body. But she must leave for work: it has begun to rain hard and she will have to drive slowly. She is a shy, cautious driver.

As she is about to leave Christopher says abruptly, "You aren't in love with anyone else, are you?" Joy laughs,

| | | | |

startled, but doesn't quite turn to him. He says, "Because you've always been happy with me. Before we met—I don't think you were happy, I think you were psychologically troubled. But you've always been happy with me."

"Yes," Joy says.

He kisses her goodbye. She feels him standing in the doorway and watching her until she is out of sight.

One evening after a dress rehearsal of Christopher's new play, an actor shows Joy the remarkably lifelike mask he wears during the final act to make him appear fifty years older than his age. "Feel this," he says, and Joy touches the rubber mask: so light, so delicate, it might be actual human skin. . . . She shivers, touching it.

On stage the actor is altogether convincing as an elderly dying man—haggard, hollow-eyed, ashen-faced. In person, smiling at Joy, he is a striking youngish man, no more than thirty-five. Joy hadn't known the technique of professional mask-making was so complex: the actor shows her not only the mask itself but the plaster mold of his face and a series of charcoal sketches. "Isn't it amazing? I frighten myself when I look in the mirror," the actor says fondly. He holds his elderly face up to his own, smiling at Joy, peering at her through the eye holes.

One April night Christopher makes love to Joy for the first time in many weeks, or has it been months? He is agitated, panting, near sobbing, but finally triumphant. Joy holds him tight and is passive and accommodating in his embrace; she isn't unfaithful to him by thinking of someone else. The years, she thinks. The seasons. Afterward she brushes his damp hair away from his forehead and makes a pretense of smoothing out the wrinkles.

He grips her tight, tight. He is trembling. He murmurs something about starting a baby at last, getting married. . . . When Joy doesn't reply he remains silent, his warm face burrowed against her neck, his ragged breath gradually growing rhythmic.

Shortly after they move to another house, a few miles north of Princeton, Rochester disappears and doesn't return for a full day and a night. But he does return, ravenously hungry. "A false alarm," Christopher says in a fond scolding voice.

Joy has enrolled in a six-week "mandala" course at the YW-YMCA, partly because her lover's wife is also enrolled in the course and she is curious about the woman. (But her curiosity is soon placated. Her lover's wife is in her early forties, slightly washed-out about the eyes but still pretty, wanly attractive, with a Virginia accent. Her manner is hopeful and zealous but she hasn't much talent for painting mandalas.)

The course is taught by a boisterous woman named Heloise who wears ankle-length gowns of coarse-woven fabric and a good deal of Navaho jewelry. She is an excellent teacher, however, filled with praise and enthusiasm, repeating many times each hour, "Free your innermost impulses, give vent to your *hidden* appetite for beauty and wholeness." She is particularly impressed with Joy's lavish mandalas, which are painted in rainbow colors with no attempt at precision or symmetry. Often she rests her beringed hand on Joy's slender shoulder. "Fantasy is beauty, beauty is fantasy," she says huskily. She carries herself well for a woman of her size though sometimes her breathing is audible. There is a faint downy mustache on her upper lip.

One evening she singles out a mandala of Joy's for especial praise. It is painted on a sheet of stiff construction paper measuring five feet by four but it looks even larger. Flamboyant fiery swaths of paint, peacock tails and cat eyes, heraldic cat figures suggestive of ancient Egyptian art. . . . Joy stands to one side, warm and flushed, her gaze veiled. Gradually she realizes that her lover's wife isn't in class that night and that she hasn't seen the woman for a while.

Christopher imagines that Joy is having a love affair though he has no proof and is too proud to quarry out proof. He has dreams in which he is clean-shaven and his face is a pink round baby's face, his skin so sensitive even the touch of the air irritates it. Dear God, simply to be *looked at* in this condition!—he is filled with chagrin, self-loathing. He has worn a beard since the age of twenty-two and cannot imagine himself without one. In his dreams it is mixed up with his plays, his "career," the woman with whom he lives whose name, in his sleep, he has temporarily forgotten. . . . When he wakes, however, it is to vast heart-pounding relief. He strokes his chin and his beard is still there. He reaches out beside him and Joy is still there, sleeping, or perhaps by now awake. Most nights the cats sleep in the bedroom, one on the bed and one beneath the bed, following an inflexible sort of protocol neither

Christopher nor Joy can always predict, though they know it must not be violated.

Christopher reaches out in the dark, toward an inert white shape pressed against his thigh. Rochester?—or Heathcliff?—no matter.

Because it is the only pragmatic thing to do *at the present time* Joy arranges to have an abortion at a clinic in New Brunswick. Christopher drives her there, waits for her, comforts her, weeps quietly with her. For many days he hugs her at odd impulsive moments. It is a queer dream-like time—the ordinary laws of nature appear suspended—a whisper can be heard throughout the house, a sigh, a stifled sob, a clearing of the throat. Even the cats are anxious and aroused and easily spooked.

A friend of Joy's asks if the procedure is painless and Joy replies at once, "I don't remember."

Christopher's new play opens to warmly enthusiastic notices. It is acclaimed as "powerful," "haunting," "lyric," "poetic"; Christopher himself is acclaimed as a "startling new talent." However, the play is not a commercial success and closes after seven weeks: not a bad run, considering the inhospitable theatrical climate.

Consequently Christopher's plans to move to New York City, to sublet a friend's loft on Vandam Street, are suspended. Consequently he may be forced to accept a playwright-in-residence position—in fact it is quite an attractive position—at the University of Connecticut. Friends congratulate him and go away puzzled by his bitterness.

"It has become so degrading," Christopher tells Joy.

| | | | |

"And I meant it to be so ennobling." He speaks with the melancholy precision of the leading man in his play.

One night, slightly high, he angrily corrects Joy's pronunciation of the word "pidgin," which she has mispronounced charmingly in the past. (She pronounces it "pidgin," as it is spelled; or, alternately, "pig-din.")

When Joy does not defend herself he becomes angrier. He accuses her of treachery and "sustained deceit." He knows she is having a love affair with someone in Princeton. He knows the baby wasn't his—if, as he says sarcastically, *there was any baby at all.*

"What do you mean?" Joy says, staring at him.

"You know what I mean," Christopher says. Suddenly he is very drunk. Suddenly, though his thoughts have a razor-sharp precision, his words are incoherent and there is nothing to do but grab Joy and shake her so that her head and shoulders strike the wall. "You want to suck out my soul—I know you!—because you have no soul of your own," he says.

Afterward they cry in each other's arms and eventually fall asleep.

Christopher and Joy have decided to separate, for experimental purposes. So they inform their friends. Perhaps Joy will move out, to live for a while with her married sister in Wilmington. Or Christopher may move out, and rent a small apartment in New York.

Then again, one balmy day in late March, they decide that they will get married after all. And put an end to it.

Christopher rocks Joy in his arms and promises they will have another baby. That is, they will have a baby. He can accept the position in Connecticut and stay there for a few years at least. Perhaps they can buy a farm in the country. An old farmhouse. With a few acres. Aren't the old farms selling very cheaply in New England? Joy sobs, and clutches at him, and grinds herself against him almost convulsively, horribly: Christopher is a little repulsed by her passion. And her physical strength.

In June Christopher makes the decision to move out of their rented house: he has been unable to work for weeks. But he is so obsessed with Joy that he hears her footfall behind him, feels the static electricity of her hair brushing against him, dreams of her constantly. . . . He drinks too much, smokes too much dope with friends who aren't really friends, who don't care about his happiness or whether he and Joy get together again. He listens to bad advice. Cruel rumors. Inflammatory news. One night, driving past his former house, now Joy's house (which is to say, a house he is still renting but in which Joy lives alone), he sees an unfamiliar car in the driveway and knows it is Joy's lover and that *she had been betraying him for a very long time.* Still, he does not wish her dead or even injured. If he had a pistol he wouldn't circle the house to get a good shot through one of the windows, he isn't that kind of man, he is far too civilized. He doesn't even write that kind of play.

That was the night he woke in his car, in a parking lot behind a tavern on Route 1, and had no idea what time it was or where he was or what had happened to him. He couldn't even remember passing out. But in the instant of waking he was suffused with a queer sense of elation because he remembered nothing. Nothing terrible had happened yet.

Or, alternately, everything had happened and he was still alive and why had he ever given a damn?

The telephone rings, rings. Joy picks it up and says carefully, "If you want to talk with me, Christopher, please talk to me. . . . Don't do this, Christopher—" she says, as the line goes dead.

Some days, Heathcliff and Rochester sleep for as many as twenty hours. (Though in different parts of the house. They rarely cuddle together or groom each other as they did as kittens: but Joy can't remember whether their estrangement was gradual or sudden.) Other days, they are skittish and forever underfoot, mewing to be fed.

Joy takes a bus to Wilmington, Delaware, to spend a weekend with her married sister, Irene, whom she decides after all not to confide in—she doesn't want news of the abortion, or the middle-aged lover, or "Lily" to get back to their mother. When she returns to Princeton it seems to her that the house has been broken into but she can't be certain. "Are you here, Christopher?" she calls out. She walks on tiptoe through the rooms, her heart beating oddly. "Christopher? Are you here? Please—" But no one answers.

Every scrap of dry cat food she left out has been devoured, and most of the water lapped up, but Heathcliff and Rochester show no interest in her return and when she tries to take him onto her lap Rochester shrinks away from her. She sits at the kitchen table, still in her raincoat, crying softly.

Christopher and Joy meet for coffee and Christopher tells her he misses her, he misses her and the cats, "and things the way they used to be." His eyes are lightly threaded with blood and his beard is grayer than Joy remembers. When she asks him if he wants to move back, however, he hesitates before saying he does. "You don't have to move back if you don't want to," Joy says, the faintest touch of irony in her voice. But Christopher says yes, yes he does, he *does* want to move back . . . except he's frightened of loving her too much.

Joy begins laughing, showing her perfect white teeth, narrowing her eyes to slits. After a moment or two Christopher lays his hand over hers as if to calm her. "People are looking at you," he whispers.

In the end it is decided that Christopher will move back, since he finds it impossible to work anywhere else; and that Joy will spend the month of September with her sister in Wilmington. (Christopher suspects that she is really going to move in with her lover—if she has a lover—but he's too proud to say anything. He doesn't love her any longer but he is still vulnerable to being wounded by her.)

When he telephones Joy in Wilmington, however, her sister tells him carefully that Joy is out at the moment, or can't come to the phone, and would he like to leave a message?—but he never does, he is sickened at the thought of making a fool of himself, of saying the wrong thing. He is also frightened of breaking down and weeping over the telephone while Joy's sister (whom he has never met) listens on, embarrassed.

One day he decides to give up the house and move to New York City after all. By delaying so long he lost the position at the University of Connecticut but he has been promised a part-time teaching job at New York University starting in January. What the hell, he thinks, excited, he will start a new life, he has begun work on his most ambitious play yet, he's only thirty-five years old. Perhaps, by the time he is thirty-six, he will have been awarded a Pulitzer Prize.

Not that prizes mean anything to him, he thinks, as if making a point to Joy, who is standing silently at the periphery of his vision.

He is ashamed to ask anyone he knows if they will take Heathcliff and Rochester; and he is fearful of turning them over to the county animal shelter—wouldn't they be put to sleep after a few days? The kindest thing to do is drive them out into the country—the deep country, away from busy roads—and give them their freedom. They are such strong healthy alert creatures, they will have no trouble hunting their food.

So he coaxes them into separate cardboard cartons, and carries them out to the car, and drives ten or twelve miles north and west of town, into farming country. The poor things are so piteous in their yowling and panting, such cowards, he doesn't know whether he should be angry with them or stricken to the heart.

In a desolate area in Hunterdon County, on a curve in a narrow unpaved road. Christopher stops the car and releases them. Heathcliff, panting, bounds into the tall grass at once but Rochester is dazed and must be urged to leave the car. (Poor "Tank" so panicked during the jolting ride, he soiled the bottom of his cardboard carton. But no matter: Christopher tosses both cartons into the ditch. He reasons that they can't be traced back to him.)

Driving slowly and cautiously away he sees both cats in his rearview mirror, staring after him. Oversized, clumsy, dumb creatures, with such blank unaccusing faces, simply staring after him. . . . Why don't they protest as any dog would, why don't they run after the car? Can it all end so abruptly? Christopher's heart lurches, he feels sickened and betrayed. He slows the car, brakes to a stop. He tells himself that, if the kittens make the smallest gesture of reconciliation, he will take them back home.

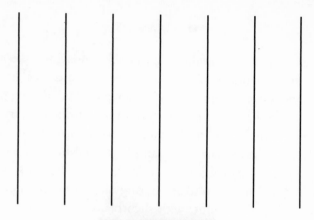

NAIROBI

Early Saturday afternoon the man who had introduced himself as Oliver took Ginny to several shops on Madison Avenue above Seventieth Street to buy her what he called an appropriate outfit. For an hour and forty-five minutes she modeled clothes, watching with critical interest her image in the three-way mirrors, and unable to decide if this was one of her really good days or only a mediocre day. Judging by Oliver's expression she looked all right but it was difficult to tell. The salesclerks saw too many beautiful young women to be impressed, though one told Ginny she envied her her hair—not just that shade of chestnut red but the thickness too. In the changing room she told Ginny that her own hair was "coming out in handfuls" but Ginny told her it didn't show. It will begin to show one of these days, the salesgirl said.

Ginny modeled a green velvet jumpsuit with a brass zipper and oversized buckles, and an Italian knit dress with bunchy sleeves in a zigzag pattern of beige, brown, and cream, and a ruffled organdy "tea dress" in pale orange, and a navy blue blazer made of Irish linen, with a pleated white linen skirt and a pale blue silk blouse. Assuming she could only have one costume, which seemed to be the case, she would have preferred the jumpsuit, not just because it was the most expensive outfit (the price tag read $475) but because the green velvet reflected in her eyes. Oliver decided on the Irish linen blazer and the skirt and blouse, however, and told the salesclerk to remove the tags and to pack up Ginny's own clothes, since she intended to wear the new outfit.

Strolling uptown he told her that with her hair down like that, and her bangs combed low on her forehead, she looked like a "convent schoolgirl." In theory, that was. Tangentially.

It was a balmy windy day in early April. Everyone was out. Ginny kept seeing people she almost knew, Oliver waved hello to several acquaintances. There were baby buggies, dogs being walked, sports cars with their tops down. In shop windows—particularly in the broad windows of galleries—Ginny's reflection in the navy blue blazer struck her as unfamiliar and quirky but not bad: the blazer with its built-up shoulders and wide lapels was more stylish than she'd thought at first. Oliver too was

| | | | |

pleased. He had slipped on steel-frame tinted glasses. He said they had plenty of time. A pair of good shoes—really good shoes—might be an idea.

But first they went into a jewelry boutique at Seventy-sixth Street, where Oliver bought her four narrow silver bracelets, engraved in bird and animal heads, and a pair of conch-shaped silver earrings from Mexico. Ginny slipped her gold studs out and put on the new earrings as Oliver watched. "Doesn't it hurt to force those wires through your flesh?" he said. He was standing rather close.

"No," Ginny said. "My earlobes are numb, I don't feel a thing. It's easy."

"When did you get your ears pierced?" Oliver asked.

Ginny felt her cheeks color slightly—as if he were asking a favor of her and her instinct wasn't clear enough, whether to acquiesce or draw away just perceptibly. She drew away, still adjusting the earrings, but said, "I don't have any idea, maybe I was thirteen, maybe twelve, it was a long time ago. We all went out and had our ears pierced."

In a salon called Michel's she exchanged her chunky-heeled red shoes for a pair of kidskin sandals that might have been the most beautiful shoes she'd ever seen. Oliver laughed quizzically over them: they were hardly anything but a few straps and a price tag, he told the salesman, but they looked like the real thing, they were what he wanted. The salesman told Oliver that his taste was "unerring."

"Do you want to keep your old shoes?" Oliver asked Ginny.

"Of course," Ginny said, slightly hurt, but as the salesman was packing them she changed her mind. "No, the hell with them," she said. "They're too much trouble to take along." Which she might regret afterward: but it was the right thing to say at that particular moment.

In the cab headed west and then north along the park, Oliver gave her instructions in a low casual voice. The main thing was that she should say very little. She shouldn't smile unless it was absolutely necessary. While he and his friends spoke—if they spoke at any length; he couldn't predict Marguerite's attitude—Ginny might even drift away, pick up a magazine and leaf through it if something appropriate was available, not nervously, just idly, for something to do, as if she were bored: better yet, she might look out the window or even step out on the terrace since the afternoon was so warm. "Don't even look at me," Oliver said. "Don't give the impression that anything I say—anything the three of us say—matters very much to you."

"Yes," said Ginny.

"The important thing," Oliver said, squeezing her hand and releasing it, "is that you're basically not concerned. I mean with the three of us. With Marguerite. With anyone. Do you understand?"

"Yes," said Ginny. She was studying her new shoes. Kidskin in a shade called "vanilla," eight straps on each shoe, certainly the most beautiful shoes she'd ever owned. The price had taken her breath away too. She hadn't any questions to ask Oliver.

When Ginny had been much younger—which is to say a few years ago when she'd been new to the city—she might have had some questions to ask. In fact she'd had a number of questions to ask, then. But the answers had not been forthcoming. Or they'd been disappointing. The answers had contained so much less substance than her own questions she had learned by degrees it was wiser to ask nothing.

So she told Oliver a second time, to assure *him,* "Of course I understand."

The apartment building they entered at Fifth and Eighty-eighth Street was older than Ginny might have guessed from the exterior—the mosaic murals in the lobby were in a quaint ethereal style unknown to her. Perhaps they were meant to be amusing but she didn't think so. It was impressive that the uniformed doorman knew Oliver, whom he called "Mr. Leahy," and that he was so gracious about keeping their package for them, while they visited upstairs; it was impressive that the black elevator operator nodded and murmured hello in a certain tone. Smiles were measured and respectful all around but Ginny didn't trouble to smile, she knew it wasn't expected of her.

In the elevator—which was almost uncomfortably small—Oliver looked at Ginny critically, standing back to examine her from her toes upward and finding nothing wrong except a strand or two of hair out of place. "The Irish linen blazer was an excellent choice," he said. "The earrings too. The bracelets. The shoes." He spoke with assurance, though Ginny had the idea he was nervous, or excited. He turned to study his own reflection in the bronze-frosted mirror on the elevator wall, facing it with a queer childlike squint. This was his "mirror face," Ginny supposed, the way he had of confronting himself in the mirror so that it wasn't *really* himself but a certain habitual expression that protected him. Ginny hadn't any mirror face herself. She had gone beyond that, she knew better, those childish frowns and half smiles and narrowed eyes and heads turned coyly or hopefully to one side—ways of protecting her from seeing "Ginny" when the truth of "Ginny" was that she required being seen head-on. But it would have been difficult to explain to another person.

Oliver adjusted his handsome blue-striped cotton tie and ran his fingers deftly through his hair. It was pale, fine, airily colorless hair, blond perhaps, shading into premature silver, rather thin, Ginny thought, for a man his age. (She estimated his age at thirty-four, which seemed old to her in certain respects, but she knew it was reasonably young in others.) Oliver's skin was slightly coarse; his nose wide at the bridge, and the nostrils disfigured by a few dark hairs that should have been snipped off; his lower jaw was somewhat heavy. But he was a handsome man. In his steel-rimmed blue-tinted glasses he was a handsome man and Ginny saw for the first time that they made an attractive couple.

"Don't trouble to answer any questions they might ask," Oliver said. "In any case the questions won't be serious—just conversation."

"I understand," Ginny said.

A Hispanic maid answered the door. The elevator and the corridor had been so dimly lit, Ginny wasn't prepared for the flood of sunlight in the apartment. They were on the eighteenth floor overlooking the park and the day was still cloudless.

Oliver introduced Ginny to his friends Marguerite

and Herbert—the last name sounded like Crews—and Ginny shook hands with them unhesitatingly, as if it were a customary gesture with her. The first exchanges were about the weather. Marguerite was vehement in her gratitude since the past winter, January in particular, had been uncommonly long and dark and depressing. Ginny assented without actually agreeing. For the first minute or two she felt thrown off balance, she couldn't have said why, by the fact that Marguerite Crews was so tall a woman—taller even than Ginny. And she was, or had been, a very beautiful woman as well, with a pale olive complexion and severely black hair parted in the center of her head and fixed in a careless knot at the nape of her neck.

Oliver was explaining apologetically that they couldn't stay. Not even for a drink, really: they were in fact already late for another engagement in the Village. Both the Crewses expressed disappointment. And Oliver's plans for the weekend had been altered as well, unavoidably. At this announcement the disappointment was keener, and Ginny looked away before Marguerite's eyes could lock with hers.

But Oliver was working too hard, Marguerite protested.

But he *must* come out to the Point as they'd planned, Herbert said, and bring his friend along.

Ginny eased discreetly away. She was aloof, indifferent, just slightly bored, but unfailingly courteous: a mark of good breeding. And the Irish linen blazer and skirt were just right.

After a brief while Herbert Crews came over to

comment on the view and Ginny thought it wouldn't be an error to agree: the view of Central Park was, after all, something quite real. He told her they'd lived here for eleven years "off and on." They traveled a good deal, he was required to travel almost more than he liked, being associated with an organization Ginny might have heard of?—the Zieboldt Foundation. He had just returned from Nairobi, he said. Two days ago. And still feeling the strain, the fatigue. Ginny thought that his affable talkative "social" manner showed not the least hint of fatigue but did not make this observation to Herbert Crews.

She felt a small pinprick of pity for the way Marguerite Crews's collarbones showed through her filmy muslin "Indian" blouse, and for the extreme thinness of her waist (cinched tight with a belt of silver coins or medallions), and for the faint scolding voice—so conspicuously a "voice"—with which she was speaking to Oliver. She saw that Oliver, though smiling nervously and standing in a self-conscious pose with the thumb of his right hand hooked in his sports coat pocket, was enjoying the episode very much; she noted for the first time something vehement and cruel though at the same time unmistakably boyish in his face. Herbert Crews was telling her about Nairobi but she couldn't concentrate on his words. She was wondering if it might be proper to ask where Nairobi was—she assumed it was a country somewhere in Africa—but Herbert Crews continued, speaking now with zest of the wild animals, including great herds of "the most exquisitely beautiful antelopes," in the Kenya preserves. Had she ever been there? he asked. No, Ginny said. "Well," said Herbert, nodding vigorously, "it really

| | | | |

is worth it. Next time Marguerite has promised to come along."

Ginny heard Oliver explain again that they were already late for an appointment in the Village, unfortunately they couldn't stay for a drink, yet it was a pity but he hoped they might do it another time: with which Marguerite warmly agreed. Though it was clearly all right for Oliver and Ginny to leave now, Herbert Crews was telling her about the various animals he'd seen—elands, giraffes, gnus, hippopotami, crocodiles, zebras, "feathered monkeys," impala—he had actually eaten impala and found it fairly good. But the trip was fatiguing and his business in Nairobi disagreeable. He'd discovered—as in fact the Foundation had known from certain clumsily fudged reports—not only that the microbiological research being subsidized there had come to virtually nothing but that vast sums of money had disappeared into nowhere. Ginny professed to feel some sympathy though at the same time, as she said, she wasn't surprised. "Well," she said, easing away from Herbert Crews's side, "that seems to be human nature, doesn't it. All around the world."

"Americans and Swedes this time," Herbert Crews said, "equally taken in."

It couldn't be avoided that Herbert tell Oliver what he'd been saying—Oliver in fact seemed to be interested, he might have had some indirect connection with the Foundation himself—but unfortunately they were late for their engagement downtown, and within five minutes they were out of the apartment and back in the elevator going down.

Oliver withdrew a handkerchief from his breast

pocket, unfolded it, and carefully wiped his forehead. Ginny was studying her reflection in the mirror and felt a pinprick of disappointment—her eyes looked shadowed and tired, and her hair wasn't really all that wonderful, falling straight to her shoulders. Though she'd shampooed it only that morning it was already getting dirty—the wind had been so strong on their walk up Madison.

On Fifth Avenue, in the gusty sunlight, they walked together for several blocks. Ginny slid her arm through Oliver's as if they were being watched but at an intersection they were forced to walk at different paces and her arm slipped free. It was time in any case to say goodbye: she sensed that he wasn't going to ask her, even out of courtesy, to have a drink with him: and she had made up her mind not to feel even tangentially insulted. After all, she hadn't been insulted.

He signaled a cab for her. He handed over the pink cardboard box with her denim jumper and sweater in it and shook her hand vigorously. "You were lovely up there," Oliver said, "just perfect. Look, I'll call you, all right?"

She felt the weight, the subtle dizzying blow, of the "were." But she thanked him just the same. And got into the cab. And wasn't so stricken by a sudden fleeting sense of loss—of loss tinged with a queer cold sickish knowledge—that, as the cab pulled away into the traffic stream, she couldn't give him a final languid wave of her hand, and even shape her mouth into a puckish kiss. All she had really lost, in a sense, was her own pair of shoes.

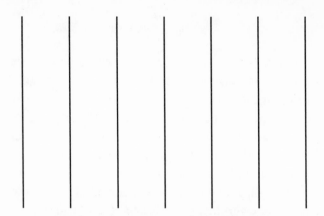

GOLDEN GLOVES

He was a premature baby, seven months old, born with deformed feet: the tiny arches twisted, the toes turned inward like fleshy claws. He didn't learn to walk until the age of three; then he tottered and lurched from side to side, his small face contorted with an adult rage, a rim of white showing above the irises of his eyes. His parents watched him in pity and despair—his father with a kind of embarrassment as well. Even at that age he hated to be helped to walk. Sometimes he hated to be touched.

Until the age of eight, when both his feet were finally operated on, he was always stumbling, falling, hurting himself, but he was accustomed to pain, he rarely cried. He wasn't like other children! At school, on the playground, out on the street, the cruelest children mocked him, called him names—Cripple, Freak—sometimes they even tripped him—but as he got older and stronger they learned to keep their distance. If he could grab them he'd hurt them with his hard pummeling fists, he'd make them cry. And even with his handicap he was quick: quick and clever and sinewy as a snake.

After the operation on his feet his father began to take him to boxing matches downtown in the old sports arena. He will remember all his life the excitement of his first Golden Gloves tournament, some of the boxers as young as fifteen, ribs showing, backs raw with acne, hard tight muscles, tiny glinting gold crosses on chains around their necks. He remembers the brick-red leather gloves that looked as if they must be soft to the touch, the bodies hotly gleaming with sweat, white boys, black boys, their amazing agility, the quickness of their feet and hands, high-laced shoes and ribbed socks halfway to their knees. They wore trunks like swimming trunks, they wore robes like bathrobes, and all with such nonchalance, in public. He remembers the dazzling lights focused upon the elevated ring, the shouts of the crowd that came in waves, the warm rippling applause when one boy of a pair was declared the winner of his match, his arm held aloft by the referee. What must it be, to be that boy!—to stand in his place!

He was seated in a child's wheelchair in the aisle, close beside his father's seat. Both legs encased in plaster from hip to toe: and him trapped inside. He was a quiet child, a friendly child, uncomplaining and perhaps even shy, showing none of the emotion that welled up in him—hurt, anger, shame—when people stared. They were curious, mainly—didn't mean to be insulting. Just ignore them, honey, his mother always said. But when he was alone with his father and people looked at him a little too long his father bristled with irritation. If anyone dared ask what had happened to him his father would say, Who wants to know? in a certain voice. And the subject was quickly dropped.

To him his father said, Let the sons of bitches mind their own business and we'll mind ours. Right?

The operation had lasted nine hours but he remembered little of it afterward except the needle going into his arm, into a vein, the careening lights, then waking alone and frightened in a room so cold his teeth began to chatter. Such cold, and such silence: he thought he must have died. Then the pain began and he knew he was alive, he cried in short breathless incredulous sobs until the first shock was past. A nurse stood over him telling him he'd be all right. He'd been a brave, brave little boy, she said.

The promise all along had been: he'd be able to walk now like any other boy. As soon as the casts were removed.

And: he'd be able to run. (Until now he'd crawled on his hands and knees faster than he'd been able to walk, like something scuttling along a beach.)

In his wheelchair at the Golden Gloves tournament he told himself he would be a boxer: he told himself at the conclusion of the first three-round match when a panting grinning boy was declared the winner of his match, on points, his arm held high, the gleaming brick-red glove raised for all to see. And the applause!—immediate, familial, rising and swelling like a heartbeat gone wild. The boy's father was in the ring with him, other boys who might have been his brothers or cousins—they were hugging one another in their happiness at the victory. Then the ring was emptied except for the referee, and the next young boxers and their seconds appeared.

He knew: he would be up there in the ring one day in the lights, rows of people watching. He would be there in the lighted ring, not in a wheelchair. Not in the audience at all.

After the casts were removed he had to learn to walk again.

They stood him carefully against a wall like a small child and encouraged him, Don't be afraid, take a step, take another step, come to them as best he could. They told him it wouldn't hurt and though it did hurt he didn't care, he plunged out lurching, swaying, falling panicked into his mother's arms. Yes, said his mother. Like that. Come *on*, said his father. Try again.

It was a year before he could walk inside the house without limping or turning his left foot helplessly inward. It was another year before he could run in the yard or in the school playground. By then his father had bought him a pair of child's boxing gloves, soft simulated dark brown leather. The gloves were the size of melons and so beautiful his eyes filled with tears when he first saw them. He would remember their sharp pungent smell through his life.

His father laced on the gloves, crouched to spar with him, taught him a few basic principles—how to hold

| | | | |

his guard, how to stand at an angle with his chin tucked against his shoulder (Joe Louis style), how to jab, how to keep moving—later arranged for him to take boxing lessons at the YMCA. His father had wanted to be a boxer himself when he was a boy, he'd fought in a few three-round matches at a local club but had won only the first match; his reflexes, he said, were just slightly off: when his opponent's jab got to him he forgot everything he knew and wanted to slug it out. He'd known enough to quit before he got hurt. Either you have the talent or you don't, his father said. It can't be faked.

He began to train at the Y, he worked out every day after school and on Saturday mornings; by the age of sixteen he'd brought his weight up to 130 pounds standing five foot six, he could run ten, twelve, as many as fifteen miles without tiring. He was quick, light, shrewd, he was good at boxing and he knew he was good, everyone acknowledged it, everyone watched him with interest. When he wasn't at the gym—when he had to be in school, or in church, or at home, even in bed—he was thinking about the gym, the ring, himself in his boxing trunks and leather gloves, Vaseline smeared on his face and his headgear on his head, he was in his crouch but getting ready to move, his knees bent, his hands closed into fists. He was ready! He couldn't be taken unawares! He couldn't be stopped! He became obsessed with some of the boys and young men he knew at the gym, their weights, their heights, the reach of their arms, could they knock him out if he fought them, could he knock them out? What did they think about *him?* There were weeks when he was infatuated with one or another boy who might be a year or two older than he, a better boxer, until it was revealed that he wasn't a better boxer after all: he had his weaknesses, his bad habits, his limitations. He concentrated a good deal on the feel of his own body, building up his muscles, strengthening his stomach, his neck, learning not to wince at pain—not to show pain at all. He loved the sinewy springiness of his legs and feet, the tension in his shoulders; he loved the way his body came to life, moving, it seemed, of its own will, knowing by instinct how to strike his opponent how to get through his opponent's guard how to hurt him and hurt him again and make it last. His clenched fists inside the shining gloves. His teeth in the mouthpiece. Eyes narrowed and shifting behind the hot lids as if they weren't his own eyes merely but those belonging to someone he didn't yet know, an adult man, a man for whom all things were possible.

Sometimes on Saturday afternoons the boys were shown film clips and documentaries of the great fighters. Jack Dempsey—Gene Tunney—Benny Leonard—Joe Louis—Billy Conn—Archie Moore—Sandy Saddler—Carmen Basilio—Sugar Ray Robinson—Jersey Joe Walcott—Rocky Marciano. He watched entranced, staring at the flickering images on the screen; some of the films were aged and poorly preserved, the blinds at the windows fitted loosely so that the room wasn't completely darkened, and the boxers took on an odd ghostly insubstantial look as they crouched and darted and lunged at one another. Feinting, clinching, backing off, then the flurry of gloves so swift the eye couldn't follow, one man suddenly down and the other in a neutral corner, the announcer's voice rising in excitement as if it were all happening now right now and not decades ago. More astonishing than the powerful blows dealt were the blows taken, the punishment absorbed as if really finally one could not be hurt by an opponent, only stopped by one's own failure of nerve or judgment. If you're hurt you deserve to be hurt! If you're hurt badly you deserve to be hurt badly! Turning to the referee to protest a low blow, his guard momentarily lowered—there was Jack Sharkey knocked out by Jack Dempsey with a fast left hook. Like that! And the fight was over. And there was aging Archie Moore knocked down repeatedly, savagely, by young Yvon Durrelle, staggering on his feet part-conscious but indomitable—how had he come back to win? how had he done it?—boasting he wasn't tired afterward, he could fight the fight all over again. Young Joe Louis baffled and outboxed by stylish Billy Conn for twelve rounds, then suddenly as Conn swarmed all over him trying to knock him out Louis came alive, turned into a machine for hitting, combinations so rapid the eye couldn't follow, left hooks, right crosses, uppercuts, a dozen punches within seconds and Conn was finished—that was the great Joe Louis in his prime. And here, Jersey Joe Walcott outboxing Rocky Marciano until suddenly Marciano connected with his right, that terrible incalculably powerful right, Let's see the knockout in slow motion, the announcer said, and you could see this time how it happened, Walcott hit so hard his face so stunned so distorted it was no longer a human face, no longer recognizable. And Rocky Marciano and Ezzard Charles fighting for Marciano's heavyweight title in 1954—after fifteen rounds both men covered in blood from cuts and gashes in their faces but embracing each other like brothers, smiling, laughing it seemed, in mutual respect and admiration and it didn't—almost—seem to matter that one man had to lose and the other had to win: they'd fought one of the great fights of the century and everyone knew it.

And *he* knew he was of their company. If only he might be allowed to show it.

He was sixteen years old, he was seventeen years old, boxing in local matches, working his way steadily up into state competitions, finally into the Golden Gloves Tri-State tournament. He had a good trainer, his father had seen to that. He had trophies, plaques, photographs taken at ringside, part of the living room was given over to his boxing as to a shrine. What do your friends think about your boxing? his relatives asked. Isn't it a dangerous sport? But he hadn't any friends that mattered and if his classmates had any opinion about him he couldn't have guessed what it might be, or cared. And, no, it wasn't a dangerous sport. It was only dangerous if you made mistakes.

It was said frequently at the gym that he was "coming along." The sportswriter for the local newspaper did a brief piece on him and a few other "promising" amateurs. He was quick and clever and intuitive, he knew to let a blow slide by his shoulder then to get his own in then to retreat, never to panic, never to shut his eyes, never to breathe through his mouth, it was all a matter of breath you might say, a matter of the most exquisite timing, momentum, a dancer's intelligence in his legs, the instinct to hit, to hit hard, and to hit again. He was a

| | | | |

young Sandy Saddler they said—but he didn't fight dirty! No, he was a young Sugar Ray. Styled a bit on that brilliant new heavyweight Cassius Clay, who'd surprised the boxing world by knocking out Sonny Liston. He hadn't a really hard punch but he was working on it, working constantly, in any case he was winning all his matches or fighting to a draw, there's nothing wrong in fighting to a draw his father told him, though he could see his father was disappointed sometimes, there were fights he should have won but just didn't—couldn't. The best times were when he won a match by a knockout, his opponent suddenly falling, and down, not knocked out really, just sitting there on the canvas dazed and frightened, blinking, looking as if he were about to cry but no one ever cried, that never happened.

You have real talent, he was told. Told repeatedly.

You have a future!

The promise was—he seemed to know—that he couldn't lose. He'd understood that years before, watching one or another of the films, young Dempsey fierce as a tiger against the giant Jess Willard, twenty-year-old Joe Louis in action, Sugar Ray Robinson who'd once killed an opponent in the ring with the force of his blows: he was of their company and he knew it and he knew he couldn't lose, he couldn't even be seriously hurt, that seemed to be part of the promise. But sometimes he woke in the night in his bed not knowing at first where he was, was he in the gym, in the ring, staring panicked across the wide lighted canvas to his opponent shadowy in the opposite corner, he lay shivering, his heart racing, the bedclothes damp with sweat. He liked to sweat most of the time, he liked the rank smell of his own body, but this was not one of those times. His fists when he woke would be clenched so hard his fingernails would be cutting into his palms, his toes curled in tight and cramped as if still deformed, secretly deformed. Cripple! Freak! The blow you can't see coming is the blow that knocks you out—the blow out of nowhere. How can you protect yourself against a blow out of nowhere? How can you stop it from happening again? He'd been surprised like that only a few times, sparring, not in real fights. But the surprise had stayed with him.

Yet there was a promise. Going back to when he was very small, before the operation.

And his father adored him, his father was so happy for him, placing bets on him, not telling him until after-ward—after he'd won. Just small bets. Just for fun. His father said, I don't want you to feel any pressure, it's just for fun.

Then of course he was stopped and his "career" ended abruptly and unromantically. As he should have foreseen. Just a few weeks before his eighteenth birthday.

It happened midway in the first round of a Golden Gloves semifinal lightweight match in Buffalo, New York, when a stocky black boy from Trenton, New Jersey, came bounding at him like a killer, pushing and crowding and bulling him back into the ropes, forcing him backward as he'd never been forced; the boy brushed aside his jabs and ignored his feints, popped him with a hard left then landed a blow to his exposed mouth that drove his upper front teeth back through his slack lower lip but somehow at the same time smashed the teeth upward into his palate. He'd lost his mouthpiece in the confusion, he'd never seen the punch coming, he was told afterward it had been a hard straight right like no amateur punch anyone could recall.

He fell dazed into the ropes, he fell to the canvas, he hid his bleeding face with his gloves, gravity pulled him down and his instinct was to submit to curl up into a tight ball to lie very still maybe he wouldn't be hit again maybe it was all over.

And so it happened.

That was his career as an amateur boxer. Twenty or so serious matches: that was it.

Never again, he told himself. That *was* it.

(The black boy from New Jersey—Roland Bush Jr.—was eighteen years old at the time of the fight but had the face of a mature man, heavy-lidded eyes, broad flat nose, scars in his forehead and fanning his eyes. An inch shorter than his white opponent but his shoulder and leg muscles rippled with high-strung nervous strength, he'd thickened his neck muscles to withstand all blows, he was ready, he was hot, he couldn't be stopped. His skin was very dark and the whites of his eyes were an eerie bluish-white, luminous, threaded almost invisibly with blood. He weighed no more than his opponent but he had a skull and a body built to absorb punishment, he was solid, hard, relentless, taking no joy in his performance just doing it, doing it superbly, getting it done, he went on to win the

Golden Gloves title in his division with another spectacular knockout and a few months later turned professional and was advanced swiftly through the lightweight ranks then into the junior welterweights where he was ranked number fourteen by *Ring* magazine at the time of his death—he died aged twenty of a cerebral hemorrhage following a ten-round fight in Houston, Texas, which he'd lost in the ninth round by a technical knockout.)

■   ■   ■

The fight was stopped, the career of "promise" was stopped, now he is thirty-four years old and it seems to him his life is passing swiftly. But at a distance. It doesn't seem in fact to belong to him, it might be anybody's life.

In his professional career, in his social life, he is successful, no doubt enviable, but he finds himself dreaming frequently these days of the boy with the crippled feet. Suppose he'd never had the operation: what then! He sees the creature on its hands and knees crawling crablike along the ground, there is a jeering circle of boys, now the terrible blinding lights of the operating room snuff him out and he's gone. And now seated in his aluminum wheelchair staring down helplessly at the white plaster casts: his punishment. Hips to toes, toes to hips. His punishment.

The adults of the world conspire in lies leaning over him smiling into his face. He will be able to walk he will be able to run he won't feel any pain he won't be hurt again doesn't he want to believe?—and of course he does. He does.

| | | | |

His wife's name is Annemarie, a name melodic and lovely he sometimes shapes with his lips, in silence: an incantation.

He had fallen in love with Annemarie seeing her for the first time amid a large noisy gathering of relatives and friends. When they were introduced and he was told her name he thought extravagantly, Annemarie, yes—she's the one!

From the first she inspired him to such extravagant fancies, such violations of his own self. Which is why he loves her desperately.

Annemarie is twenty-nine years old but has the lithe small-boned features of a girl. Her hair is light brown, wavy, silvery in sunshine, her eyes wide-set and intelligent, watchful. Most of the time she appears to be wonderfully assured, her center of gravity well inside her, yet in the early weeks of the pregnancy she cried often and asked him half angrily, Do you love me? And he told her, Yes, of course. Of course I love you. But shortly afterward she asked him again, as if she hadn't believed him, Do you love me—*really?* More than before, or less? and he laughed as if she were joking, as if it were one of her jokes, closing his arms around her to comfort her. This was Annemarie's second pregnancy after all: the first had ended in a miscarriage.

Don't be absurd, Annemarie, he tells her.

Most of the time, of course, she is good-natured, sunny, uncomplaining; she loves being pregnant and she is eager to have the baby. She chooses her maternity outfits with care and humor: flowing waistless dresses in colorful fabrics, blouses with foppish ties, shawls, Indian beads, cloth flowers in her hair. Some of the outfits are from secondhand shops in the city, costumes from the forties and fifties, long skirts, culottes, silk pants suits, a straw boater with clusters of artificial berries on the rim: to divert the eye from her prominent belly, she says. But the childlike pleasure Annemarie takes in dressing is genuine and her husband is charmed by it, he adores her for all that is herself, yes, he'd fight to the death to protect her he'd die in her place if required.

Odd how, from the start, she has had the power to inspire him to such melodramatic extravagant claims.

The miscarriage took place in the fifth month of the first pregnancy. One night Annemarie woke with mock-labor pains and began to bleed, she bled until nothing remained in her womb of what was to have been their son. And they were helpless, helpless to stop it.

They'd known for weeks that the fetus was impaired, the pregnancy might not go to term; still, the premature labor and the premature death were blows from which each was slow to recover. Annemarie wept in his arms and, he thought, in his place: her angry childish mourning helped purge his soul. And Annemarie was the first to recover from the loss for after all—as her doctor insisted—it wasn't anything personal, *it's just physical.* The second pregnancy has nothing at all to do with the first.

So we'll try again, Annemarie said reasonably.

And he hesitated saying, Not now. Saying, Isn't it too soon? You aren't recovered.

And she said, Of course I'm recovered.

And he said, But I think we should wait.

| | | | |

And she said, chiding, *Now*. When if not *now?*

(Twenty-nine years old isn't young, in fact it is "elderly" in medical terms for a woman pregnant with her first child. And they want more than one child, after all. They want a family.)

So they made love. And they made love. And he gave himself up to her in love, in love, in a drowning despairing hope, it's just physical after all it doesn't mean anything. Such failures of the physical life don't mean anything. You take the blow then get on with living isn't that the history of the world? Of course it is.

He's an adult man now, not a boy any longer. He knows.

He cradles his wife's belly in his hands. Stroking her gently. Kissing her. Fiercely attentive to the baby's secret life, that mysterious interior throb, that ghostly just-perceptible kick. Through the doctor's stethoscope each listened to the baby's heartbeat, a rapid feverish-sounding beat, *I am, I am, I am.* This pregnancy, unlike the first, has been diagnosed as "normal." This fetus unlike the first has been promised as "normal."

Approximately fifteen days yet to go: the baby has begun its descent head first into the pelvic cavity and Annemarie has begun, oddly, to feel more comfortable than she has felt in months. She assures him she is excited—not frightened—and he remembers the excitement of boxing, the excitement of climbing through the ropes knowing he couldn't turn back. Elation or panic? euphoria or terror?—that heartbeat beating everywhere in his body.

For months they have attended natural childbirth

classes together and he oversees, genially but scrupulously, her exercises at home: he will be in the delivery room with her, he'll be there all the while.

This time, like last time, the fetus is male, and again they have drawn up a list of names. But the names are entirely different from the first list, Patrick, William, Alan, Seth, Sean, Raymond; sometimes Annemarie favors one and sometimes another but she doesn't want to choose a name until the baby is born. Safely born.

Why hasn't he ever told Annemarie about his amateur boxing, his "career" in the Golden Gloves?—he has told her virtually everything else about his life. But it is a matter of deep shame to him, recalling not only the evening of his public defeat but his hope, his near-lunatic hope that he would be a hero, a star! a great champion! He has told her he'd been a premature baby, born with a "slight deformity" of one foot which was corrected by surgery immediately after his birth: this is as near to the truth as he can manage.

Which foot was it? Annemarie asks sympathetically.

He tells her he doesn't remember which foot, it isn't important.

But one night he asks her to caress his feet. They are in bed, he is feeling melancholy, worried, not wholly himself. He has begun to profoundly dislike his work in proportion to his success at it and this is a secret he can't share with Annemarie; there are other secrets too he can't share, won't share, he fears her ready sympathy, the generosity of her spirit. At such times he feels himself vulnerable to memory, in danger of reliving that last fight, experiencing moments he hadn't in a sense experienced at the time—it had all happened too swiftly. Roland Bush Jr. pressing through his defense, jabbing him with precise machinelike blows, that gleaming black face those narrowed eyes seeking him out. White boy! White boy who are *you!* Bush was the true fighter stalking his prey. Bush was the one.

He hadn't been a fighter at all, merely a victim.

He asks Annemarie to caress his feet. Would she hold them? Warm them? Would she . . . ? It would mean so much, he can't explain.

Perhaps he is jealous of their son so cozy and tight upside down beneath his wife's heart but this is a thought he doesn't quite think.

Of course Annemarie is delighted to massage his feet, it's the sort of impulsive whimsical thing she loves to do, no need for logic, no need for explanations, she has wanted all along to nourish the playful side of his personality. So she takes his feet between her small dry warm hands and gently massages them. She brings to the intimate task a frowning concentration that flatters him, fills him with love. What is she thinking? he wonders. Then suddenly he is apprehensive: What does she know of me? What can she guess? Annemarie says, smiling, Your feet are so terribly cold! But I'll make them warm.

The incident is brief, silly, loving, quickly forgotten. One of those moments between a husband and a wife not meant to be analyzed, or even remembered. It never occurs a second time, never again does Annemarie offer to caress his feet and out of pride and shame he certainly isn't going to ask.

The days pass, the baby is due in less than a week, he keeps thinking, dreaming, of that blow to his mouth: the terrible power of the punch out of nowhere. His skull shook with a fierce reverberation that ran through his entire body and he'd known then that no one had ever hit him before.

It was his own death that had crashed into him—yet no more than he deserved. He was hit as one is hit only once in a lifetime. He was hit and time stopped. He was hit in the second minute of the first round of a long-forgotten amateur boxing match in Buffalo, New York; he was hit and he died and they carried him along a corridor of blinding lights, strapped to a stretcher, drooling blood and saliva, eyes turned up in his head. Something opened, lifted, a space of some kind clearing for him to enter, his own death but he hadn't had the courage to step forward.

Someone whose face he couldn't see was sinking a needle deep into his forearm, into the fleshy part of his forearm, afterward they spoke calmly and reassuringly saying it isn't really serious, a mild concussion not a serious fracture, his nose wasn't broken, only his mouth and teeth injured, that could be fixed. He flinched remembering the blow flying at him out of nowhere. He flinched, remembering. It happens once in a lifetime after that you're dead white boy but you pick yourself up and keep going.

There followed then the long period—months, years—when his father shrank from looking him fully in the face. Sometimes, however, his father examined his mouth, wasn't entirely pleased with the plastic surgeon's work. It had cost so damned much after all. But the false

teeth were lifelike, wonderfully convincing, some consolation at least. Expensive too but everyone in the family
was impressed with the white perfect teeth affixed to their
lightweight aluminum plate.

All that the old tales of pregnancy promise of a female
beauty luminous and dewy, lit from within, was true: here
is Annemarie with eyes moist and bright as he'd rarely
seen them, a skin with a faint rosy bloom, feverish to the
touch. Here is the joy of the body as he had known it
long ago and had forgotten.

There were days, weeks, when she felt slightly unwell yet the bloom of pregnancy had held and deepened
month following month. A woman fully absorbed in herself, suffused with light, heat, radiance, entranced by the
plunge into darkness she is to take. Pain—the promised
pain of childbirth—frightens yet fascinates her: she means
to be equal to it. She doesn't shrink from hearing the
most alarming stories, labors of many hours without anesthetic, cesarean deliveries where natural childbirth had
been expected, sudden losses of blood. She means to
triumph.

Within the family they joke—it's the father-to-be,
not Annemarie, who is having difficulty sleeping these past
few weeks. But that too is natural, isn't it?

One night very late in her term Annemarie stares
down at herself as if she'd never seen herself before—the
enormous swollen belly, the blue-veined stretched skin
with its uncanny luminous pallor—and because she has
been feeling melancholy for days, because she is fatigued,
suddenly doubting, not altogether herself, she exclaims

with a harsh little laugh, God look at me, at this, how can you love anything like—*this!*

His nerves are torn like silk. He knows she isn't serious, he knows it is the lateness of the hour and the strain of waiting, it can't be Annemarie herself speaking. Quickly he says, Don't be absurd.

But that night as he falls slowly asleep he hears himself explaining to Annemarie in a calm measured voice that she will be risking something few men can risk, she should know herself exalted, privileged, in a way invulnerable to hurt even if she is very badly hurt, she'll be risking something he himself cannot risk again in his life. And maybe he never risked it at all.

You'll be going to a place I can't reach, he says.

He would touch her, in wonder, in dread, he would caress her, but his body is heavy with sleep, growing distant from him. He says softly, I'm not sure I'll be here when you come back.

But by now Annemarie's breathing is so deep and rhythmic she must be asleep. In any case she gives no sign of having heard.

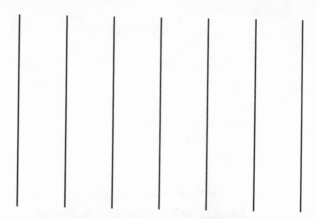

HARROW STREET
AT LINDEN

They have been married one hundred and eight days and have been living less than a week in the buff-brick house on Harrow Street at the corner of Linden (a fifteen-minute walk from the southeasterly edge of the university campus) when Drew Stickney is discovered by his young wife with his ear splayed flat against the bathroom wall of their three-room apartment—against the cheery yellow plastic "tile" that carries certain noises so clearly from the adjoining bathroom. Drew is later discovered examining their neighbors' mail in the downstairs front hall, where mail has been left in an unsorted heap by the substitute postman. (The situation invites trouble, Katherine Stickney thinks. She has been watching her husband from the first-floor landing but thinks it prudent not to call out a warning to him: she has always been a reserved girl.)

Katherine has been counting the days since she has been Mrs. Drew Stickney: one hundred and eight, one hundred and nine, one hundred and ten. . . . She has been counting without her conscious knowledge, sometimes even against her will, but how do you control your thoughts?—except for extinguishing them at certain times. She is still a bride, she doesn't think of herself as a wife, she is tall and graceful and very pretty with pale blond hair and wide-spaced hazel eyes and a faint blue vein in her throat. Since earliest childhood it has been Katherine's strategy to shut herself up like a telescope at night so that she can sleep undisturbed by bad thoughts. Now in the night, in the dark of the bedroom on the third floor, rear, of Harrow Street, Katherine shuts herself up to sleep while her husband touches himself secretly, in rhythm with the noisy lovers a few yards away, on the other side of the bedroom wall. Katherine is not a graduate student like Drew—in fact she needs fifteen more credits to graduate. But she is confident that she will receive her bachelor's degree if she works steadily enough and isn't impatient. She also has a part-time job, mainly typing and filing, in the law library. (Drew is extremely grateful for her willingness to work because, by his estimation, it will enable him to earn his master's degree a full year ahead of schedule; and then he will continue without hesitating, to get his Ph.D. "It's the least I can do," Katherine says. "I love you." Drew says, "Well I love *you*.")

They were married in the last week of May in a

university town in the Midwest, on a wide flat mud-colored river; in early September they drove a U-Haul to another university town in the Midwest, on the same river, approximately three hundred eighty miles to the south. There is so much space in the center of the continent, Katherine thinks, it hardly matters which direction you move. Very little changes. If she didn't know from the Rand McNally Road Atlas that they had moved in a southerly direction she could not have deduced it from her surroundings. SINNER DO YOU KNOW THAT JESUS DIED FOR YOUR SINS? is a billboard poster general in the Midwest.

There are only eight apartments for rent in the house on Harrow Street, which was converted from a private residential dwelling to a multifamily rental property some years ago. Though the exterior is hearty and stolid, and the peaked roofs inspire confidence, the interior walls are somewhat thin and the plumbing is noisy on all floors. "Just ignore them, Katherine," Drew says stiffly, when their neighbors begin to quarrel and every word, or nearly, communicates itself through the wall. At such times Drew hurriedly puts a record on their phonograph and turns the volume up, or switches on the radio. Classical music is played much of the day on the campus FM station.

Drew and Katherine Stickney live in Apartment 3A, and Mack and Holly Cott live in Apartment 3B. No one lives overhead but sometimes, in the very early morning, there are odd soft thumps like footsteps on the roof, and sliding noises like snow or sand. When she hears these sounds Katherine has to resist succumbing to alarm. She is a naturally reserved girl, not excitable or high-strung. She has been in excellent health for years. Neither Katherine nor Drew chooses to call attention to the overhead noises because they are probably imaginary.

"I can sleep through anything," Drew has begun to say, yawning and stretching boyishly in the mornings. "If I'm tired enough. If I'm *dead* enough." Katherine supposes he is lying but does not contradict him.

Drew is from Allentown, Pennsylvania, a city Katherine has never visited. He is tall and thin and self-conscious, with ash-blond hair lighter than Katherine's, and chill unblinking gray eyes behind glasses with black plastic rims. At the present time he takes classes and laboratories most of the day, five days a week, and is research assistant in the monkey lab on the sixth floor of Fenner Hall. His interests, he told Katherine when they first met, have always centered upon the "life sciences." ("For instance," he said, frowning and staring past Katherine's shoulder, a faint blush coloring his cheek, "the problem of what life is, what we mean when we say 'life'; whether it's just warmth, and breath, and a heartbeat, and an electrical charge, or something more.") He has always been a scholarship student despite his weak eyes and his susceptibility to headaches; he would have had an all-A average except for a B+ in a required English course and a string of C's in Physical Education. He is the only son of fairly aged parents who are both active in the Bible Baptist Church Independent of Allentown-Bethlehem. Though his birth was considered a miracle by his parents, an answer to their prayer of many years for a son, Drew himself is not religious: he hasn't prayed to God, he told Katherine, since the age of nine, and considers the subject closed.

So far as Katherine knows her single remaining

parent—her mother—has no religious ties. In the company of two or three other widows she often plays bingo on Thursday evenings at St. Joseph's Church hall in Lake Forest, Illinois, but she doesn't belong to that church. Her advice to Katherine has been general but enthusiastic. "The best of life is always ahead," she tells Katherine when they speak on the phone every few weeks. "You have to believe that, otherwise you're finished."

Drew and Katherine fell in love during the long midwinter break, when most of the student population had departed and only foreign students remained on campus. Every other face glimpsed on the street was dusky-skinned if not frankly black. There were exotically colored native costumes beneath quilted jackets, there were many turbaned heads. Katherine, tall and blond and frequently alone, knew herself followed closely when she hurried back to her dormitory from the library after dark, but nothing happened of a specific sort, and after she and a senior biology major named Drew Stickney fell in love she was in no danger.

Now danger is present again in her life though Katherine cannot name it. She is a young bride with a plain gold wedding band on her finger, her husband is a research assistant in the field of neuroendocrinology, she takes meticulous and unfailingly complete notes in her lecture classes and will graduate from college in another year or two; there is little likelihood that she will become pregnant; life is a matter of semesters, weeks, days, fifty-minute hours, and hurried lunches in the student union. These things Katherine reasons she can negotiate, though Drew sometimes looks at her oddly through his glasses and says, "Do you regret it? Are you having second thoughts? Are you telephoning your mother when I'm not here? Do you compare notes with other wives?"

Katherine tells him quietly that she doesn't know any other wives.

"There's the one next door," Drew says.

Mack and Holly Cott intrude upon the Stickneys at unanticipated hours of the day, but particularly in the early morning between 6:30 A.M. and 8, and in the evening from approximately 6 P.M. to 1 A.M. or even 2. Their footsteps are heavily jocular on the stairs. Their key tears into the lock on their door and twists it brutally open. Books are dropped, duffel bags, cartons of groceries, undefined cartons and weights. Perhaps there are actual weights, Drew has speculated—barbells and such. The Cotts walk heavily on their heels, and the floorboards in the Stickneys' apartment creak. Sometimes the lights flicker. There are shouts from next door that carry through even distant walls, there are exchanges of ribald laughter, quarrels that flare up like tiny fires and immediately subside, longer and more baroque quarrels that take up the better part of a weekend. The Cotts' oven door thumps heavily open, their refrigerator drones loudly, their faucets screech, their teakettle whistles obtrusively. There are drum strokes, trills, strings, and percussion. There are cadenzas of pure sound. Gargling, energetic toothbrushing, spitting, singing and humming, and every variety of foul noise in the bathroom, including toenail clipping. Katherine has imagined she hears the rushed uneven notes of an xylophone, Drew has imagined he hears castanets or bones being shaken. There are long expectant silences, often in the latter half of the evening, that are broken suddenly by inexplicable sounds—marbles rolling across the floor, a flurry of tiny scuttling claws against the wall? In bed Drew holds his bride so tight her frail ribs begin to ache. "I can't breathe," she says nervously. Even at such times she speaks with a faint air of apology. "You're hurting me, I can't breathe," she whispers. Drew says reproachfully, "Don't move."

As a girl in early adolescence Katherine had sometimes fainted. There is truth to the expression "light-headed" because at such times Katherine's skull was both suffused with light and queerly weightless. She fell as gracefully as possible, always sinking forward as if in a curtsy, her knees finally giving way—no strength to them at all. She had fainted perhaps less than a dozen times between the ages of thirteen and seventeen but she worried about the possibility of fainting at any time, in one of her enormous lecture classes, perhaps, or while preparing a meal in the tiny kitchen where the floor space wasn't large enough to accommodate her and where she might strike her head on the edge of the stove or the refrigerator. She worried too that she might lose consciousness while her husband was making love to her because without knowing it he was sometimes rather impatient and overenergetic. At the same time the idea of fainting exerts its appeal. It is a place that is *there* and not *here,* a world parallel to this world, very near, contiguous, but only rarely accessible. But Katherine has not fainted in some time.

"You think of *him,* don't you," Drew says accusingly.

"Of who?" Katherine asks.

"Of him. Them. The two of them," Drew says.

"Why should I think of them?" Katherine says in a faltering voice. "*When* do I think of them?"

"You know when," Drew says.

The Cotts communicate with the Stickneys through the thin plasterboard walls of the bedrooms that are side by side and parallel in a way Katherine cannot quite imagine. There are coughs, sneezes, nose-blowings, the raucous clearing of throats, every variation of snore: light cracklings, hums and purrs and rasping whirs, violent snorts that wake all four of them like an alarm. There are giggly exchanges, there are murmurous conversations at all hours, outbursts of incredulity and laughter, love moans, love demands, grunts, guttural exclamations, choked sobs (or laughter?), outcries that probably erupt from Holly Cott without her awareness, but that might come from Mack Cott too. Katherine shuts herself up like a telescope and sleeps. She doesn't hear, she doesn't allow herself to become disgusted or excited. Sometimes she is nearly asleep when Drew takes hold of her. She never turns from him because it is easier to give in though she cannot always understand his incoherent words as he kisses, sucks, pokes, pries into her. "Did I hurt you last night?" Drew may inquire in the morning with a boyish air of guilt. "I didn't mean to," he will say.

Sometimes Katherine slips from bed to lock herself in the bathroom and wash as thoroughly, though as quietly, as possible. She loves these times and thinks of them as secret times: the plumbing in the adjoining bathroom is silent for once, the shower isn't on, the toilet

| | | | |

isn't being robustly flushed. "I live alone here," Katherine tells her steamy mirror image. Her neck aches, her spinal column is afire, the skin of her breasts and inside her thighs is raw and chafed, something is running down her leg . . . semen or blood. . . . But she is alone in the little bathroom with the "bamboo" plastic shower curtain and the green throw rug from Sears and no one can interrupt.

Once or twice her reverie has been rudely violated, however, by one or the other of the Cotts. Bare heels sounding heavily on the floor, the bathroom door opened, the light switched on, a noisy and bubbling and protracted urination, the flush of the toilet, and then a second flush, perhaps, as if the first were ineffectual. Katherine switches off the light and retreats to her sleeping husband. "These are bonds we are establishing," she says. "These are trials we will cherish in later years."

Early October is sunny and humid enough to breed maggots in the unlidded and untidy garbage pails belonging to the Cotts, so that Drew spends much of an otherwise pleasant Saturday morning vomiting in the bathroom and murmuring repeatedly, so that Katherine can hear, "They can't do this. I won't let them. I'll kill them. This is my home, this is my wife."

After a while the gagging and retching stopped but Drew refused to open the door. Katherine knocked shyly. She told him she would take care of the garbage from now on. "Get away," Drew said savagely through the door. "I can't stand you always spying on me."

The Cotts are having a party, evidently. The sounds of laughter, music, gay high spirits, crowding and lunging, go on until very late: the last guest doesn't leave until after 4 A.M., the Cotts don't collapse into bed until 4:30. Drew guides Katherine's chill unresisting hand to him in the dark. She is made to stroke, squeeze, stroke again, and finally release. On the other side of the wall a confusion of bedsprings, grumpy chatter, Holly Cott's amusing sneeze—which is to say, a series of absurdly dainty high-pitched sneezes at odds with her fleshy bovine self. "Why did you marry me," Drew asks in a bitter panting voice, "if you don't love me? My father and mother were the same way," he says, but does not elaborate. Upon this occasion Katherine and the Cotts sink into sleep within a half hour but Drew lies moodily awake, thinking that it was unnatural of his parents to wish to have, and then actually to have, a baby at their age. His mother had been in her late forties, his father eight years older. Now they are elderly and becoming a problem to themselves and others. For instance, Mr. Stickney wears a hat and gloves to bed and insists on playing the radio at all times of the day and night, with the volume turned up high. According to Mrs. Stickney he is concerned that Jesus Christ may try to make contact with him over the radio and what if he hasn't turned it on . . . ? "It's too much responsibility for one person," Mrs. Stickney has said. She is thinking of turning her husband over to the Bible Baptist Church Independent Home for Aged and Unwell Persons in Bethlehem, Pennsylvania. Drew has neither consented nor protested: he considers the matter of his parents closed.

| | | | |

Katherine sits in her eight o'clock lecture class taking notes in her small precise hand. She has never fainted while taking notes, she suddenly realizes. After a while, however, she wakes to discover that her pen has drifted off the page and there is a growing ink blot on her skirt. She continues taking notes. At ten o'clock she returns to the same amphitheater, which is always slightly confusing. Holly Cott is sitting nearby. Her thick red-brown coil of hair has been flung back over her shoulder with a certain dash. She wears blue jeans that fit her plump buttocks snugly and a bright red cotton shirt with nothing beneath it. She waggles one foot in boredom and rarely takes notes. Her profile is porcine, puggish. Perhaps this isn't Holly Cott but a young woman who resembles her. Perhaps they are sisters: that slight hint of a double chin, just beginning. Katherine tries to clear her head of drowsiness and faintness by wondering at Holly Cott's calm placid *ordinary* manner in public. Katherine has observed her in the A&P on Linden, and in the student union, and in the university library—the young woman with the thick-coiled hair and the damp smile, groaning and sobbing and crying out in ecstasy, greedily thumping her head against the wall, clawing at Mack's shoulders, every night, or nearly every night, on the other side of the bedroom wall. "I don't hate you," Katherine tells Holly, "but your heart might burst one of these nights." But perhaps the young woman in Katherine's ten o'clock sociology class isn't Holly Cott after all. Drew has learned from somewhere that Mack Cott's wife is a swimmer of near Olympic status, and this young woman has flaccid shoulders and upper arms. In any case Katherine doubts that they will ever meet: it's mysterious, how the residents of 3A and 3B avoid one another.

"Once you're married and moved away," Katherine's mother has said, "you'll see things differently. You'll never see things the same again."

Later that day Katherine spies Holly Cott hand in hand with her lusty big-bellied husband, Mack, running up the steps of the side entrance to Shadrick Gymnasium where Red Cross volunteers are draining blood from donors. Mack Cott is perhaps six feet five inches tall, weighs two hundred twenty pounds, has wiry hair just perceptibly darker than his wife's, a rich loud guileless baritone laugh. He snores with zest; his lungs must have an enormous capacity. Katherine doesn't know whether she envies Holly Cott her light wet rasping snore in that man's arms, or whether she is revulsed by the thought. Once, lying sleepless and listening to them, Drew said wistfully, "Don't you hate *people* . . . ?" Katherine said, "But they can't help it, they're probably exhausted." Drew was too demoralized to reach for her and to bury himself in her, as he often did, blinking back tears, half sobbing and grunting. Katherine would have been pliant: she has never been high-strung or selfish or "strange." These are important vows we are making, she tells herself. A bond we are establishing for the rest of our lives.

She would have followed the Cotts into Shadrick Gymnasium to watch their bright red blood being drained from their arms, but the fear of growing light-headed and crashing to the floor amid strangers discouraged her. She has always been sickened by the sight of blood, even her own. In any case perhaps that couple wasn't the Cotts—

she has never really allowed herself a direct observation of Mack.

There are red-brown hairs in the Stickneys' bathroom, in the sink and at the bathtub drain. (The bathtub is also dirtier than Katherine remembers.) In the next-door apartment someone is scuffling. There are low delighted shouts, surprised giggles. Of course it is only puppyish grappling. Love play. Holly seizes Mack by his hair and wags his big head vigorously up and down; Mack seizes Holly by one of her thick ankles and twists it until she screams. He chases her around the apartment, through the three and a half rooms, his trousers unzipped and his rodlike penis in his hand. They are delirious, shameless, overgrown children. By accident Holly's nose is bloodied; even the beige wallpaper is splattered. When Katherine tells Drew, much later that night after he has returned exhausted and haggard from the monkey lab, he shakes his head and says primly, "That would never happen to us." For some reason Katherine is disappointed that he doesn't break into boyish laughter.

He *is* a handsome young man from the front, she *does* love him as she has never loved anyone before, male or female. It's a pity he has to work so hard, however; and such disagreeable things are being printed in the local newspaper as well as in the student newspaper, concerning "ethics" and "sanitation" in Fenner Hall. (Charges have been made that animals, including monkeys, are being unnecessarily tortured. Their eyes are removed from their sockets, their spinal columns sawed into segments, electrodes are introduced into their brains. Also, animal excrement and bloody matter sometimes back up in the plumbing in Fenner Hall. Monkey feces have dribbled down the walls of classrooms, lecture halls, and professors' offices on the fifth floor of the building. But Drew has nothing to do with these matters since he is only a research assistant under the supervision of Professor Tucker.) Katherine prepares chili con carne for her young husband, and spaghetti with Italian sauce, and chicken cooked with sage, tarragon, and onions. His favorite dish is veal but the Stickneys don't think they can afford veal. Sometimes when they sit at their candlelit table they can hear the Cotts sitting at *their* table only a few yards away. "They're having veal tonight," Drew says, sniffing. "Veal with peppers and mushrooms. A red wine sauce." Katherine says nothing. She lifts her slender trembling hands to cup the candle's flame, to keep it from being extinguished in the small fierce exhalation of her husband's breath.

Katherine's part-time typing and filing job at the law library is terminated but she doesn't tell Drew because she is afraid he will be angered. He has lost ten or twelve pounds in recent weeks, working all day in the laboratory, typing up his notes at night, sometimes not stumbling to bed until three in the morning. "I hope you will never lie to me," he whispers at such times. His lips are cracked and dry, his skin burning. "I hope *you* will never betray me," he says. Katherine wonders if having lost her job and being absent from her classes sporadically since the beginning of winter (the first sleet storm intimidated her, she hung behind with a half-dozen other young women

| | | | |

in the laundromat on University Place, staring out at the street and making no effort to move) constitute betrayal: and, if so, what punishment her husband will exact from her. He can be cruel. He can be impatient. Of course he is often gentle as well, and even romantic in the old sense of the word. "I don't want to live without you," he said when he proposed. His strained expression, his unblinking bloodshot gaze, his air of reproach convinced her. He forces her onto him as they lie in their bed snug against the wall, a few yards from the sleet-splattered windowpane. "Like this," he whispers. "God, you're clumsy." But his tone is good-natured, affectionate. She has begun to ache deep inside where her flesh is tight and dry but she is careful to give no indication. She is still a bride, she needn't worry about pregnancy, there is scandalous talk too about monkey, dog, and cat fetuses in Fenner Hall, unfortunate (and not very amusing) jokes about these things, but Katherine takes no notice. Drew fits her in place atop him. His skin burns but his hands are cold on her small tight buttocks. She is made to grind and circle, her face swelling and reddening like a boil, just like Holly Cott's on the other side of the wall. To calm herself she thinks of an enormous needle sunk into her forearm, draining her of blood; she thinks of her bearded sociology professor—a popular campus eccentric with a jocularly ridged face and beringed busy hands—lecturing animatedly on the family as a social institution (with emphasis upon the demographic determinants of its structure and life cycle); she thinks of a quarrel she'd heard between the Cotts as they were descending the stairs to the front hall and she was rapidly sorting through the mail, an exchange that was hardly more than ". . . you," "You . . ." and ". . . you!" with the connective tissue missing. There are a half-dozen letters for the Cotts nearly every day, sometimes handwritten, sometimes typed, to *The Cotts* or to *Holly & Mack Cott* or to *Mack Cott* or to *Mrs. Mack Cott,* letters from friends in some cases and from prospective employers, it seems, in other cases, though Katherine doesn't hold the envelopes up to the light, she wouldn't dream of prying open an envelope with her fingernail or allowing it to fall down behind the radiator to be lost forever amid the dust balls and other forgotten cards and letters and notices from the library regarding overdue books. (For one thing, she might discover that Mack Cott has been offered a job. And Drew is frantic about summer employment. And employment in general. If he brings the subject of the "future" up with any of his professors, even kindly and paternal Professor Mac-Murray, who is director of all the animal laboratories—vertebrates and otherwise—at the university, he is likely to be met with a stony silence, in his own bitter words. "They won't give me a chance to prove myself," Drew says, standing shivering in his underwear in the kitchen very late at night, his face creased and pallid in the light of the opened refrigerator—for at such times Katherine has followed him out into the kitchen, where he stands devouring slices of bread and jam without appetite, a guilty little boy. Wordlessly Katherine embraces her husband despite the rigidity of his posture and his air of subtle contempt. She feels her mother's presence and her mother's approval, though they have never discussed the situation in so many words.)

| | | | |

One lightless December dawn when the temperature in both 3A and 3B is 63 degrees F and the radiators are stone cold, Holly Cott gags and retches into the toilet, barefoot in her long soiled flannel nightgown, shadows and tucks beneath her eyes, and the Stickneys whisper together about her "condition": whether it might be considered by any stretch of the imagination as deliberate; whether Mack will let her have the baby or press for an abortion. "It would mean a severe drain on their finances if they had the baby," Drew observes. Katherine, her eyes half closed, feels the seepage of blood or semen in her own loins and gives thanks that *that* particular worry need not be hers, she knows how such an issue can injure a marriage irreparably. And then too if the wife insists upon having the baby isn't the husband displaced in her affections?—the visible evidence being the infant sucking at the milk-heavy breasts. She soothes Drew; she strokes his narrow sides, his smooth back, his wiry ash-blond hair. Some weeks before she had discovered him holding aloft a lighted match and regarding it with an odd half-smiling quizzical expression and she'd simply stood on tiptoe to blow it out coquettishly—she knew he wasn't serious and would never consider so extreme an act as arson, to rid them of their hateful neighbors. Aroused, Drew had snatched her wrist and turned it until her arm turned with it and was about to snap: or so it seemed in the excitement of the moment. Katherine begged for mercy and Drew lavishly granted it for he *did* love her, he claimed to have fallen in love with her at first sight, though such romantic excesses are foreign to his upbringing in the Bible Baptist Church Independent. She is encouraged to straddle him, for warmth. She is encouraged to fit herself to him while he grips her small tight buttocks with his kneading hands and whispers instructions into her ear. Sometimes he groans, sometimes he utters shocking words, but Katherine pretends they aren't for her ears—perhaps they are for the benefit of eavesdroppers? In any case Drew's cupped hands grip her tight as if she were precious to him and his upright rod is affixed to her, a shaft driven up deeply into her with no time to dwell idly and unproductively upon monkey convulsions or monkey excrement fouling the bottom of a clean cage, or whether important letters of his have been stolen from the downstairs foyer. The Cotts have been smoking more than usual in recent days—the Stickneys' apartment stinks of their cigarettes—and Drew knows from having examined their garbage that they consume inexpensive red wine and at least a case of beer a week and packaged frozen meals including Italia Pizza, trash foods with very little nourishment: in *that* area of life the Cotts are deficient! Drew has discovered too that Mack Cott is highly regarded in the engineering college but he tries not to feel a pang of envy at this precarious moment. After Katherine rolls from him and lies very still beside him, a strand of pale hair caught in her mouth, Drew says, "I think I'm strong enough now, I mean if my father dies." Katherine does not contradict him.

Katherine realizes she has missed any number of classes—but what has she done with her time, has she been wandering aimless around the campus?—when her mother telephones late one evening. The Cotts' phone has been

| | | | |

ringing off and on for hours, Mack isn't home, Holly must be curled up watching television, she pads heavily over to the phone and snatches it up and says, "Yes? Hello? Who is it?" in a singularly abrasive voice. The telephone rings in the Stickneys' apartment and Katherine hurries to answer it so that Drew won't be disturbed, he is typing out lecture notes on their faulty typewriter and drinking black coffee though the caffeine will keep him awake half the night. Katherine's mother is distraught and tearful. She tells Katherine that she has terrible news for her: Katherine wasn't her firstborn, as all the world believes, and she wasn't on purpose. She hadn't been a premeditated baby. "I don't understand," Katherine says. She keeps her voice neutral to spare Drew. "Why are you telling me this now?" Katherine's mother says that her firstborn was "out of wedlock," a darling little boy named Bobby who was given out to adoption but (she later discovered) died before his first birthday as his tiny heart was defective. "After that I got sick and was sick for a long time," Katherine's mother says. Her voice has gained strength but sounds unfamiliar. "For years," she says. "Then I got married and had you and though I loved you from the first you can see that there has been a curse over us both. . . ." Katherine lets her ramble on for a few minutes. The telephone in the Cotts' apartment is ringing. Katherine wonders if her fainting spells and her habit—a self-defeating habit, Drew has affectionately called it—of crowding all her lecture notes together *in one paragraph* might not spring from her uncertain relationship with her mother. She has never brought up the subject with Drew because she senses his embarrassment regarding certain intimate subjects. "It might be better for us to remain mysteries to each other," Drew has said. He particularly dislikes her spying on him: though when she opened the bathroom door to see him standing with his ear against the wall, slender and shivering in his underpants, it had not been deliberate and she had been as embarrassed as he. As for Katherine's father, he had been a car salesman who wore a cardboard bowler hat while on duty. He developed cancer of the mouth and throat at an early age (thirty-six) as a consequence, Katherine's mother said accusingly, of his "filthy habit" of pipe smoking. The house was fouled with pipe smoke for years. Clothes, hair, linens. . . . Katherine's father spoke infrequently around the house because he was always sucking on his pipe, but after the cancer began he wasn't able to talk, whether he had wanted to or not. *This,* Katherine thinks suddenly, might account for her fainting spells. She says goodbye to her mother politely and hangs up. Holly Cott is still talking on her phone.

Katherine's notes are a single paragraph broken by such notations as *Tuesday, Friday a.m.,* etc. She has stopped attending classes. She seems not to have made a decision—a conscious decision, as the saying goes—to stop attending classes, but one morning she realizes that there is an examination in her Introduction to Anthropology class and she hasn't attended lectures or quiz sections for a considerable period of time. The thought of taking this exam makes her feel faint so she erases it from her consciousness. She *does* attend classes, lectures, slide demonstrations, symposia. Her days are remorselessly filled. Her notebook paragraph grows longer, denser, filled with unfamiliar and provocative expressions like "vector squares," "matrix symbology," "Tacitus," "Morte d'Arthur," "diagenesis," and "excitable membranes." She attends lectures every afternoon at 4:30, sometimes slipping out of one amphitheater to run across the snowy campus to another, where "emerging African nations" are being discussed, or "current developments in symbolic logic." She attends a lively symposium on Sir Gawain and mingles with the guests at a wine and cheese party in honor of a distinguished visitor from Oxford, though she isn't hungry: her appetite has been depressed of late, perhaps because of the vomiting. She wears her long brown coat, her gray wool slacks, her beige sweater. Often she forgets to take her beige wool cap off her head and is (perhaps) becoming a familiar and fond sight at the lectures. She is usually intense, though her mind might wander too. In the midst of a slide lecture on quattrocento art she remembers that she left the front burner of the stove on beneath the teakettle and by now all the water must have whistled away and both apartments filled with steam: so it's necessary to excuse herself, tripping over legs and feet. Drew isn't home in any case, nor is Mack: but Holly might be home in bed: she is sick often these days, the toilet is always flushing, there are queer sounds like Ping-Pong balls flying about and striking surfaces. Katherine's menstrual period is more or less continuous these days so she knows that *she* cannot be pregnant.

"I'm sorry," Katherine whispers.

But Drew turns away with a bitter tremulous smile. He has been a young husband now for more than two hundred days.

Katherine is becoming familiar with the women's rooms of certain university buildings. She feels an odd nostalgic kinship with the loneliness peculiar to the fourth-floor women's room in the Hall of Languages; she recognizes at once the cloudy mirrors and littered sinks of the basement women's room in Lyle Hall (where the toilet's flushing mechanism is operated by a chain); she admires the tricky geometrical pattern in the tile floor of the larger of the two women's rooms in Brattle Hall. (She and Holly Cott have nearly collided in this lavatory when Holly rushed in with a nosebleed and Katherine was pressing paper towels soaked in cool water against her forehead. But in the confusion of the moment neither seems to have noticed the other.) Katherine spends a moderate amount of time reading the scrawled messages on the lavatory walls because she has a superstitious fear that one might be for her. There are also doodles, drawings, puzzling riddles *(What has five sides and a top but no bottom?)*, prayers *(Dear Jesus take my side)*. If she were not so shy and reserved she might add one or two sentences of her own, but the problem is: to write a single message means to exclude all the rest, and how can she choose? There is also the worry that she might become overwhelmed and continue writing until the entire wall was filled.

Katherine isn't afraid to go home because of Drew or the next-door neighbors. She has made a healthy adjustment to changing circumstances. (For instance, the Cotts' acquisition of a television set. It seems to be placed against the Stickneys' living room wall, directly behind their sofa; but, since it is portable, it is sometimes moved into the bedroom.) In the meantime Katherine is supplementing her education in a way her late father would have approved of. She takes complex notes on kinship customs in Bali, and the significance of the cockfight; she is deeply moved, though of course does not join in the animated discussion, at an open symposium on the subject of the interplay between free enterprise and nuclear armaments. She rarely frequents Fenner Hall except for the vending machine canteen on B-level because of the poor ventilation system and the dampness underfoot, but one afternoon by accident she sees a skinny tight-faced young man in a stained laboratory apron standing brooding by a window, and it is a moment or two before she realizes that it is her husband, Drew. How haggard he looks these days, and how his silky ash-blond hair is thinning! Katherine feels a pang of remorse. She will make it up to him tonight: perhaps she can prepare a veal stew with peppers, onions, and carrots. He is sweet despite his occasional temper outbursts, and he never means to hurt her. Afterward he is always convincingly repentant. They lie together in their private bed weeping quietly and rocking in each other's arms. Katherine wipes her eyes on Drew's cotton undershirt. Drew becomes aroused and burrows eagerly into her body. "These are vows we are making in the flesh," Katherine murmurs. "There is no sin involved."

Still, she does not reveal herself to Drew when she comes upon him in Fenner Hall because he is angry if he suspects he is being spied upon. "There's enough of that sort of thing going on next door," he says, with a brusque nod of his head toward 3B.

Katherine has observed Mack Cott in the Rexall's Drugstore at the foot of Linden. He is tall and husky and, she supposes, handsome, if one's taste runs in that direction. His hair is windblown because, unlike Drew, he refuses to wear a hat. His quilted khaki windbreaker has many mysterious pockets, zippers, and buckles. When he looks at Katherine his eyes are revealed as a surprising steely blue but he doesn't appear to recognize her. Why are you and your wife systematically destroying my marriage? Katherine would like to ask. Why have you poisoned our happiness? But of course she says nothing. She watches him covertly as he pays for his purchases—a package of razor blades, a vial of prescription capsules—and strides out of the store. He is uncouth and bearish despite his reputation as a promising engineer. In fact he is an impersonal force of nature, Katherine thinks, and it's absurd to take him seriously.

Not long afterward, when Drew loses control of his patience and raps sharply against the bedroom wall to reprimand the shameless couple a few yards away, Mack Cott responds by pounding furiously against the wall for fifteen or twenty seconds. There are also muffled expletives from both Cotts. The Stickneys are so shaken by the episode that they spend the remainder of the night on the living room sofa, where Drew cannot sleep at all. A powerful artery throbs in his forehead and his fingers twitch with the desire to do violence: but of course these are only wayward and insubstantial fancies.

An atavistic impulse, Drew thinks calmly. One not worthy of him.

Sometimes, alone in the apartment, Drew presses his ear against the wall and hears only the uncertain beat of his own heart. Or perhaps it is his neighbor's heart, if

| | | | |

Mack Cott is similarly pressed up against the wall . . . ? Sometimes he hears a faint sigh, and the silky sound of cloth swinging against voluptuous female flesh. Holly Cott hums mindlessly under her breath and pads about barefoot in her underwear, her freshly shampooed hair wild about her shoulders. Despite his repugnance for her Drew begins to feel aroused. He wonders if her soft plump belly has begun to bulge in pregnancy; or whether she has secretly had an abortion. As for Katherine—often they lie side by side in their rumpled bed, against the wall, sleepless and hostile to each other's warmth. "No," Katherine says. "I don't want to, I don't feel well," Katherine says stiffly. "Why did you marry me, then?" Drew asks, grinning up at the ceiling. "Why did you marry anyone, then?" But the bitch has no answer—of course.

Still, they are quickly reconciled. This phase of their marriage is still the "honeymoon phase," so many gray gritty featureless winter days propel them into each other's arms, no matter that the Cotts are having another drunken party, or stinking up the entire third floor with Holly's incense. Katherine dissolves often in tears, perhaps because the strategy is so becoming. Drew dries his bride's eyes with his undershirt, kisses her breasts reverently, whispers in triumph, "We are married—*married*," in her ear, and, after a certain number of minutes, rises trembling above her in the dark to fit himself into her and to make husbandly love. Her thighs are unresisting, her belly warm and flat, her mouth a dark floating oval, she rarely cries out in alarm or pain. Between her smooth pale thighs she is moist and ready for him, though sometimes dry and tight and unprepared for him, but she embraces him passionately and rarely shrinks away. "We aren't really married—are we?" she asked once, with a catch in her throat Drew could not interpret: lascivious amusement, somnolent alarm, he couldn't have said. His pleasure in his bride's body is roughly equivalent to a gunshot that is slow, even sluggish at first, and then suddenly violent, unstoppable, with the risk of pain: then again it is (perhaps) equivalent to the electrically induced convulsions in certain mammals in the animal laboratories of Fenner Hall. But in general, enraptured with his bride and his own vigorous lovemaking, Drew does not trouble himself over such quibbles.

When he thinks of his father, Drew remembers expert advice given to him by one of his biology professors at his undergraduate college. The gist of it is that while mourning is "natural" and certainly not to be disregarded, one must understand that the earth—its land surface, its vast seas, its very atmosphere—would be choked beyond calculation by millions upon countless millions of creatures that refused to die and decompose. *That refused to die and decompose.* "The clock alone is a means of biological salvation," this professor said gnomically. "Time simplifies." Drew did not fully comprehend these words but he broods over them often. In recent weeks he has brooded over them very often.

Someday, perhaps, he will share them with his young wife. At the present, however, he fears becoming too intimate with her—too weakly dependent upon her. He has even begun to wonder if he married at too young an age.

| | | | |

Katherine frequently walks in the little park at the far end of Harrow Street. She is timid about returning to the apartment because the Cotts' schedules and her own husband's schedule have become erratic of late. (She cannot remember with confidence when Drew has an early day—Tuesday, is it, or Thursday?—or when he has a two-hour break between classes and laboratory and might drop back at the apartment for a brief fatigued nap.) In recent days too the Cotts have been exchanging sharp if not altogether intelligible words.

Hello, she will say shyly when she sees Holly Cott sitting on one of the park benches, I'm your next-door neighbor in that terrible house. But I wish you no harm.

Perhaps Holly will invite Katherine to sit beside her. Embarrassed, tongue-tied, she will be gradually drawn out of her solitude by the more gregarious young woman: before long they will be comparing notes on their husbands, exchanging recipes, laughing uproariously. Oh but aren't we *awful,* one will say, wiping her eyes. Do you think this constitutes marital betrayal . . . ?

But the park is empty at this time of year. There are no lovers strolling hand in hand, no mothers with small children, only a middle-aged woman with frazzled blond hair and a vacant stare—a woman Katherine remembers having seen at a number of the university lectures. She is always seated prominently in the front row, her thick legs crossed. She wears a long shapeless black coat and her stockings are badly wrinkled. Katherine senses that she must avoid this woman, who is doubtless insane.

("Is something wrong? Why are you crying? Would you like me to hold you?" etc. These are the things the madwoman would probably say to Katherine.)

Katherine walks briskly along the graveled paths. She is a tall, poised, very pretty young woman. She wears a beige knit cap pulled low on her forehead, and her pale blond hair falls to her shoulders. Her breath steams daintily. Her eyes are bright and alert. Perhaps the wind from the northeast is blowing unwanted thoughts out of her head. . . . Perhaps in fifteen or twenty years she will revisit this park on a balmy May afternoon, having walked along Harrow Street past "that" house of grimy buff-colored brick where her marriage (her first marriage?) came to an end. . . . After all, she consoles herself, there *is* another Katherine.

SOMETIMES I AM SICK & ASHAMED OF THE WHOLE HUMAN RACE a young woman has written in careful block letters on the wall of the Lyle Hall women's room. Katherine then discovers the same message in the same block letters in the women's room on A-level in the library, with these words added: JESUS CHRIST OR ANYONE (!!!) HELP ME.

"Why did you marry me if you don't love me?" Drew asks wistfully.

Katherine tries to laugh airily. She uncurls herself from the sofa and goes to his chair to kiss him on the forehead, or on the crown of his head where his hair is thinning.

In 3B someone walks heavily on his heels. A telephone is being dialed: every *click* is recorded.

Katherine whispers, "I don't know what you mean."

"You know what I mean," Drew says with a bitter little smile.

| | | | |

"Why did you marry me if you don't love me?" Drew asks.

Katherine is playing with a strand of hair, biting it, as if she were an innocent little girl and not a married woman. She tries to keep her fear from sounding in her voice. "What do you mean?" she says.

"You know," says Drew neutrally.

"I don't," Katherine whispers. "I don't know."

They stare at each other helplessly. In the apartment next door someone is yanking a vacuum cleaner around. The mechanism roars and then is shut off for a minute or two: then begins again. Despite the companionable noise, fear is general in both apartments. The air is tinged with panic, simply to breathe it is to risk terror.

"You know," Drew whispers, staring at his bride.

It is the improvised nature of human life that accounts for the prevalence of unhappiness, Katherine writes in her notebook. She is attending a lecture in the Hall of Languages. *But this factor also contributes to instances of "oceanic feeling,"* Katherine faithfully transcribes. She had shut herself up like a telescope for the sake of peace but these words of wisdom penetrated her solitude. *The improvised nature,* Katherine writes again. She underlines the words in red ballpoint ink.

The next time she lies sleepless on the third floor of the house on Harrow Street, Katherine promises herself, she will remember this. It is useless to worry about other things, things beyond her control: for instance, she is probably not pregnant, despite the occasional seizures of vomiting. These nights, Drew sleeps fitfully because of his worries about the future. His breathing is feathery and damp and sometimes there is a sharp catch in his throat that wakes her, though he continues sleeping. Mack Cott's snoring is abrasive and sometimes erupts into a snort. As for Holly—her breathing is hoarse and arrhythmic and Katherine often suspects she isn't asleep at all but only pretending.

It is in late January when the Stickneys are jolted awake by a terrible commotion in the apartment next door.

They clutch each other beneath the covers, frightened. What on earth is happening? It is just past two o'clock in the morning and there are shouts, poundings, the sound of splintering wood, footsteps on the stairs. Doors are slammed open and shut. Very shortly a siren screams up Harrow and more voices and footsteps are heard on the stairs. Then there is another siren, an ambulance. Drew stands cringing at the window but can only see a reflection of the flashing rotation red light in the windowpane of the house next door.

"Is it a fire? Has someone set a fire? What will happen to us?" Katherine whispers.

Drew tiptoes back to bed. They lie together huddled beneath the covers. In the apartment next door ambulance attendants are carrying Holly Cott out on a stretcher and dazed weeping unshaven Mack is trotting ineffectually behind. He has thrown on his quilted khaki windbreaker with the many zippered pockets and buckles over his pajamas; he has jammed his bare feet into his boots. "I was afraid something like this might happen," Katherine says, shivering convulsively in her husband's protective embrace. The Stickneys wonder if seepage from the blood in the Cotts' bathtub will manifest itself in their own. Drew has promised to check first—to spare Katherine the shock.

"I think things will work out," he whispers into her neck.

Before the next tenants move into 3B in mid-February the Stickneys enjoy a second honeymoon. Like newlyweds they hold hands frequently—when their schedules coincide and they are home together in their apartment they sometimes hold hands *constantly,* like high school sweethearts who realize they are being excessive and sentimental but don't care. Katherine has decorated the apartment with crudely gay and uplifting color posters of certain paintings of Van Gogh, including "Sunflowers"; she indulged herself in a dime-store spree and brought home a plastic bowl containing three beautiful goldfish, and an inexpensive but attractive bathroom shag rug to replace the one that was stained, and a half-dozen incense candles dipped "by hand." When Drew isn't at the monkey laboratory until midnight they often curl up on the living room sofa, the brushed velvet pillows (also from the dime store) propped up behind them, each reading a book and making underlinings. Often Katherine allows her touseled head to sink into Drew's accommodating shoulder; often he slides his arm around her slender waist. It is very quiet next door.

If in secret one of the Stickneys presses an ear against the wall it's mainly silence that pervades—even the alarm clock in the Cotts' bedroom has run down. There are faint indecipherable pulsations and footsteps, the sounds of toenails being clipped, a teakettle lifted from the stove just as it begins to whistle, and the usual shiftings of snow or sand on the roof: but the Stickneys have long since learned to ignore such distractions. "I have no doubt but they are imaginary," Katherine has said.

One afternoon when Drew is at the laboratory Mack Cott, or a bearish young man resembling him, returns to 3B with two friends and clears the apartment out, packing books, plates, household items, and every sort of miscellaneous trash in cardboard cartons and carrying the furniture downstairs to a rented U-Haul van. Katherine does not step out into the hall to express her sympathy to Mack Cott, or to say goodbye, because she has just shampooed her hair and is wearing a bathrobe. She is very shy in any case and shrinks from forcing herself on other people even to offer condolences. "What the hell did you do with the keys?" one of the men shouts down two flights of stairs to another. The answer is inaudible. Katherine stands with her ear against the just-opened door of 3A but cannot hear any reply, or even discern who has spoken—Mack Cott or an anonymous buddy.

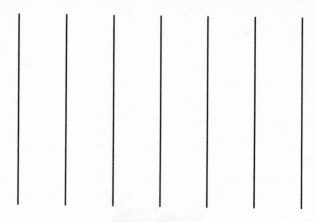

HAPPY

She flew home at Christmas, and her mother and her mother's new husband met her at the airport. Her mother hugged her hard and told her she looked pretty, and her mother's new husband shook hands with her and told her, Yes, she sure did look pretty, and welcome home. His sideburns grew razor-sharp into his plump cheeks and changed color, graying, in the lower part of his face. In his handshake her hand felt small and moist, the bones close to cracking. Her mother hugged her again—God I'm so happy to see you—veins in her arms ropier than the girl remembered, the arms themselves thinner, but her mother was happy, you could feel it all about her.

The pancake makeup on her face was a fragrant peach shade that had been blended skillfully into her throat. On her left hand she wore her new ring: a small glittering diamond set high in spiky white-gold prongs.

They stopped for a drink at Easy Sal's off the expressway, the girl had a club soda with a twist of lime (*That's* fancy, her mother said), her mother and her mother's new husband had martinis on the rocks which were their "celebration" drinks. For a while they talked about what the girl was studying and what her plans were, and when that subject trailed off they talked about their own plans, getting rid of the old house, that was one of the first chores, buying something smaller, newer, or maybe just renting temporarily. There's a new condominium village by the river, the girl's mother said, we'll show you when we drive past; then she smiled at something, took a swallow of her martini, squeezed the girl's arm, and leaned her head toward hers, giggling. Jesus, she said, it just makes me so happy, having the two people I love most in the world right here with me. Right here right now. A waitress in a tight-fitting black satin outfit brought two more martinis and a tiny glass bowl of beer nuts. Thanks, sweetheart! her mother's new husband said.

The girl had spoken with her mother no more than two or three times about her plans to be remarried, always long distance; her mother kept saying, Yes, it's sudden in your eyes but this kind of thing always is, you know right away or you don't know at all. Wait and see. The girl said very little, murmuring Yes or I don't know or I suppose so. Her mother said in a husky voice, He makes me feel like living again, I feel, you know, like a woman again, and the girl was too embarrassed to reply. As long as you're happy, she said.

Now it was nearly eight-thirty and the girl was light-headed with hunger, but her mother and her mother's new husband were on their third round of drinks. Easy Sal's had entertainment, first a pianist who'd been playing background music, old Hoagy Carmichael favorites; then a singer, female, black, V-necked red spangled dress; then a comedian, a young woman of about twenty-six, small bony angular face, no makeup, punk hairdo, dark brown, waxed, black fake-leather jumpsuit, pelvis thrust forward in mock-*Vogue*-model stance, her delivery fast brash deadpan in the nature of mumbled asides, thinking aloud, as if the patrons just happened to overhear, The great thing about havin' your abortion early in the day is, uh, like y'know the rest of the day's, uh, gonna be fuckin' uphill, right? There's these half-dozen people in a, uh, Jacuzzi—uh, lesbians in a hot tub, hot new game called "musical holes," uh, maybe it just ain't caught on yet in New Jersey's why nobody's laughin', huh?—the words too quick and muttered for the girl to catch but her mother and her mother's new husband seemed to hear, in any case they were laughing though afterward her mother's new husband confided he did not approve of dirty language issuing from women's lips, whether they were dykes or not.

They stopped for dinner at a Polynesian restaurant ten miles up the Turnpike, her mother explaining that there wasn't anything decent to eat at home, also it was getting late wasn't it, tomorrow she'd be making a big

dinner, That's okay honey isn't it? She and her new husband quarreled about getting on the Turnpike then exit-
ing right away, but at dinner they were in high spirits
again, laughing a good deal, holding hands between courses,
sipping from each other's tall frosted bright-colored trop-
ical drinks. Jesus I'm crazy about that woman, her mother's new husband told the girl when her mother was in
the powder room. Your mother is a high-class lady, he
said; he shifted his cane chair closer, leaned moist and
warm, meaty, against her, an arm across her shoulders.
There's nobody in the world precious to me as that
lady, I want you to know that, he said, and the girl said,
Yes, I know it, and her mother's new husband said in a
fierce voice close to tears, Damn right, sweetheart: you
know it.

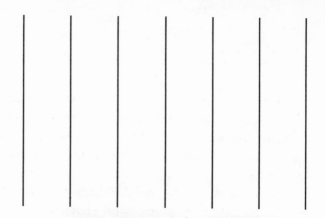

ANCIENT AIRS, VOICES

TIMESPEEDEDUP: *November 22, 1983*

Eighteen years and five months will be a matter of (as the coroner afterward estimates) forty minutes' erasure. There is beauty in such economy. There is nobility of a sort. There is also, as Mikey had not dared to anticipate, a leisurely pace to the procedure because the heart's frightened pumping grows progressively weaker (and less frightened) as the pressure of the blood decreases.

A mathematical equation, an inverse ratio of some sort?—Mikey settles himself into the tepid bathwater, eyes closed, to think about it.

SUPERSTITION

When Mikey's mother, Helen, was much younger than he is at the time of his death, when she was in fact a slightly precocious eleven or twelve, she played at scaring herself and her girlfriends with: *What is the worst thing that can happen?*

Whatever they said, whatever horror (usually personal and domestic) they came up with, Helen would say, But isn't there something worse?

Yes, okay, but isn't there something worse?

Yes, but—

But—

She saw that it was more powerful to be in control of questions, not answers. *What is the worst thing that can happen?*

When she was twenty-four years old and pregnant with her unknown yet-to-be-named baby, when her sharp angles and jumpy nerves were plumped out in a ripe rosy blood-warm well-being that couldn't be hers yet *was*— when she thought secretly of herself as swollen with love (love *for,* love *of,* both her husband and the yet-to-be-named baby)—it occurred to her one day, crossing Harvard Square at an imprudent angle and at an ill-calculated moment (cautionary yellow about to change to red) precisely what the worst thing would be.

She told Neil about it that night in bed, whispering. She expected him to comfort her though it was late, past midnight, and he had a moot court session the next morning at eight. (He so often comforted her these days. These weeks. He was, as both his parents commented,

| | | | |

not quite approvingly, "growing up fast.") But he responded impatiently, rubbing his forearm against his face, snorting with exasperation, as if Helen brought up such morbid things all the time now, and he'd had enough. That's superstition, he said angrily. You don't know it but that's superstition: trying to define the very worst so that it can't happen because if you define it it *can't* happen as you have defined it.

That isn't true, Helen said, drawing away from him.

What isn't true—that it's superstition, or that, if you define something to yourself, it can't happen? Neil asked.

She fashioned a little cocoon for herself of the bedclothes, at the very edge of the bed. She doubled the pillow up uncomfortably beneath her head. She was waiting to cry—tears had their own authority now—but nothing happened. When she and Neil quarreled a curious sort of flamelike rage shot up between them, instantaneous and unpremeditated, heart-stopping in its virulence. Yet it meant nothing, they loved each other; they were in fact—were to be for five, six more years—deeply in love with each other.

DESIRE

These are the classic years of romance, of adulterous romance, when to think of desire is to immediately experience desire; and to think of (nobly, contemptuously) resisting desire is to immediately experience desire. Though Neil and his friend Garrett's wife are not conscious, at the time, of their good fortune.

These are the years of romance, bittersweet in memory; and of desire so potent it plucks at the roots of one's being. But these are not, in retrospect, years of love. (Neil is waiting, he tells himself, for desire to shade into love. Desire *must* shade into love. But he waits impatiently, resentfully. At times he fantasizes dying with Yvette—by accident, only by accident—while driving on the Turnpike, for instance, crashing into a retaining wall.)

Neil is thirty-seven when the affair begins, Yvette is thirty-one, Neil's son Mikey is ten years old, Yvette's daughter Sonya is seven. Guilty, flushed with pride, the lovers talk about their children often: each pretends a genuine interest in the other's child. Mikey is the brightest boy in his fifth-grade class; Sonya is a sweetheart, so pretty. Mikey doesn't seem to make friends easily; Sonya is so *spoiled*. Does Mikey sense that something is . . . strained between his parents? Sonya, fortunately, cheerful chattering Sonya, notices nothing.

They agree that they love their children, they love their children more than, well, their own lives. Neil grows vehement on the subject, Yvette frequently cries. Sweet, bittersweet, agitated, *poignant*. . . .

THE UNFORGIVABLE

You aren't thinking, God damn you, Neil whispers, so that Helen, who is sobbing, cannot quite hear. It is one of their minor quarrels: no one will be slapped, pummeled, thrown shrieking across a bed, banged against a closet door; no one will pull books or records off a shelf, or smash china in the kitchen, in a trance of hysteria. In-

| | | | |

deed, the quarrel is so minor, it will soon be forgotten; except, perhaps, by the Schuelers' son.

Again, whispering, panting, Neil says, *You're thinking with your—womb.*

These are the frantic jumbled months of 1975, the era of unforgivable insults that are not quite said out loud; and not quite heard.

(Except, perhaps, little Michael hears. Dark-eyed spiky-haired little Michael, Mikey as his grandmother calls him, who soon becomes an expert in things said and not said, heard and not heard. Michael, who gets uniformly high grades in school—*very* high grades in arithmetic, then math—with an aristocratic sort of contempt for the mere act of performing, competing, *earning.* Mikey, of whom both his parents appear to be nervously proud—no, of course they *are* proud, excitedly informed by one of the boy's teachers that his I.Q. has been measured at 183 and his "creative potential" is in the very highest percentile.)

Of course the guilty lovers insult each other as well, say unforgivable things, things calculated to do great injury—to lacerate, pierce, penetrate, demolish. Simply by accusing Neil of not loving her, Yvette has the power of rendering him frantic; simply by walking out, slamming a door (not by design, that's the frightening thing, but furiously, helplessly), Neil Schueler the amiable, the congenial, the entirely *reliable* husband-father-son-brother-colleague-citizen) has the power to reduce Yvette Held to an anguish so physical, so overwhelming, she imagines her bodily gravity has increased tenfold. What to do on such days but crawl into bed, hide away her misery, allow Garrett to console her without knowing why he is consoling her . . . without knowing whom, precisely, he consoles. What's wrong Yvette, what's wrong please tell me, are you sick Yvette should I call a doctor Yvette please tell me what's *wrong*—the lament of many a kindly husband, in the year of romance 1975. While across town at the Schuelers' Helen discerns but cannot bring herself to name the love abscess working in her husband's gut; and one evening it is Mikey, cautious little Mikey, who plays suddenly at being a much younger child and huddles in his pajamas in his daddy's lap, burrowing into Daddy's chest, begging, giggling, begging, You aren't going to go away are you Daddy . . . You *aren't* going to go away *are* you Daddy . . . ?

Guilt, improvisation, despairing delight, O delightful bowel-wrenching despair. The usual. Yet it's the first time, such fancies: telephone calls hot and breathless as bouts of love made from, for instance, a forgotten hotel in a forgotten midwestern city, when Neil, sick with love, anxious to "finally get things straight," excuses himself in the awkward midst of a luncheon meeting, an important luncheon meeting, to rush away to his room on the forty-ninth floor and dial the Held residence back home—to speak with Yvette, with whom he'd spoken (and quarreled) at eleven-thirty that very morning. Yet another instance: Yvette, feverish, sleepless, slips away from her sleeping husband, walks barefoot past the door (always slightly ajar, to accommodate her nighttime fears) of her sleeping daughter, descends into the darkened kitchen to dial the number, *that* number, of her presumably

||||

sleeping lover some three or four miles away . . . and the phone is answered on the first ring . . . by Neil? or by Helen? or little Mikey? And she quickly hangs up.

November 1973

In Cunningham's Drugs beneath the too-bright fluorescent lighting she stands tall and splendid in a camel's-hair coat, her blond hair glittering as if with chips of mica, lightly scolding her pouting little girl (such a beautiful child!—Neil feels an actual pang of loss, why hadn't he and Helen had another child, a girl, to balance Mikey), unaware of Neil Schueler a few yards away. Yes, she's the one, that woman, *her,* though he knows himself invisible and harmless, her husband's friend Neil, married to pretty dark Helen whom he loves and whom he would no more think of betraying than . . . than he would betray the confidence of the prestigious law firm for which he works.

Parties, dinners, accidental meetings in other people's homes, occasional (increasingly frequent) sightings in town, the public library, the dry cleaners, the Village Market, and always he's invisible, supremely innocent, he isn't spying on Yvette Held (*he* isn't that sort of man, happily married, thoroughly content with his life) . . . and she isn't aware of him. Except, perhaps, obliquely.

A wintry November afternoon, pitch dark at five-thirty, and again Neil happens to see her by accident, at the Texaco station, again in the camel's-hair coat, a sporty striped scarf wound around her throat, she's upset, she's arguing with one of the mechanics, he had promised her car for five o'clock but now he tells her it won't be ready for another hour, maybe an hour and a half, and she doesn't know what to do, it's so trivial and demeaning a thing but what should she *do:* sit in the freezing waiting room and wait for her car, or call Garrett, have him pick her up, get the car in the morning. . . .

Neil offers to drive her home. Of course.

It's so trivial and demeaning, says Yvette, wiping angrily at her nose, and Neil says gravely, happily, I don't think it is.

THE WIVES

. . . are not friends though they might be said to have been, at one time, "friendly acquaintances."

Helen is nearly forty-four when the Master of Mikey's residential college at Yale telephones with the news (two days before Thanksgiving of 1983); Yvette is thirty-nine. Both women are invariably "young for their age" whatever their current age: the remark (generally made by a man) is of course meant to be flattering.

Helen, who thinks of herself as numb, hollow, emptied out, as if (for instance) she'd had a massive gynecological operation, is a very attractive woman: small-boned, olive-skinned, with damp dark eyes and a delicate high-bridged nose, a small mouth. She becomes starkly visible to her husband only when something in the household goes wrong *and someone is to blame.* Otherwise, she is invisible to him and he loves her. He loves her well enough. No—he doesn't love her at all (why lie about it?) but he is responsible for her, a little frightened of her (her drinking, her spasms of cruel silent laughter, her *eyes*),

| | | | |

worried about her effect (her "neurotic" behavior) upon their son.

Yvette, the beloved, the object of desire, is tall, rangy, blond, with a wide oval face and strong cheekbones, gray-green eyes, a fleshy mouth. She mugs, she jokes, she makes faces, her gestures are loose and casual, her confidence in herself (her beauty, her power) is absolute: is it possible she has never grown up? She dresses with a stylish silly chic, Chinese woolen jackets, suede trousers and vests, high-heeled boots, fur-lined caps, white silk dresses, and pale hair in tiny tight braids coiled prettily about her head. Her secret is a terrifying craving for forbidden foods (Planters peanuts devoured in fistfuls, M&M's by the bag, French fries lurid with salty grease), which she combats by going on impromptu fasts, once or twice a month, losing so much weight (what exhilaration, to starve herself!—it's better than sex) her pelvis bones begin to show through her tightest pair of jeans and her cagey eyes are all shadow. At such times she exults in feeling light-headed, transparent, angelic. She exults in the fact that two highly attractive men—her husband and her lover—watch anxiously over her.

Even before Helen learned specifically of the affair she bravely asked Neil whether he wanted a divorce; whether he wanted a trial separation; whether he might be happier without her. (Don't be ridiculous, Neil said at once, frightened, excited, you don't know what you're talking about.) Helen has a master's degree in biology, Helen plans to return to graduate school soon, she is fully capable (as she says, often) of living her own independent life.

As for Yvette: she intimidates Garrett simply by *hinting* . . . if he isn't entirely happy (with her moods, her treatment of Sonya, her circle of youngish friends) . . . he has the "option" of moving out.

Yvette is *loved,* Helen is *not-loved,* and is there any logical reason? There is not. There is not. As Neil would be the first to admit.

(Indeed, he sometimes imagines closing his fingers, hard, around Yvette's throat. The squirming eel-like body, the magnificent muscled legs, all that *blondness* . . . erased forever. This is the woman who deserves pain, humiliation, rejection, and not poor Helen, who is so . . . undeserving.)

The wives, the wives. So many. Yet they are not interchangeable parts, that's the problem. As Neil would be the first to admit.

THE SEVEN BRIDGES OF KÖNIGSBERG

She is awake, walking about the house in the dark, he knows she is touching things, groping, trying to keep her balance; he feels the tension, tightening, in her head. She has become a blind woman, prowling downstairs in the dark, sometimes her eyes *are* shut tight, does he dare to approach her?—touch her?—take her cold limp hand in his?

Mother I hate you. Mother please die.

But no: Mother I love you, *Mother please don't die.*

Michael Schueler's father is away: a conference in Brussels, a meeting in Frankfurt, confidential business in Tokyo. He telephones home dutifully, talking five minutes to Helen, five minutes to Mikey. He's a good father, he calls home. (It's true that he moved out for a while—a few weeks when Mikey was fourteen—but that's ancient history now, that's long forgotten.) There are Occasions: Thanksgiving, Christmas, the usual birthdays, Easter Sunday, Grandma's funeral, Mikey's First Prize at the State Science Fair. There are comradely father-son Saturday mornings in the car, doing errands, taking Mikey to the dentist, stopping by the public library, that sort of thing, afterward raking leaves (in season), shoveling snow (in season), digging up the flower beds (in season) for Mother to plant her wax begonias and impatiens. Mikey calmly notes the *routine,* the *logic,* the *normalcy.* The Schuelers are (are *almost*) a television family, they strike the observing eye as so routine and so normal, and clearly they're an attractive threesome: mother and son dark and ferret-faced, father tall sandy-haired embarrassed scowling smiling, the skin crinkling heartily about his eyes. Hey Dad!

Mikey listens hard, but no longer hears the quarrels.

Were they a fiction of his boyhood?—his childhood?

Had he imagined everything?

Little Michael Schueler who isn't precisely popular at school—so taciturn, so solemn, yet with that sarcastic look, as if he knows the answer to the question (he knows the answers to *all* the questions) but won't condescend to raise his hand. His teachers pretend to be fond of him, his classmates make no pretense. (A shy kid. Scared. Weird. Has a temper. A nice enough kid but, well, maybe a little . . . unbalanced? One day another boy flicked water into Mikey's face at the drinking fountain and Mikey went crazy—hitting, kicking, screaming, *swearing*—every sort of foul word you can imagine. He bloodied the other boy's nose, had to be half carried to the principal's office, sobbing, hysterical—*I'll kill anyone who touches me, I'll kill anyone who touches me*—a small kid but, God, really strong.)

But he doesn't know all the answers, he doesn't even know all the questions. He's frightened of what he doesn't know. *And there is so much.* At the age of twelve he investigates analytical geometry and calculus, at the age of thirteen he invents (not very successfully) his own geometry, at the age of fourteen he broods over the Möbius strip with its *single edge* and *single side,* a logical impossibility. (Or, as he tells his mother, an illogical possibility.) At the age of fifteen he amuses himself by making a model of the famous Seven Bridges of Königsberg to tape on his bedroom wall, with the intention (he's joking of course) of solving the problem within a year.

He won't solve it because as the Swiss mathematician Euler demonstrated centuries ago *it is insoluble,* yet, still, he's having fun, he likes to lie propped up on his elbows on the bed, staring, blinking, thinking hard, thinking very very hard, until his forehead is covered with an itchy film of perspiration and his eyes burn. Don't make yourself ill, Mother cautions, brushing his damp hair out of his face, don't make me worry about you, all right?

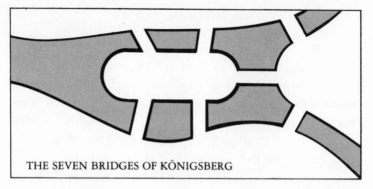

THE SEVEN BRIDGES OF KÖNIGSBERG

It's a hoary old puzzle, an ancient conundrum, a bit of Infinity to tape to the wall, and simple enough: Can you cross each bridge in turn *in one unbroken path* without crossing any of the bridges twice?

Yes. Sure. *He* (secretly) thinks so. Just give him time.

(A front-page story in the *New York Times,* which Daddy and all of Daddy's friends read: FIFTEEN-YEAR-OLD MATHEMATICAL GENIUS SOLVES CLASSIC PROBLEM.)

So Mikey dreams of the Seven Bridges of Königsberg, he squints, shuts his eyes hard, opens them again, stares at the sheet of construction paper on the wall, feels his heartbeat accelerate with the . . . certainty . . . that he is going to succeed where hundreds, thousands, of mathematicians have failed. Oh yes he's going to solve it! Maybe by accident, intuition, the way he beats his father at chess if he can get his father to play (Mikey beats him nine games out of ten now, though he hasn't any chess strategy per se); the way he guesses what his mother is thinking though she stands with her back to him, calm and rigid, unaware of his presence. Oh yes he's going to solve it, just give him time.

One bridge and then another and then another. A clockwise then a counterclockwise motion. And now he doubles back shrewdly on himself to travel on land. And now he twists about, in a surprising maneuver. And now . . . no, he's been on this bridge already . . . or has he . . . ?

THE LOVERS, PAST & PRESENT

The baby was born, there were no complications or ugly surprises, they named him Michael after Neil's father's father, they saw that he was a beautiful baby, a perfect baby, mother's and father's flesh mysteriously conjoined. A gasping fish's mouth, tiny fingers that clutch, eyes clear with hunger, then cloudy with the need to sleep: so sweet, so funny, hot with life: theirs. One of the stories Neil told for years was that he'd been communicating with his boy before the birth, oh as many as eight weeks before the actual birth; one of the stories Helen told, which she will begin to tell again after Mikey's suicide, was that she couldn't . . . quite . . . bring together the fact of being pregnant with the fact of having, being in the possession of, being responsible for, this particular baby. Not that she didn't, doesn't, love him; not at all. She loves him, or loved him, the way you love . . . your own flesh . . . ? No, your own self. No. It is, yet it isn't, *you:* actually you love it better than you love yourself.

Especially, says Helen with her breathless near-inaudible laugh, if you don't love yourself.

One of the stories Neil tells Yvette is that he and Helen "had very little to say to each other," that they were each

| | | | |

lonely, a little angry, baffled, she spent a good deal of time by herself, by herself or with Mikey, sometimes she'd take a nap when Mikey took his, Neil would find the two of them together, upstairs, lying beneath an afghan, sleeping or not quite sleeping, drowsing, dozing, dreamy-peaceful, the boy sucking a corner of the afghan in his sleep, Helen's eyes snapping open as Neil—the husband after all, *the* man—entered the room in the twilight, wondering, well, how long Helen had *been* there, comatose with a year-old child.

Helen dislikes lovemaking, Helen has become obsessed with lovemaking, Helen lies tight and clenched and inaccessible, Helen clutches at her alarmed husband with a need so ravenous, so enormous, no one (so he tells himself angrily) could satisfy it. But he complains to Yvette of his wife's . . . indifference; the cold sluggish feel of her flesh; the fact that, for more than a year after Mikey's birth, she refused to make love with him and stiffened in response even to his wayward casual affectionate questioning harmless touch. It was all baby, Neil says, his voice lightly mocking, puzzled—it was baby this baby that all *baby*.

(He does not tell Yvette—of course he does not tell Yvette, or anyone—that the new violence of his wife's passion, the rawness of her sexual need, has become disgusting to him. These past few years. These past months especially. It is repulsive, sickening, that concentrated self-absorbed thrusting . . . insisting . . . demanding . . . the smell, the sweat, the anguish . . . the willfulness of flesh. Why should I service *you,* Neil thinks, mean and gloating and frightened, why should I perform this task with *you,* I don't even know who *you* are.)

Whereas Yvette: the rather wild rather flamboyant rather outsized passion she displays (or in fact actually feels) excites him enormously. Enormously. At any time, at any hour, in her presence or apart. Oh, enormously. *Isn't this what life is all about?*

The baby *was* born, the young father *did* communicate with it (in a poetical manner of speaking) before the birth— yes it was all a miracle, it is miraculous still, but Neil feels a natural masculine resentment at being expected to contemplate a miracle for the rest of his life.

Neil Schueler, in love, is angry much of the time though he would call it happy. In Yvette Held's presence he is a *lover;* elsewhere he is, it might be said—though who but Neil could say it?—a *hater.*

His breath comes short and quick, he walks heavily, aggressively, bangs into chairs, the corners of tables, an ugly bruise on his left knee, shaving cuts on his chin, head slightly lowered, eyes narrowed. He opens his mail impatiently, rips the envelopes more than they require being ripped, draws out letters to scan in midair as if it's a task he resents, applying his energy and attention and goodwill to something so inconsequential. But then isn't everything not Yvette inconsequential? The lover's dilemma, the lover's delight.

It's clear that he resents, generally, his hours in this house, the company of his wife, his frightened adoring problem son, clear that he yearns to be elsewhere, but where?—no one dares inquire. Are you angry with me? Helen asks. Why are you angry with me? Helen sometimes asks, please *answer* me; and Neil turns his distracted gaze upon her as if he has never seen her before. Though the questions are preposterous—though it is absurd for Helen to take herself this seriously—Neil manages, most of the time, a civil reply. No.

No, of course not, certainly not, he says, absently, kindly, sometimes stroking her thin shoulder, her arm. Of course not, honey—a soft consoling drawl, gaze already retreating.

(One afternoon he tells Yvette a story they both find sad, pitiable: Helen did not accuse him of being in love with another woman, Helen very carefully *declared* that he was in love with another woman, and if he wanted a divorce, if he wanted a trial separation, she would agree, she wouldn't cause legal or domestic difficulties, she wasn't, isn't, that kind of woman. Yvette, listening closely, wipes at her eyes, laughs nervously, says with a strained smile, I guess *I'm* that kind of woman.)

Should-they-get-married is a story adulterous lovers tell.

A long exotic convoluted story. With variations, modulations.

Yes he says; but I don't think so, she says, not right now. Or, *yes* he says and *yes* she says too; but do they dare hurt so many people? he worries. She is hurt, stung; You don't care about hurting me, do you, she says, surprising him with her emotion. Plans are made, vague, like words written in steam on windows, bathroom mirrors, the other wife is this, the other husband is that, in another month one lover will be, and Yvette is planning to (planning to spend a few weeks with her ailing mother in Sarasota, Florida, as she tells Neil, though in truth, as she can't bring herself to tell him, she is going to be operated on for a cyst, yet surely it will prove to be a harmless cyst, in her uterus; she simply can't *tell* him because she fears his fear and she fears his, well, possibly manly repugnance, she doesn't entirely trust him), and it's a difficult time right now, the stock market, interest rates so high, by the end of the year as Garrett predicts the rates are sure to start downward, it will make a considerable difference. Then perhaps they shouldn't indulge themselves in making plans except Neil is one afternoon so wounded, so furious, he leaves her without even making love to her, though in truth (as he isn't about to tell her) he's so upset he surely could not make love to her, not in his customary robust supremely triumphant way; and another afternoon Yvette begins to sob uncontrollably, Yvette hides her contorted face from her lover, Yvette is ashamed, ashamed . . . but of what? All these lying little maneuvers, all these games. Or, conversely, the fact that nothing means anything to her except Neil.

The story has to do with Garrett, good-natured sweet-tempered Garrett, Garrett of whom everyone is fond and whom Neil dreads alienating, injuring, wounding in his pride (since Neil knows how he would feel, losing his wife to another man—and the other man a *friend*); the story has to do, yet more painfully, with Helen, poor Helen, who tells Neil that he should move out if he wishes then begs Neil not to move out, she loves him, she loves him so much, she and Mikey love him so much, doesn't he know? . . . of course he knows. Helen who has begun to see "some sort of analyst" in a nearby city, another woman (Neil says almost dismissively, not knowing how he sounds to Yvette), the two of them spending five hours a week (at $100 a session) poking about in the frayed inconsequential memories of Helen's childhood, as if *her* childhood matters in the slightest to anyone. Helen, poor Helen, of whom Yvette has grown obliquely fond, in fact Yvette is one of the few women in their circle who still like, or can tolerate, Helen Schueler: that brittle sardonic woman with the bruised eyes, the twisty little mouth, Neil Schueler's wife who has developed a truly bizarre mannerism of laughing silently, her eyes shut tight, and laying a meek little weighty little hand on her listener's arm . . . as if to beg sympathy, solicitude, she's actually in *pain* this is all so funny, aren't those tears running down her cheeks . . . ? And then there's the problem of her coughing spells, her smoker's breath, her slightly weaving just perceptibly *floating* air after she's had, maybe, a single glass of dry white wine and her big accusing eyes are black with pupil. She reports to Neil that she and her analyst sometimes discuss *his* childhood, but Neil hasn't any idea what they discuss since, after turning forty, he can barely remember having been an actual child, in the sense in which, more recently, his own son has been a child.

But the story they tell each other has most to do with children because of course they *genuinely love their children, wouldn't hurt them for the world, they're innocent victims after all, they must come first.* Neil's son, Yvette's daughter. The precocious sixteen-year-old, the rather silly thirteen-year-old. One is obsessed with mathematical puzzles and games, and working with his computer; the other is obsessed with friends, telephone calls, clothes, whether she is pretty enough, whether she is pretty at all . . . whether she is *popular.* (She doesn't give a damn about her father and me, Yvette says sullenly, she doesn't know we exist.) Mikey is childish, demanding, emotional, unpredictable, a tough little shit as Neil calls him, a troubled boy as his mother calls him, boasts of having no friends, boasts of being hated even by his teachers, locks himself away in his room for hours at a time, for complete Saturdays, Christ knows what he is doing apart from the computer, the math . . . the thinking. Neil has long given up trying to make sense of his son's preoccupations (what the hell *is* Infinity after all, isn't it just a pretentious word?—and what *is* Space/Time if you can't experience it?), he finds himself growing agitated, annoyed, if he's forced to listen to the boy's whining, self-absorbed, always subtly reproachful voice. Well, it's a sad story. It's a hell of a sad story. Spoiled by his mother and grandmother, made to think he's the center of the goddam universe, too smart for his own good, a born show-off, no wonder he hasn't any friends, no wonder he's never invited to anyone's house . . . and always that sly little air of reproach, reproach.

| | | | |

Still (as the story continues, month following month) both Neil and Yvette are acquainted with parents who have troubled adolescents, suicidal adolescents, kids who bring their friends home when their families are away and very nearly wreck the house . . . yet it's rage, raw aggression . . . yes some of these domestic situations are really tragic.

In which context it might be said (though who but Neil might say it?) that Mikey Schueler's problems are not so *very* serious.

Yes but should they get married, the lovers ask.

Yes but when. But how.

At what cost.

And isn't there a deadly risk in bringing the story to an end . . . ?

THE BITTER WOMAN

Actually it is wonderful to be alive like this, says Helen's mother softly, actually it is . . . enough of a miracle . . . to be able to breathe deeply . . . to sit here in the sun-shine and watch the birds at the feeder.

Yes, says Helen, alert, attentive, staring out the window: two cardinals, several chickadees, a small cheery flock of juncos. God's in his heaven and all's right with the world, she isn't bitter, she isn't sick with hatred, she *is* grateful that her mother has been recovering steadily from the operation; hasn't she been smiling since her arrival?

Smiling for three weeks, smiling dry-eyed, empty as a drum.

Poor Helen Schueler: she's the last, isn't she, to know.

. . . vowed I would never be one of those people, says Helen's mother bravely, her fingers clasping Helen's, one of those older people, like your grandmother, you know, your poor grandmother . . . vowed I would *not* . . . be filled with self-pity . . . recriminations . . . talk of health, operations, who has died and who is going to die. . . . No indeed I am happy to be alive. Like this. Oh dear God just like this.

The warm dry bony hand, the thin thin old-woman hand, delicate as a sparrow's skeleton.

Helen is in White Plains taking care of her mother, Helen is trying not to think of Neil and his love affair (she's fairly certain by now, in September 1978, that the woman is Yvette Held—who else could it be?), and of Mikey, cruel impatient Mikey, who has told her she is "neurotic," "an old bore." Mikey, who knows about his father, who has perhaps known for years. The shame, the disgust. The *shame*.

What shall I do, Mother? Helen wants to ask, holding her mother's hand hard, hard, feeling her throat constrict with the terrible need to cry, what shall I do, I love you but my love isn't enough to save you, to keep you forever, I love Mikey but it won't be enough to save *him*.

LYRIC

Neil, partly undressed, turns to see Yvette sprawled gracelessly across the bed, her hair in a tangle and her eyelashes matted, that coarse fleshy lovely mouth distended by a yawn, something kicks inside him, it has all been worth it, he thinks, both women, all of it, *all* of it, he'd do it over again, right now he'd like to tear the hot bitch open with his teeth and have done with all this ceremony.

THE EXPERIMENT

It's only a Thought Experiment, it isn't "real."

Mikey's computer is programmed to emit signals *into the past.*

Mikey's computer is equipped with a self-detonating device.

Mikey's computer is instructed to blow itself up at, say, 9 A.M., the signal having gone out at, say, 11 A.M. *Will the instruction be obeyed?*

"THOSE BOTTICELLI EYES"

Methodically, cruelly, she fasts; she is triumphing these days in the disciplining of the "animal appetites"; proud and secretly gloating at the delicate pulsing of a blue vein in her forehead, the new intensity of her gray-green eyes. A cup of bitter black coffee trembles in her hand, she zips up an old pair of her daughter's jeans (too tight now for Sonya), she hears the telephone ringing but declines to answer (for what if it is Neil's crazy wife—she *won't* answer), she's already on her way out: a white-hot energy compels her, *is* her. She feels weightless, near bodiless, innocent.

She fasts, it is her pleasure to fast, preparing herself, rehearsing, for a final—*final*—conversation with her lover (at this moment flying home from Atlanta, their plan is to meet at the new Hyatt Regency fifteen miles away, or is it at the new Hilton, so splendidly tacky, by the Turnpike?—there have been so many), though in fact they seem to have had this conversation before. But now she is in the ascendency, now she is suffused with power, *now* she can make the necessary break.

And they will—or won't they?—make love a final time.

A ceremony of sorts. Romantic ritual.

Pots of strong black coffee, the telephone that must not be answered (though there's the risk that it is Garrett who is calling, or even Neil with a modification of their plans), the sudden revelation in one of the household mirrors (though not a mirror Yvette customarily looks into) that her ash-blond hair has been turning gray, silvery gray, in secret, especially near the nape of her neck: that this is a fact about her others have observed in silence.

Yvette makes the observation with a wry shrug of her shoulders, tells herself she doesn't give a damn, she isn't after all the sort of woman who cares to deny her age, fight feebly against whatever age she *is*—she thinks too well of herself for that. (Also, she is still in her mid-thirties, six years younger than her lover and nine years younger than her husband. She may even be under the unexamined impression that this is middle age and she has already conquered it by an act of will.)

To think of herself is to think well of herself, for

how could it reasonably be otherwise?—Yvette in one of her skinny translucent phases, looking anemic, fragile, something hot and tremulous about her mouth. (Beautiful, her lover says, has been saying for so long—beautiful, he claims, a litany she takes for granted, worship of a sort, familiar and consoling—a beautiful woman. As if it were an accomplishment of his own, to claim her.) The story she tells herself is in itself consoling, though largely improvised, fantastic. The story she tells herself is that one day, years ago, she was introduced to an attractive young couple, a very attractive young couple—husband sandy-haired, smiling, funny, wife quick and bright and dark and *sweet;* a female sort of flirtation—shall we—*can* we—be friends?—and she simply thought, even while shaking hands, exchanging pleasantries, joking with her husband, she thought: Him. It will be him. Whenever we are both ready.

She will, or will not, recover readily from the break with Neil; she will, or will not, know herself the victor (for, all sentimentality aside, all this crap about romance aside, there *is* inevitably a victor in such affairs); she will, or will not, feel intense guilt a few years later, when the Schuelers' son kills himself. She will in any case urge her husband to accept his company's remarkable offer, made to all the top attorneys this year, of a six-week trip to Europe: yes they will take the Orient Express, yes they will stay in a perfect hotel in Venice, certainly they will fly to Morocco for a few days. . . .

No, they won't take the daughter, Sonya and her mother don't get along very well these days, Sonya has her own circle of friends, a very tight circle of friends, Sonya wouldn't have any interest in touring Europe with Mother and Father. *Not on your life.*

MOTHERSON

Mikey denies it all, denies everything, shrugging his skinny shoulders, giggling his mirthless laugh, the usual mannerisms—picking at his blemished skin, rolling his eyes as if he's in the presence of idiots, going suddenly mute, stubborn, a catatonia of the will. No he did not threaten thusand-such, yes his teacher is full of shit, *yes* the whole school is full of shit, or does he mean (a contemptuous flutter of his eyelashes) *shits:* he's had enough of them.

And they've had enough of you, says Mother.

Okay I've had enough of *them*—that's the point.

But the point is also that they've had enough of you, they don't want you back unless—

I'm not going back. I said, *I'm not going back.*

Your father and I think—

I said—

Your father and—

Mikey begins to hum, his head bowed, bobbing, a queer rhythmic motion, hearing and not-hearing. The school won't take him back unless he apologizes and promises, etc., but how can he apologize when he did *not* say those juvenile things (wiring the place with dynamite, setting it off by way of a computer hookup, Christ!—he's beyond *that*) or threaten (why is the word "threaten" always used, so corny, banal) to kill himself in such a way as to bring adverse publicity upon the school, any asshole (and the school is filled with assholes) would know he was only joking . . . he does a lot of joking . . . to relieve the boredom.

Don't lie to me, Mother says.

"I'm not lying to you," says Son.

Please don't lie to *me,* Mother says.

"I said I'm not lying to you," says Son.

I think you're cruel to make me so miserable. . . . I think you're sick, you need help . . . you've been contaminated by your father.

"I think you're sick, you need help," says Son, singsong.

You need professional help. . . .

"You need professional help. . . ."

Stop! Stop that!

"Stop! Stop that!"

Mikey, please—

"Mikey, *please—*"

A giggling fit, a fit of hot enraged tears, Motherson pummeling each other, Mother slapping Son and Son shoving Mother, it looks like an embrace, an awkward dance step, and what of that frenzied giggling?—as Father enters the twilit room.

THE FORGIVING WIFE

The mother-grandmother-mother-in-law in White Plains dies at the age of seventy-six, Helen discovers herself dry-eyed (she *is* empty as a drum and damn glad of it), while Mikey moons about the house sniffling and dazed . . .

but tractable, civilized, *courteous* for once. And even Neil is struck by the loss, saddened, mourning (had he thought *her* mother was obliged to live forever just because *his* died years ago?), tender with Helen, and consoling, and so forth, as if Helen needs, now, consolation, *now*.

It's a relief that Mother is dead, Helen thinks cynically, because it spares her from knowing . . . certain details Helen would not wish her to know . . . now that the affair is over (Yes I can say that it's really over, yes I can say that I love you and I'm ashamed, says the repentant husband, frightened by something in his wife's face, oh yes *sincerely* frightened there's no mistaking it) . . . now that certain truths, specific and general, are being revealed. Such as: Neil had not really loved Yvette, he'd been going through a (is the word crisis?—psychic maladjustment?)—a difficult period in his life, professional primarily, all that pressure, that insane *competition*, too many aging Harvard Law boys under one roof, perhaps even some neurotic jealousy of his wife and son, *their* closeness, and wouldn't any father (murmured with a faint faltering laugh, a crinkling of blood-threaded eyes) be uneasy about having a son who is so—bright? So mercilessly bright? So much the whiz kid? So much the—not smart aleck, but what is the word—precocious intelligence, brain—ah yes: *wunderkind.*

Helen laughs, forgiving. All forgiveness.

Helen has it in her power to forgive, thus why not forgive? So she forgives.

She forbids herself to think *what it must mean* that her mother has died despite the fact that she loved the

| | | | |

woman so very much . . . so painfully childishly much . . . despite the fact that her mother loved *her*. (And who after all loves *her*, baby is all growed up, or nearly.)

A lonely predicament here in the Void. Familiar but still lonely, not very comforting. She examines the Milky Way photographed and taped to Mikey's wall, these are lonely prospects, permanent-seeming though ostensibly ephemeral (how long *has* she been alive after all?), and next year Mikey too will be gone, he'll make his escape, wait and see, already he flushes at the name Mikey saying Mother I *told* you my name is Michael my name is *Mi*chael for Christ's sake *please*. A lonely predicament, wife-and-husband together at last.

She wants to cry for her mother but it's difficult, it isn't easy, this is a knotty convoluted "ephemeral" story she tells herself, raking her nails experimentally over her flesh to get a little . . . sensation: raw, throbbing, primitive, healthy. Her left forearm, her breasts, her soft flaccid belly. Numb for so long. Well why not be numb, dead inside, dead inside where it counts, not like Y. who luxuriates in lovemaking, laughs gasping for air, is drowning, dying amid the smelly bedclothes, greedy for what he has to give her, tireless, insatiable, those hips bucking, pelvis frantic, old tricks Helen deftly performed a lifetime ago, oh don't leave me don't stop don't leave me oh Christ: *I love you.*

I love you, says Neil, only you, says Neil, and Helen says gently, her eyes turning in their sockets, I love *you*. It has always been you, says Neil, sobbing, huddling in her arms, you know it has always been you, I'd be nothing without you, and Helen says, suppressing her laughter, I know, I know, I've always known.

THE SEVEN BRIDGES OF . . .

It is Infinity of a kind: you begin (for instance) with the bridge at the upper left, proceed to cross the island, cross the bridge at the lower left; you then turn to the right, proceed to cross the next bridge, cross the island, cross the *next* bridge. . . . You don't get very far, however, before the terrifying nature of the problem strikes you; and then it's too late. Then you must go back. Then you must go back and begin again, this time perhaps with the horizontal bridge leading to the island.

Mikey hasn't given a thought to the Königsberg puzzle for years, at least it seems like years, he has stopped thinking about many useless things, it is a function of growing up. In fact he isn't Mikey now but Michael Schueler, respected if not greatly liked by his suitemates at Yale, admired in a way for his industry, seriousness, maturity . . . and for the astounding fact that, at midterm, he has straight A's except for his course in algebraic topology, in which he has an A+. But suddenly he's tired.

Among his parents' circle back home he is, he's been told, a model of sorts, an exemplum: living proof should such proof be desired that a brattish neurotic *wunderkind* can make adjustments to ordinary life after all, laying aside certain childish obsessions forever, behaving normally, pulling up his socks and so forth, some stories have happy endings. Never too late in America.

| | | | |

Never too late in the upper middle class. His high school teachers and his guidance counselor are after all the sort of people who ache to be proven wrong, to be surprised in their dreary predictions, they *want* to see a lost cause suddenly find himself: and then the father Neil Schueler is such a nice guy, and the mother, that poor nervous woman—actually she's an *attractive* woman if you can see past the god-awful mannerisms—she's said to have a Ph.D. or is it an M.A. in something like organic chemistry. . . .

Mikey Schueler the somber whiz kid buckled down as the saying goes, applied himself diligently and tirelessly to his studies during his senior year, did so well on his SAT tests he was accepted at each of the four universities to which he applied: some stories *have* happy endings. So he went away to New Haven. So he is in New Haven at this very minute.

Feeling suddenly, unaccountably, very tired.

(Why aren't you applying to Harvard they asked him—teachers, father—and he said something vague and flippant like, I was *born* there after all, why press my luck and go back?)

It's Thanksgiving recess and his suitemates have gone home, in fact the college is nearly deserted, the silence is luxurious, why not stay another day or two?—Yale has an entire week off. He is scheduled to take the train home on Tuesday afternoon at two-fifteen but suddenly he's tired, exhausted really, there is bliss in his empty suite and in a bathroom solely his, he *is* tired from working so hard: four A's and an A+ but he'll be embarrassed if Mother and Father make a fuss over him because (as he has been admitting to himself for weeks) the grades didn't come easily . . . no they didn't come easily . . . and he isn't certain that he wants to live it all again . . . yes he's pretty certain he doesn't want to live it all again. His record is so very perfect, why press his luck and keep going?

In any case he can't go back home. Not to that house.

No, he *can't* go home, that's his first premise.

A perfectionist to the end, Mikey knows how to skillfully sever (not merely slash at) the arteries in his left arm: a strong unflinching grip on the razor with the fingers of his right hand, the blade drawn lengthwise, deep and pitiless, exhilarated at the feat that can't be done (as Spinoza teaches all things desire to persist in their being) yet is being done, only observe. If this is dying it feels after a few minutes like goofing off as Mikey rarely allows himself, hiding under the shower in steaming hot water, or in this case hiding in the tub, the water spashing in as water drains out, cleverly timed, he has everything cleverly timed, he isn't going to be found until early evening when everything will be over. The door is locked, the steam is consoling, he's sprawled out ungainly (nearly six feet tall, only one hundred thirty-five pounds) but curiously relaxed in the tub, as if he has done this before, oh many times before, it isn't at all difficult once you've stated your first premise. Too cowardly or too shrewd to open his eyes for a while, he wonders whether there will be sinewy cords of blood, skeins that won't blend in with the water, or whether it is all a pale tepid washed-out pinkish-red, and then, suddenly, he isn't interested, he can't be bothered to check, he notes the peaceful unexcited heartbeat that feels like wisdom, suddenly he is crossing one of the Königsberg bridges, he's simultaneously in the tub amid the noisy water and on the bridge above *that* water, he sees himself crossing the first of the bridges . . . and then the island . . . and then the second bridge . . . and this time he'll try something unexpected, how about proceeding at once to the horizontal bridge . . . and proceeding onward. . . .

THE HAPPY ENDING

This is the final story they tell, this is *the* story, surprising and placating them both, one mild Saturday morning in early September 1983 when by accident Neil Schueler and Yvette Held meet in the Village Market, not having spoken together since approximately June of 1982: a story with a happy ending.

. . . so absurd, so *extreme,* Yvette says in a lowered voice, there were times I actually prayed for . . . well, *both* of us . . . you think such crazy things . . . for instance once when you were driving on the Turnpike I think and driving quite fast . . . and I had this little fantasy of pulling at the steering wheel . . . something, anything, you know . . . to make an end of it.

Neil listens fascinated, believing and not-believing, staring at a woman he no longer loves despite her Botticelli eyes (hadn't he once called them that?) and her slender snaky body and something secret and sly and at-the-edge-of-frenzy in her voice; Neil murmurs, God did you really, God I'm glad you *didn't*. . . .

Well of course I *wouldn't,* it was just a fantasy, anything, you know, to make an *end,* Yvette says, smiling to show her good strong damp white teeth, you get in these extreme states of mind when you're in love or are convinced you're in love, it's something I have to remember now that Sonya has a boyfriend I mean a *steady* boyfriend. . . .

Sonya must be how old now? Neil asks, though he isn't interested: he wants to hear more about Yvette's crazy fantasy and maybe, just maybe (well, maybe not) he'll tell her about *his* . . . strangling her with her hair . . . when she wore it long, long and loose, falling past her shoulders. Oh is she really that old, he says, slightly perplexed, I think of her as such a little . . .

And Mikey's at Yale, someone said? says Yvette brightly.

And Mikey's at Yale, says Neil, grinning, swiping at his nose, thank *God.*

So they talk, chat. Laugh. A shock for them to meet after so long (and Neil isn't altogether certain how much Garrett knows) but after a few minutes it seems, well, quite casual, even ordinary, two friendly acquaintances meeting in the Market, lounging over their grocery carts, a familiar sight. Yvette is wearing something that resembles a burlap tunic cinched in severely at the waist, a belt with a big Navaho buckle, sandals, her hair is close-cropped, a mass of stylish frazzled curls, she's given to smiling a good deal, laughing huskily, not at all embarrassed or uneasy. Neil is wearing khaki shorts and a sweatshirt, he's sporty, tanned, unshaven, hopes Yvette won't inquire after Helen, who is in one of her lethargic phases, staying at home day after day, unwashed hair, bathrobe, bare feet, grainy flaccid skin but she's *all right,* it's just a cyclical thing by now . . . hopes Yvette won't notice the soft roll of flesh at his waist . . . or the fact that his hair is thinning at the crown.

. . . working out for the best, after all, says Yvette.

Yes, says Neil, after all.

Those Botticelli eyes!—hadn't he once called them that, in absolute dazed sincerity, framing the woman's face with his hands?—and now he sees the fine white lines at the eyes' edges, now he sees the smudge of brown eyeliner on the lids, in any case he is immune, he certainly *is* immune, it's such an old hacked-over pondered-over story.

The thing is, Neil says carefully, his voice still lowered—that nobody was hurt. That's the important thing.

Oh I know, says Yvette at once.

That's the thing that matters most, says Neil, licking his lips, calculating when he should begin to edge his cart past hers, that's really it, you know, all the rest was—

Oh I know, says Yvette, brightly, I *know.*

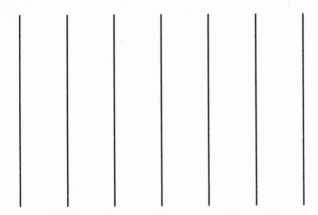

DOUBLE SOLITAIRE

They were sisters but they had never been friends, so when the telephone call came late one weekday evening Anita didn't recognize Miriam's voice at first. Mirian was calling to say she was scheduled to check into Detroit General the next day, she'd be operated on the following morning, yes it was serious but she didn't expect to die, nobody expected her to die, she just thought that Anita, being her sister, should be informed.

Anita wasn't certain she had heard correctly, Miriam's voice was so hoarse and muffled. She turned down the radio volume, her hand trembling, and asked Miriam what was wrong, what kind of operation was it?—and Miriam repeated that it was serious but not all that serious, an operation many women have, she just thought that Anita should be informed. Anita said at once, "I'd better drive over, I can get off work if it's an emergency," and Miriam said quickly, "It isn't an emergency, nobody expects me to die or anything. I don't want Wayne and the kids upset," and Anita heard herself say for some reason, "No don't *die,*" and from that point on the conversation was out of control: she and Miriam interrupted each other, spoke at the same time, misheard, misunderstood, came close to seriously quarreling. Anita was almost in tears, saying, "Look, please, I want to come—I'm coming." Miriam's words were beginning to slur, she might have been drunk, she might have been drugged, saying it wasn't an emergency, she knew Anita had a life of her own.

But by the time they hung up ten minutes later it was all settled: Anita would drive to Detroit, Anita would stay with them for as long as Miriam and the children needed her. "Please, I *want* to come," she insisted.

Afterward, Anita noticed that she had broken out in perspiration, her hands were shaking badly. She resented that she should be so frightened when she'd spent half the days of her childhood wishing her sister would die.

There were two vivid memories from childhood that had to do with Miriam, Anita and Miriam together. Alone together.

Anita, five or six years old, being pushed in a playground swing by Miriam, who must have been about ten at the time: Anita, for fun, leaping from the swing in midair, not guessing how the swing seat would fly back and strike Miriam on the side of the head. (Had she cried? Anita wondered. She must have cried, it must have hurt her badly. But Anita hadn't any memory of Miriam crying—only of herself crying, in Miriam's presence.)

Anita, older, in seventh grade maybe, sitting in the kitchen with Miriam, playing double solitaire. Slapping the cards down. Noisy, silly, on the verge of bursting into wild laughter, because it was so late at night and no one knew or cared what they did, their father was dead and their mother was in bed drunk, their mother spent much of her time in bed, drunk, and she hadn't more than a few years more to live, and both Anita and Miriam seemed to know this fact. All one winter they'd played double solitaire at the kitchen table, drinking diet cola and eating doughnuts covered in confectioner's sugar, not minding that both decks of cards were sticky, frayed. Miriam won most of the games and though Anita guessed she was cheating—Anita herself cheated occasionally—she never said anything.

Anita left home at six-thirty in the morning and arrived at Miriam's house on the west side of Detroit in the early afternoon, in time to help her get ready for the hospital. When they embraced Anita smelled cigarette smoke and sweet red wine on her sister's breath.

She shook hands self-consciously with Miriam's husband, whom she'd met only once before, at the wedding. He was Miriam's second husband and no one in the family knew him very well. His name was Wayne; he was tall, stiff, silent, frightened; he had long narrow suspicious eyes and Indian-sharp facial bones. He thanked Anita for coming without moving his mouth and without exactly looking at her, and Anita heard herself say again, in a faltering voice, that she wanted to come. She wanted to help out with the children. It was the least, she said, not knowing what she said, she could do.

Both Anita's parents were dead now, her only brother had moved to Oregon eight years before, Anita supposed she went for weeks without thinking of Miriam though sometimes, in a weak, melancholy mood, she found herself thinking about Miriam's children—*her* little niece Julie, *her* little nephew Bobby—and wondering if they remembered her. Both the children were from Miriam's first marriage, which had ended when Miriam was twenty-six and Anita was finishing her last semester of college. The marriage had been a mistake from the start so Anita was relieved when it ended but she'd felt sorry for Julie and Bobby—Miriam hadn't told her any details about the divorce except that, at one point, she'd had to get a court injunction against her husband, to keep him from breaking into the house. "Once a man lives in a house," Miriam would say, as if giving Anita warning, "he won't just walk out the door. Nothing's that easy."

The children didn't remember her, or pretended they didn't, which hurt Anita at first. She was their *aunt,* wasn't she? Their only *aunt.*

But she was careful with them, cheery, playful, soft-spoken, not pushing herself on them, knowing her time would come.

The operation, Miriam's doctor said cautiously, had turned out well. Barring post-op complications.

Such words as *tumor, uterus, hysterectomy* sounded faintly comical, obscene, uttered so frankly in fluorescent-lit rooms and corridors. *Fibroid. Nonmalignant. Complete removal of.* Anita noted how Wayne shrank from speaking them, how he hunched his heavy shoulders when he heard them, how his face went hard and neutral . . . as if he happened to be part of these exchanges only by accident. As if, in his sheepskin jacket, his hands in his pockets, he'd only wandered in to hear the tail end of a conversation between strangers.

Anita and Wayne had spent most of the long morning together in the hospital coffee shop, waiting for Miriam to come down from surgery.

Anita wasn't frightened, Anita knew that Miriam couldn't die, but still she heard her voice vague and faltering and falsely bright, talking about the children, talking about Miriam "back home," while Wayne glanced through newspapers left behind by other customers. Where was Wayne from, was he from Detroit? . . . how had he and Miriam met? . . . was she still married at the time? . . . what sort of business did he own? . . . could she have a cigarette? . . . and she saw how automatically he pushed the pack toward her, how natural it was that, just for an instant, she touched his wrist, closed her fingers lightly about his wrist.

Afterward, after the consultation with the doctor, they went out for a drink at a place Wayne knew, just off the expressway, and both Anita and Wayne got pleasantly high. Just beer. One or two tequilas.

"Okay," said Wayne, "this is a celebration."

His spiky black hair was disheveled, there were deep depressions at the corners of his mouth, Anita liked

| | | | |

the way he leaned forward against the bar and then turned, on his elbow, lazily, to face her. They'd been doing this for years, maybe. Anita and Wayne. Coming to this place off the expressway where the late-morning light didn't quite penetrate the grimy front windows and where everyone seemed to know Wayne but didn't waste his time by coming over.

Wayne's smile was slow and mocking. "You don't know how to drink tequila?" he said.

"Sure I do," said Anita.

For three days Miriam was so heavily sedated she didn't feel pain but then, on the fourth morning, it hit. She screamed at Wayne and Anita to get out, to take the children away, she didn't want anybody to see her like this.

They'd scooped out her insides, she said, and now there was nothing left.

"Hey don't *say* that," Anita said, embarrassed.

The incision was ten inches long and she was filled with staples—Christ, with *staples,* would you believe it!— and she had to sleep sitting up because it hurt too much to stretch out flat. Right now she didn't care whether she lived or died so don't anybody hand her bullshit about being lucky. "You think I'm *lucky,*" she said, staring at Anita, tears in the corners of her eyes, "you get in this fucking bed and take my place."

Wayne had to be away, most days, from ten in the morning until late at night. He had business problems, he said. People he couldn't always trust. So he wasn't able to make it down to the hospital more than twice, or was it three times, in the eight days Miriam was there. During that time Anita did all the visiting. Driving back and forth on the expressway, learning all the exits, which lanes to avoid and why, sometimes with Julie and Bobby, sometimes alone. When she was alone she turned the car radio up as loud as she could stand it. Weird spaced-out Detroit sounds, a heavy black beat, country-and-western, an announcer with an Ozark drawl whose voice sometimes dropped to a whisper. Anita knew them all.

When she was alone in the car her face felt elastic, she might have been a little girl again, her mouth just naturally turning up in a secret smile.

Closets. What was there about other women's closets.

Anita seemed always to be looking in them, didn't she, barefoot and half dressed and her hair in her eyes, fingering the sleeve of a black velveteen dress, pushing hangers aside to stare, critically, at a silk blouse with a ruffled front, jersey dresses, wool skirts, sweaters on hangers that are ruining the shoulders, pairs of shoes on the floor, neat, or jumbled together, depending. She never put on another woman's clothes, never even held anything (this maroon blazer, for instance, more Anita's style than Miriam's) up against her, looking in a mirror, not because none of the clothes appealed but because they all did.

In this case the closet belonged to her sister, not a stranger, but it made no difference because all the clothes were new to her.

Strange, Anita thought, brushing her sticky hair out of her eyes, how you only remember certain things at certain times. There'd been a married lover in Cleveland when she was just out of college, and another married lover in Pittsburgh, and, for the past three years, intermittently, the man who supervised her office. (She worked at a social welfare agency in Buffalo but she'd had to go on part-time salary because the state legislature had cut their budget, yes she was fortunate she had a job at all, yes she knew enough to be grateful.) One December day when it was dark at five in the afternoon this man brought her to his house on Delaware Avenue because his wife and children were away and they could be alone together. One of the things he said was, It's good you're here in this bed because God knows it's a place where I think about you all the time. In a while Anita was crying, though she wasn't unhappy, and then she was coming out of the shower, out of the adjoining bathroom, a towel wrapped around her, barefoot, her skin glowing, her eyes wild and darting . . . because her lover loved her so much . . . because she was alone for the moment in a room in which strangers slept . . . there was a mahogany bureau whose contents she didn't know, there were photographs on the wall of people she didn't know, there was a closet that ran the entire length of the room with white louvered doors, filled with clothes she didn't know. . . .

She went to the closet and looked through it hurriedly, a woman's clothes, so many clothes, a faint scent of wool, mothballs, stale perfume, expensive-looking shoes arranged in neat pairs on the floor, she had to move quickly, quickly, for fear her lover would discover her, for fear (was this possible?) he'd forget and call her by another woman's name.

Of course that never happened. He never called her anything but Anita.

Tomorrow Miriam was being discharged from the hospital and tonight why not go out for a few drinks, Wayne had completed a deal he felt good about, why not celebrate, why not make a night of it, as long as the kids were asleep (though Anita wondered if Julie, nervous little Julie, ever slept at all now); and Anita said, But is it safe to leave them all alone?—they're so little; and Wayne, car keys rattling in his hand, said, You coming or not?

An hour earlier, in his and Miriam's bed, he'd gripped Anita's buttocks hard, squeezing hard, his fingers had come away bright with blood, Anita was in the second day of her period. The hottest time, Wayne kept saying, c'mon, c'mon, it's the hottest time isn't it? short of breath, excited as she hadn't seen him before, not caring (as other men did) if he was hurting her, wasn't Anita a pool into which he plunged, exhilarated and wild and vengeful, no you couldn't say he was vengeful, he was just . . . what he was doing right now; and Anita was what was being done to her. She strained and strained until her heart hammered but the dim little kernel of sensation he'd aroused deep inside her never got any stronger and when they were finished she started crying, really sobbing, though she knew Wayne would hate it, Wayne was the kind of man who got bored with tears—hadn't Miriam said, Don't cry in front of him?—but she couldn't help crying because this was something he and Miriam knew to do and maybe one day (was *this* possible?) he'd tell Miriam about it, to hurt her feelings or to make her laugh.

The *Detroit News* had been running a series on fires in the city, suspected arson, a high percentage of the fires suspected arson, maybe for insurance purposes, maybe to get welfare tenants out of buildings, though of course—many of the houses being old, in disrepair—there were blameless fires as well, "blameless" in the sense of being no one's specific criminal intention.

Anita heard sirens in the night, Anita's head was buzzing, her heartbeat pleasantly quickened. Wayne knew more ways of getting high than Anita had read about or had been told at the social welfare agency but he was sparing, it might be said he had a certain professional discretion. She nudged her forehead against his and said, What if the house burns down while we're out, and Wayne laughed and said, Sweetheart that isn't going to happen, and Anita said, But what *if,* and Wayne said, Y'know you worry more than Miriam, and Anita said, That's because I'm not Miriam, and Wayne said, irritated, Okay sweetheart but you aren't their mother, are you, and Anita, stung, but remembering to keep it all light, said, *You* aren't their father, are you.

She lost track of the drinks, the bars, the parking lots, the men who greeted Wayne, there were two or three who actually called her Miriam, she lost track of the sirens she couldn't always hear fully, to know if they were fire trucks or just police or ambulances. It was a weekday night in Detroit but it wouldn't shut down for a long, long time. What if, Anita said under her breath, what *if,* but Wayne wasn't in the mood to humor her, anyway she knew she was being silly, a house doesn't catch fire so quickly, most of the time it has to be someone's fault. Miriam was the kind of mother who'd slap her kids if she caught them playing with matches, no nonsense about *her,* she'd said the other day in the hospital when Anita came, alone, to visit and was holding her hand for a while, just holding her hand, she'd said, trying not to cry, If it wasn't for Julie and Bobby, shit, I don't *know.* . . .

Anita told her it was natural to feel bad, to feel depressed, following surgery. It wasn't just the pain, it was the anesthetic too.

Wayne was crazy about her, he said, and wanted her to move to Detroit, couldn't she get a job here, couldn't she get an apartment here, maybe even move in with them, she and Miriam got along all right, didn't they? Anita had been thinking she wouldn't be able to leave Detroit just yet but she didn't want to take any of this too seriously because, well, she didn't want to take any of this too seriously, there she was crying and gagging in Wayne's arms in a cinder parking lot, just past closing time, four in the morning; then, making a joke of it, he gripped her under the arms like a big rag doll and tried to walk her to the car.

That was the night they pulled up in front of the darkened house Anita couldn't recognize, and Wayne said, nudging her, "See?—no fire," and Anita, blinking and squinting, couldn't remember what the subject was.

In Wayne's car on the way home from the hospital Miriam had her first cigarette, and her first glass of red wine

| | | | |

she had in the kitchen, and her hands were shaking when she hugged the kids, hugged and kissed them. Julie said, Don't you never *never* go away, Mommy, and Bobby was sniveling over some worry, Bobby wasn't getting enough attention, in a few minutes he'd turn back to Aunt Anita, whom he'd gotten to like a lot, Aunt Anita who loved him more than Mommy did, but right now things were confused, right now it was strange, it was frightening, that Mommy should be crying but trying to laugh at the same time.

Wayne kept saying, Jesus it's good to have you back, Wayne was almost shy around her, fearful of touching her and hurting her. She had a three-week recovery period to get through, she said, and that was just the beginning. But, God, she *was* glad to get home, she felt a thousand times better just being home. . . .

Anita helped her walk, Anita helped her in the bathroom, dressing and undressing, getting ready for bed. Anita made dinner and Anita cleaned up afterward and Anita gave the kids their baths and Anita put them to bed and a half hour later Anita put Julie to bed again—Julie you little sneak, *I* see you!—and Anita slept on the sofa except she couldn't sleep, she put on the television, the volume low, and watched old movies, the tail end of the Carson show, her feet curled up beneath her. Very early in the morning when she finally fell asleep she heard someone, it must have been Wayne, in the bathroom, she heard the toilet flush, she wasn't asleep and she wasn't awake but she was telling him, laughing, "Look please honey *no,* Miriam will hear us."

| | 152 | |

Anita helped Miriam lower herself into the bathtub and Anita shampooed Miriam's hair and Anita set up a board—a breadboard, actually—so that Miriam could play solitaire in bed, propped up in bed, and Anita quieted the kids when they ran wild and Anita let Bobby sleep curved in her arms on the sofa and Anita went shopping at Kroger's on Livernois and Anita did the laundry and Anita tried to vacuum the place but the vacuum cleaner bag was clogged, stuffed full with dirt, and she'd never changed one quite like this before, and Miriam said, "Let me do it for Christ's sake," but of course she didn't dare bend over; she had a long way to go before she'd be able to bend over like that.

Anita said, "I guess I'd better make plans to leave."

Anita said, shakily, not looking at Wayne, "I don't think I should stay much longer," not looking at Wayne to read his expression, to see why he didn't answer.

And, hearing her, Miriam said with a sharp little laugh, "Hey, what do you *mean?*—you just came."

Anita became wise, even fussy, in the ways of the household; she learned how to scold the kids, even to "discipline" them (Bobby required a slap, Julie a light pinch), but she couldn't gauge how much her sister knew about her, not just her and Wayne but Anita's own life back in Buffalo. She had a job there, an apartment, even a lover. She had a life, there. It was real, it was waiting for her to come back to resume it.

Still, when she thought suddenly of her apartment—a certain angle of vision when she dressed hurriedly in the morning, looking slantwise into the mirror on the back of a closet door which reflected a window with a patched venetian blind—she felt a stab in her belly hard and frightening as sex. It *was* real, her life back there, her life alone, waiting for her.

One evening she and Miriam, putting the kids to bed, couldn't help overhearing Wayne on the telephone in the next room.

Was he angry?—no, maybe pretending.

Laughing, too.

But angry, yes.

His voice rose in a curious way—rage, elation, resignation—but Anita couldn't make out anything except: *"I'll be right over, you!"*

After he went out Anita asked Miriam, whom she didn't want to annoy (Miriam had been feeling rotten since morning), "What is Wayne's business exactly?" and Miriam looked at her and said, "Hasn't he told you?" and Anita felt the corners of her eyes tighten but she went on; she said, "No, he doesn't tell me much, I mean we don't talk much," and then, because Jesus God that sounded bad, she said, "I just mean Wayne and I don't see that much of each other."

Miriam was staring at her but she *was* smiling, so it must have been all right. She said, "Ask him, sometime. Maybe he'll tell you."

Two and a half weeks, and then three weeks, and Miriam had good days and bad days, and Anita learned to know (or was it to sense?) when her sister was feeling pain though they might be in separate rooms.

And one morning when the sisters were sitting in the kitchen, drinking coffee, eating stale cherry-jelly doughnuts, and playing at their old game of double solitaire, Miriam said suddenly, as if it had something to do with a card she'd just turned up, "Hey. I hope you don't think it means a damn thing."

"What means a damn thing . . . ?" Anita asked.

"You and Wayne," Miriam said.

Anita felt that stab of fear in her bowels but she continued with the cards, a jack of clubs, an ace of spades, she didn't miss a single beat though Miriam was watching. But her voice was faint, her voice gave everything away, when she said, *"What? Me and Wayne . . . ?"*

The apartment was always drafty these days so they'd put the oven on, had the oven door down, the kitchen was warming up nicely, the coziest room of all despite the loose-fitting windows. The place was quiet— no radio right now, no television, not even any noise from the street—Julie and Bobby were at school—Wayne was away on business, wouldn't be back until the end of the week, in Toledo Anita remembered him saying but Miriam said it was Chicago: his most important contacts were in Chicago.

Anita had never asked Wayne what his business was, maybe she'd been afraid he would tell her.

"This is the coziest room I know," Anita said, about to giggle, "and it's only a *kitchen*."

Then she cleared her throat. She said in a low

careful voice, "I don't know what the hell you're talking about, Miriam, but it isn't funny."

"It *is* funny, in its way," Miriam said.

"I mean, I just don't know what you're talking about."

"Just so you don't think it means anything," Miriam said. She was no longer watching Anita, she was watching her cards, a single sharp crease between her eyes. "I've been through this before with that bastard and he always comes back whining, he always says he loves *me*."

Anita wanted to say, But that was before you were operated on, wasn't it!—but of course she kept quiet. After a while she said, "I really don't know what you're talking about, but I don't think it's funny."

"You're the one who said it was funny."

"I'm *not*."

For a few minutes they continued with their games, their double game, slapping down the cards. Anita thought as she'd thought many times in childhood that a special card—the queen of diamonds, for instance, the handsome jack of clubs—had to come a long way to get to her. She heard herself say suddenly, about to cry, "Look—I don't think I can leave here yet."

"I've been through it before," Miriam said. "He always comes back."

"Yes," said Anita. "But I don't think I can leave yet. For Buffalo."

"The kids aren't his but he loves them and they love him, he's very close to them," Miriam said, not looking up, "he just isn't the kind of man to show it. What do *you* know—you don't know a damn thing."

Miriam was breathing hard, her cheeks flushed. Anita held a six of clubs she didn't know what to do with, it seemed to be a card she'd drawn out of nowhere. She had forgotten how to play the game.

If Miriam reached out suddenly to touch her hand, to grab hold of her wrist, she knew she'd embarrass them both by crying but she wanted very badly for Miriam to reach out and touch her and tell her she couldn't go back home yet, it wasn't time.

"What do you know about it," Miriam whispered. Her breath had become audible.

"I don't know anything," Anita protested. She was staring at the card in her hand, not recognizing it, waiting.

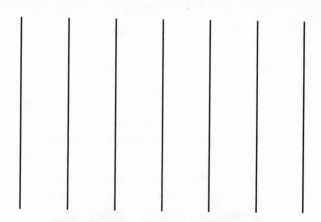

MANSLAUGHTER

Eddie Farrell, twenty-six, temporarily laid off from Lackawanna Steel, had been separated from his wife, Rose Ann, for several months, off and on, when the fatal stabbing occurred. This was on a January afternoon near dusk. Most of the day snow had been falling lightly and the sun appeared at the horizon for only a few minutes, the usual dull red sulfurous glow beyond the steel mills.

According to Eddie's sworn testimony, Rose Ann had telephoned him at his mother's house and demanded he come over, she had something to tell him. So he went over and picked her up—while he was driving his brother's 1977 Falcon—they went to the County Line Tavern for a drink—then drove around, talking, or maybe quarreling. Suddenly Rose Ann took out a knife and went for him—no warning—but he fought her off—he tried to take the knife away—*she* was stabbed by accident—he panicked and drove like crazy for twenty, twenty-five minutes—until he was finally flagged down by a state trooper out on the highway, doing eighty-eight miles an hour in a fifty-five-mile zone. By then Rose Ann had bled to death in the passenger's seat—she'd been stabbed in the throat, chest, belly, thighs, thirty or more times.

"I guess I lost control," Eddie said repeatedly, referring to the drive in the "death car" (as the newspapers called it), not to stabbing his wife: he didn't remember stabbing his wife. It seemed to him he had only defended himself against her attack, somehow she had managed to stab herself. Maybe to punish him. She was always criticizing him, always finding fault. She called up his mother, too, and bitched over the telephone—*that* really got to him.

When asked by police officers how his wife had come into possession of a hunting knife belonging to his brother, Eddie replied at first that he didn't have any idea, then he said she must have stolen it and hidden it away in the apartment. He really didn't know. She did crazy things. She threatened all kinds of crazy things. The knife was German-made, with an eight-inch stainless steel blade and a black sealed wood handle, a beautiful thing, expensive. Lying on a little table at the front of the courtroom, beneath the judge's high bench, it looked like it might be for sale—the last of its kind, after everything else had been bought.

At first Eddie Farrell was booked for second-de-

| | | | |

gree murder, with $45,000 bail (which meant 10 percent bond); then the charges were lowered to third, with $15,000 bail. Midway in the trial the charges would be lowered further to manslaughter, voluntary.

In was Beatrice Grazia's bad luck to happen to see the death car as it sped along Second Avenue in her direction. She was on her way home from work, crossing the street, when the car approached. She jumped back onto the curb, she said. The driver was a goddamned maniac and she didn't want to get killed.

Sure, she told police, she recognized Eddie Farrell driving—she got a clear view of his face as he drove past. But it all happened so quickly, she just stood on the curb staring after the car. Her coat was splashed with slush and dirt, he'd come that close to running her down.

At the trial five months later Beatrice swore to tell the truth, the whole truth, and nothing but the truth, but it all seemed remote now—insignificant. Her voice was so breathless it could barely be heard by the spectators in the first row. She was the tenth witness for the prosecution, out of twenty-seven, and her testimony seemed to add little to what had already been said. She hadn't wanted to appear—the district attorney's office had issued her a subpoena. Yes, she'd seen Eddie Farrell that day. Yes, he was driving east along Second. Yes, he was speeding. Yes, she had recognized him. Yes, he was in the courtroom today. Yes, she could point him out. Yes, she had seen someone in the passenger's seat beside him. No, she hadn't recognized the person. She believed it was a woman—she was fairly certain it was a woman—but the car passed by so quickly, she couldn't see.

Her voice was low, rapid, sullen, as if she were testifying against her will. Both the district attorney's assistant and the defense lawyer repeatedly asked her to speak up. The defense lawyer grew visibly irritated, his questions were edged with malice: How could she be certain she recognized the driver of the car?—wasn't it almost dark?—did she have *perfect* vision?

Blood rushed into her cheeks; she stammered a few words and went silent.

Eddie Farrell was sitting only a few yards away, staring dully into a corner of the courtroom—he didn't appear to be listening. His hair was slickly combed and parted on the side. He wore a pin-striped suit that fitted his skinny body loosely, as if he had put it on by mistake. His eyes were deep-set, shadowed; there was a queer oily sheen to his skin. Beatrice wasn't sure she would have recognized him, now.

Though everyone waited for Eddie to take the stand, to testify for himself, it wasn't his lawyer's strategy to allow him to speak: this disappointed many of the spectators. In all, the defense called only six people, four of them character witnesses. They spoke of Eddie Farrell as if they didn't realize he was in the courtroom with them; they didn't seem to have a great deal to say.

The most articulate witness was a young man named Ron Boci who had known Eddie, he said, for ten, twelve years, since grade school. He spoke rapidly and fluently, with a faint jeering edge to his voice; his swarthy skin had flushed darker. Yeah, he was a friend of Eddie's, they went places together—yeah, Eddie'd told him there was trouble with his wife—but it wasn't ever serious trouble, not from Eddie's side. He loved his wife, Ron Boci said, looking out over the courtroom, he wouldn't ever hurt her, he put up with a lot from her. Rose Ann was the one, he said. Rose Ann was always going on how she'd maybe kill herself, cut her throat, take an overdose or something, just to get back at Eddie, but Eddie never thought she meant it, nobody did—that was just Rose Ann shooting off her mouth. Yeah, Ron Boci said, moving his narrow shoulders, he knew her, kind of. But not like he knew Eddie.

Ron warmed as he spoke; he crossed his legs, resting one high-polished black boot lightly on his knee. He had a handsome beakish face, quick-darting eyes, hair parted in the center of his head so that it could flow thick and wavy to the sides, where it brushed against his collar. His hair was so black it looked polished. He too was wearing a suit—a beige checked suit with brass buttons—but it fitted his slender body snugly. His necktie was a queer part-luminous silver that might have been metallic.

During one of the recesses, when Beatrice went to the drinking fountain, Ron Boci appeared beside her and offered to turn on the water for her. It was a joke but Beatrice didn't think it was funny. "No thank you," she said, her eyes sliding away from his, struck by how white the whites were, how heavy the eyebrows. "No thank you, I can turn it on myself," Beatrice said, but he didn't seem to hear. She saw, stooping, lowering her pursed lips to the tepid stream of water, that there was a sprinkling of small warts on the back of Ron Boci's big-knuckled hand.

It was shortly after the New Year that Beatrice's husband, Tony, drove down to Port Arthur, Texas, on the

Gulf, to work for an offshore oil drilling company. He'd be calling her, he said. He'd write, he'd send back money as soon as he could.

A postcard came in mid-February, another at the end of March. Each showed the same Kodacolor photograph of a brilliant orange-red sunset on the Gulf of Mexico, with palm trees in languid silhouette. Not much news, Tony wrote, things weren't working out quite right, he'd be telephoning soon. No snow down here, he said, all winter. If it snows it melts right away.

Where is Tony? people asked, neighbors in the building, Beatrice's parents, her girlfriends, and she said with a childlike lifting of her chin, "Down in Texas where there's work." Then she tried to change the subject. Sometimes they persisted, asking if she was going to join him, if he had an apartment or anything, what their plans were. "He's supposed to call this weekend," Beatrice said. Her narrow face seemed to thicken in obstinacy; the muscles of her jaws went hard.

He did call, one Sunday night. She had to turn the television volume down but, at the other end of the line, there was a great deal of noise—as if a television were turned up high. A voice that resembled Tony's lifted incoherently. Beatrice said, "Yes? Tony? Is that you? What?" but the line crackled and went dead. She hung up. She waited awhile, then turned the television back up and sat staring at the screen until the phone rang again. This time, she thought, I know better than to answer.

"What are you doing about the rent for July?—and you still owe for June, don't you?" Beatrice's father asked.

Beatrice was filing her long angular nails briskly

with an emery board. Her face went hot with blood but she didn't look up.

"*I* better pay it," Beatrice's father said. "And you and the baby better move back with us."

"Who told you what we owe?" Beatrice asked.

She spoke in a flat neutral voice though her blood pulsed with anger. People were talking about them—her and Tony—it was an open secret now that Tony seemed to have moved out.

"Tony won't like it if I give this place up," Beatrice said, easing the emery board carefully around her thumbnail, which had grown to an unusual length. To provoke her father a little she said, "He'll maybe be mad if he comes back and somebody else is living here and he's got to go over to our house to find me and Danny. You know how his temper is."

Beatrice's father surprised her by laughing. Or maybe it was a kind of grunt—he rose from his chair, a big fleshy man, hands pushing on his thighs as if he needed extra leverage. "I can take care of your wop husband," he said.

It was a joke—it really *was* a joke because Beatrice's mother was Italian—but Beatrice hunched over the emery board and refused even to smile. "You wouldn't talk like that if Tony was here," she said.

"I wouldn't need to talk like this if Tony was here," her father said. "But the point is, he isn't here. That's what we're talking about."

"That's what *you're* talking about," Beatrice said.

When her father was leaving Beatrice followed after him on the stairs, pulling at his arm, saying, "Momma wants Danny with her and that's okay, Momma is wonderful with him, but, you know, this was supposed to be . . ." She made a clumsy pleading gesture indicating the stairs, the apartment on the landing, the building itself. She swallowed hard so that she wouldn't start to cry. "This was supposed to be a new place, a different place," she said, "that's why we came here. That's why we got married."

"I already talked to the guy downstairs," her father said, rattling his car keys. "He said you can move any time up to the fifteenth. I'll rent one of them U-Hauls and we'll do it in the morning."

"I don't think I can," Beatrice said, wiping angrily at her eyes. "I'm not going to do that."

"Next time he calls," Beatrice's father said, "tell him the news. Tell him your old man paid the rent for him. Tell him to look me up, he wants to cause trouble."

"I'm not going to do any of that," Beatrice said, starting to cry.

"It's already halfway done," her father said.

One night around ten o'clock Beatrice was leaving the Seven-Eleven store up the street when she heard someone approach her. As she glanced back an arm circled her shoulders, which were almost bare—she was wearing a red halter top—and a guy played at hugging her as if they were old pals. She screamed and pushed him away—jabbed at him with her elbow.

It was Ron Boci, Eddie Farrell's friend. He was wearing a T-shirt and jeans, no shoes. No belt, the waist of the jeans was loose and frayed, you could see how lean he was—not skinny exactly but lean, small-hipped. His hair was a little longer than it had been in the courtroom but it was still parted carefully in the center of his head; he had a habit of shaking it back, loosening it, when he knew people were watching.

"Hey, you knew who it was," he said. "Come on."

"You scared the hell out of me," Beatrice said. Her heart was knocking so hard she could feel her entire body rock. But she stooped and picked up the quart of milk she'd dropped, and the carton of cigarettes, and Ron Boci stood there with his knuckles on his hips, watching. He meant to keep the same kidding tone but she heard an edge of apology in his voice, or maybe it was something else.

"You knew who it was," he said, smiling, lifting one corner of his mouth, "you saw me in there but you wouldn't say hello."

"Saw you in where?" Beatrice asked. "There wasn't anybody in there but the salesclerk."

"I was in there, I stood right in the center of the aisle, where the soda pop and stuff is, but you pretended not to see me, you looked right through me," Ron Boci said. "But I bet you remember my name."

"I don't remember any name," Beatrice said. Her voice sounded so harsh and frightened, she added quickly, "It's just a good thing I wasn't carrying any bottles or anything, it'd all be broke now." She said, "Well, I know the name Boci. Your sister Marian."

"Yeah, Marian," Ron Boci said.

Beatrice started to walk away and Ron Boci followed close beside her. He was perhaps six inches taller than Beatrice and walked with his thumbs hooked into the waist of his jeans, an easy sidling walk, self-conscious, springy. His smell was tart and dry like tobacco mixed with something moist: hair oil, shaving lotion. Beatrice knew he was watching her but she pretended not to notice.

He was a little high, elated. He laughed softly to himself.

"Your telephone got disconnected or something," Ron Boci said after a pause. He spoke with an air of slight reproach.

"I don't live there anymore," Beatrice said quickly.

She saw a sprinkling of glass on the sidewalk ahead but she didn't intend to warn him: let him walk through it and slice up his filthy feet.

"Where do you live, then, Beatrice?" he asked casually. "I know Tony is in Texas."

"He's coming back in a few weeks," Beatrice said. "Or I might fly down."

"I used to know Tony," Ron Boci said. "The Grazias over on Market Street—? Mrs. Grazia and my mother used to be good friends."

Beatrice said nothing. Ron Boci's elbow brushed against her bare arm and all the fine brown hairs lifted in goose bumps.

"Where are you living now, if you moved?" Ron Boci asked.

"It doesn't matter where I live," Beatrice said.

"I mean, what's their name? You with somebody, or alone?"

"Why do you want to know?"

| | 167 | |

| | | | |

"I'm just asking. Where are you headed now?"

"My parents' place, I'm staying overnight. My mother helps out sometimes with the baby," Beatrice said. She heard her voice becoming quick, light, detached, as if it were a stranger's voice, overheard by accident. She was watching as Ron Boci walked through the broken glass—saw his left foot come down hard on a sliver at least four inches long—but he seemed not to notice, didn't even flinch. His elbow brushed against her again.

He was watching her, smiling. He said, in a slow, easy voice, "I didn't know Tony Grazia had a kid, how long ago was that? *You* don't look like you ever had any baby."

Beatrice said stiffly, "There's lots of things you don't know."

"I saw you last night at the Hi-Lo but you sure as hell didn't see me," Beatrice's father told her across the supper table. His face was beefy and damp with perspiration. "Ten, ten-thirty. You sure as hell didn't notice *me*."

It was late July and very hot. They'd had a heat spell for almost a week. Beatrice and her mother had set up a table in the living room, where it was cooler, but the effort hadn't made much difference. Beatrice's arms stuck unpleasantly to the surface of the table and her thighs stuck against her chair. She could see that her father was angry—his face was red and mottled with anger—but he didn't intend to say much in front of Beatrice's mother.

"I wasn't at the Hi-Lo very long," Beatrice said. "I don't even remember."

"Wearing sunglasses in the dark, *dark* glasses," Beatrice's father said with a snort of laughter, "like a movie star or something."

"That was just a joke," Beatrice said. "For five minutes. I had them on for five minutes and then I took them off."

"Okay," her father said, chewing his food. "Just wanted you to know."

"I just went out with some friends," she said.

"Okay," her father said.

After a while Beatrice said, "I don't need anybody spying on me, I'm not a kid. I'm twenty years old."

"You're a married woman," Beatrice's father said.

Beatrice's mother tried to interrupt but neither of them paid her any attention.

"If I want to go out with some friends," Beatrice said, her voice rising, "that's my business."

"I didn't see any *friends,* I saw only that one guy," Beatrice's father said. "As long as you know what you're doing."

Beatrice had stopped eating. She said nothing. She sat with her elbows on the table, staring and staring until her vision slipped out of focus. She could look at something—a glass saltshaker, a jar of mustard—until finally she wasn't seeing it and she wasn't thinking of anything and she wasn't aware of her surroundings either. In the past, when she lived at home, lapsing into one of these spells at the supper table could be dangerous—her father had slapped her awake more than once. But now he wouldn't. Now he probably wouldn't even touch her.

| | | | |

"Do you like this?" Ron Boci was saying.

Beatrice woke slowly. "No," she said. "Wait."

"Do you like *this?*" Ron said, laughing.

"No. Please. Wait." Her voice was muffled, groggy, she had dreamed she was suffocating and now she couldn't breathe. "Wait," she said.

After a while he said, "Christ, are you crying?"— and she said no. She was sobbing a little, or maybe laughing. Her head spun, Jesus she was hung over, at first she almost didn't know where she was, only that she didn't ever want to leave.

At work in the post office those long hours—waiting for the Clinton Street bus—changing the baby's diaper, her fingers so swift and practiced my God you'd think she had been doing this all her life—she found herself thinking of him. Of him and of it, what he did to her. That was it. That was the only thing. Sometimes the thought of him hit her so hard she felt a stabbing sensation in the pit of the belly, between her legs. She never thought of her husband, sometimes she went for hours without thinking of her baby. Once, changing his diaper, she pricked him and he began to cry angrily, red-faced, astonished, furious; she picked him up she held him in her arms she buried her face against him begging to be forgiven but the baby just kept crying: hot and wriggling and kicking and crying. Like he doesn't know who I am, Beatrice thought. Like he doesn't trust me.

Ron Boci's driver's license had been suspended for a year but in his line of work, as he explained, he had to use a car fairly often, especially for short distances in the city. He needed to make deliveries and he couldn't always trust his buddies.

He made his deliveries at night, he told Beatrice. During the day there was too much risk, his face was too well known in certain neighborhoods.

He usually borrowed his brother's '84 Dodge. Not in the best condition, it'd been around, Ron said, had taken some hard use. His own car, a new Century, white, red leather inside, wire wheels, vinyl roof, stereo—he'd totaled it last January out on the highway. Hit some ice, went into a skid, it all happened pretty fast. Totaled, Ron said with a soft whistle, smiling at Beatrice. He'd walked away from the crash, though, just a few scratches, bloody nose—"Not like the poor fuckers in the other car."

Beatrice stared. "So you were almost killed," she said.

"Hell no," Ron said, "didn't I just tell you? I walked away on my own two feet."

(Once Beatrice had happened to remark to Tony that he was lucky, real lucky about something. The precise reason for the remark she no longer remembered but she remembered Tony's quick reply: "Shit," he said, "you make your own luck.")

Manslaughter should have meant—how many years in prison? Not very many compared to a sentence for first-degree murder, or even second-degree murder, but, still, people in the neighborhood were astonished to hear that a governing board called the state appeals court had over-

| | | | |

turned Eddie Farrell's conviction. Like that!—"over-turned" his conviction on a technicality that had to do with the judge's remarks while the jury was in the court-room!

"Christ, I can't believe it," Beatrice's father said, tapping the newspaper with a forefinger. "I mean—*Jesus.* How do those asshole lawyers do it?"

So Eddie Farrell was free, suddenly. Released from the county house of detention and back home.

It was no secret that Eddie had killed his wife but people had been saying all along she'd asked for it, she'd asked for it for years, knowing Eddie had a nasty temper (like all the Farrells). Beatrice was stunned, didn't know what to think. And didn't want to talk about it. Her father said, laughing angrily, "It says here that Eddie Farrell told a reporter 'I was innocent before, and I'm innocent now.'"

Word got around the neighborhood: Eddie hadn't any hard feelings toward people who'd testified against him at the trial. He guessed they had to tell the truth as they saw it, they'd been subpoenaed and all. He guessed they didn't mean him any personal injury.

Now, he said, he hoped everybody would forget. *He* wasn't the kind of guy to nurse a grudge.

Beatrice's mother heard from a woman friend that Tony was back in town—someone had seen him with one of his brothers over on Holland Avenue. One day, pushing Danny in the stroller, Beatrice thought she heard some-one come up behind her, she had a feeling it was Tony, but she didn't look around: just kept pushing the stroller.

In Woolworth's window she saw the reflection of a young kid in a T-shirt striding past her. It wasn't Tony and she was happy with herself for not being frightened. You don't have any claim on me, she would tell him. I'm twenty years old. I have my own life.

The rumor that Tony Grazia was back in town must have been a lie, because Beatrice received another post-card from him at the beginning of August. He'd written only hello, asked how she and Danny were, how the weather was up north—it was hot as hell, he said, down there. *Hot as hell* was underscored. Since there was no return address Beatrice couldn't reply to the card. I have my own life, she was going to tell him, all her anger gone quiet and smooth.

It was meant to be a joke in the household, Tony's three postcards Scotch-taped on the back of the bath-room door, each the same photo of a Gulf of Mexico sunset.

"You're getting a strange sense of humor," Be-atrice's father told her.

"Maybe I always had one," Beatrice said.

Later that week Beatrice was in the shower at Ron Boci's, lathering herself vigorously under her arms, between her legs, between her toes, when she felt a draft of cooler air—she heard the bathroom door open and close. "Hey," she called out, "don't come in here. I don't want you in here."

He'd said he was going out for a pack of cigarettes but now he yanked open the scummy glass door to the stall and stepped inside, naked, grinning. He clapped his

| | | | |

hands over his eyes and said, "Don't you look at me, honey, and I won't look at you." Beatrice laughed wildly. They were so close she couldn't see him anyway—the skinny length of him, the hard fleshy rod erect between his legs, the way coarse black hairs grew on his thighs and legs, even on the backs of his pale toes.

They struggled together, they nipped and bit at each other's lips, still a little high from the joint they'd shared, and the bottle of dago wine. Beatrice wanted to work up a soapy lather on Ron Boci's chest but he knocked the bar of soap out of her hands. He gripped her hard by the buttocks, lifted her toward him, pushed and poked against her until he entered her, already thrusting, pumping, hard. Beatrice clutched at him, her arms around his neck, around his shoulders, her eyes shut tight in pain. It was the posture, the angle, that hurt. The rough tile wall of the shower stall against her back. "Hold still," he said, and she did. She locked herself against him in terror of falling. "Hold still," he said, grunting, his voice edged with impatience.

Later they shared another joint, and Beatrice cut slices of a melon, a rich seedy overripe cantaloupe she'd brought him from the open-air market. Though it was on the edge of being rotten it still tasted delicious; juice ran down their chins. Beatrice stared at herself in Ron Boci's bread knife, which must have been newly purchased, it was so sharp, the blade so shiny.

"I can see myself in it," Beatrice said softly, staring. "Like a mirror."

One Saturday night in the fall Ron Boci played a sly little trick on Beatrice.

They were going out, they were going on a double date with another couple, and who should come by to Ron's apartment to pick them up but Eddie Farrell? He was driving a new green Chevy Camaro; his girlfriend was a slight acquaintance of Beatrice's from high school, named Iris O'Mara.

Beatrice's expression must have been comical because both Eddie and Ron burst out laughing at her. Eddie stuck out his hand, grinning, and said, "Hey Beatrice, no hard feelings, okay? Not on *my* side." Ron nudged her forward, whispered something in her ear she didn't catch. She saw her hand go out and she saw Eddie Farrell take it, as if they were characters in a movie. Was this happening? Was she doing this? She didn't even know if, beneath her shock, she was surprised.

"No hard feelings, honey: not on *my* side," Eddie repeated.

He was cheery, expansive, his old self. Grateful to be out, he said, and to be *alive.*

The focus of attention, however, was Eddie's new Camaro. He demonstrated, along lower Tice, how powerfully it accelerated—from zero to forty miles an hour *in under twenty seconds.* Hell, these were only city streets, traffic lights and all that shit, he'd really cut loose when they got out on the highway.

Ron and Beatrice were sitting in the backseat of the speeding car but Ron and Eddie carried on a conversation in quick staccato exchanges. Iris shifted around to smile back at Beatrice. She was a redhead, petite, startlingly pretty, Beatrice's age though she looked younger. Her eyelids were dusted with something silvery and glittering and her long, beautifully shaped fingernails were painted frosty pink. To be friendly she asked Beatrice a few questions—about Beatrice's baby, about her parents—*not* about Tony—but with all the windows down and the wind rushing in it was impossible to talk.

Eddie drove out of town by the quickest route, using his brakes at the intersections, careful about running red lights: he wasn't going to take any chances ever again, he said. It was a warm muggy autumn night but Beatrice had begun to shiver and couldn't seem to stop. She wore stylish white nylon trousers that flared at the ankle, a light-textured maroon top, open-toed sandals with a two-inch heel, she looked good but the goddamned wind was whipping her hair like crazy and it seemed to be getting colder every minute. Ron Boci noticed her shivering finally and laid his arm warm and heavy and hard around her shoulders, pulling her against him in a gesture that was playful, but loving: "Hey honey," he said, "is this a little better?"

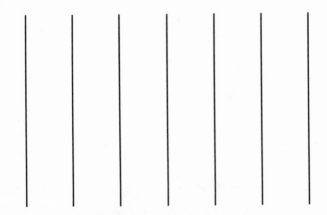

LITTLE WIFE

I

Damn his soul to hell, Judd was the first to notice the girl
across the street from the café though he was too sleepy
to know that he was watching her especially or even, at
first, that she was a girl. She might have been a boy his
age or a few years older. Hanging out, alone, by the bus
station; not by the lighted drive where buses pulled up
every half hour or so but by the entrance to the darkened
garage where the buses were parked overnight and ser-
viced during the day. She must have arrived on the eight-
thirty bus because after it pulled away Judd noticed her
standing there, waiting by the curb, a purse or duffel bag

slung across her shoulder. At first she seemed to be looking across the street at the café. Then it appeared she was
waiting for somebody. If Judd had given it much thought
he would have supposed she was waiting for a car to drive
up, it would slow, stop, the headlights on, he'd see her
open the door on the passenger's side and get in, the driver
would be her father, maybe, or an older brother, they'd
drive away and be home in a few minutes. It was a time
of day when people were going home.

Then he noticed that she was panhandling, or trying
to. Standing back in the shadows until somebody came
walking by. But she didn't know how to go about it. She
was slow and clumsy and maybe frightened. When she
saw somebody she would advance with her hand held out
and the man would just quicken his pace and hurry past
without looking at her. She made it too easy for them to
get away, Judd thought. Once he had panhandled himself
for a day or two, in a town upriver, after his mother had
kicked him out and before he'd gone back to live with
his father. He wasn't any fool, was Judd, shrewd like a
fox or a monkey his mother used to say—it was the kind
of remark you couldn't always figure out, did it mean good?
bad? or was it just funny?—but he had known enough to
study the older panhandlers and see how they went about
their business. First of all you need to place yourself on
a busy corner, by an intersection if you can with a traffic
light so that people can't rush by, you need to get them
to look you direct in the eyes, if you got them direct in
the eyes you had them, usually. At that time Judd hadn't
looked much more than ten years old. Small-boned, runty,
with grayish skin, damp squinting eyes, his nose running

and his face dirty. It had been winter, after Christmas, and he hadn't any hat or gloves. Or boots: he was wearing sneakers. If he managed to get people to look at him, men or women, it didn't seem to matter which, then they'd give him something most of the time, a dime or two or a quarter or a half-dollar dropped into his hand, rarely anything larger, the sons of bitches. The main feeling was them wanting to get away, and giving Judd a coin or two was payment for getting away but he hadn't cared, he'd made almost twenty dollars in those two days, which was the most money he had ever held in his hand at one time. Later almost half the money was stolen away from him but that wasn't the point, that was another story.

Twenty minutes. Half an hour. Now it was past nine-thirty and dark, and the girl was still across the street by the Greyhound station. Judd was a little nervous waiting for something to happen. A car to drive up after all and take her away. Maybe a police patrol car. As near as he could see she'd approached only five or six people in all this time and only one of them had given her something. The others carefully avoided her. When a bus pulled up to let passengers off she stood back in the shadows waiting, the duffel bag at her feet. Judd leaned against the window and stared out, he hadn't anything better to do. It was early, not even ten o'clock yet, his father and his father's friends Vern and Al and Ryan were drinking beer and had a long way to go, Judd would be lucky if he got to bed by one. In any case they weren't going home—it wasn't clear these days where "home" was—they were staying with Vern Decker out in the country, Decker's parents' old place, most of the acreage sold off and only the farmhouse and a few outbuildings left. Judd's eyes ached with the need to sleep and his stomach ached from the cheeseburger he'd eaten so fast. The French fries and sugary cole slaw. Lukewarm Pepsi-Cola. He could feel something moving low in his bowels like a snake uncoiling and pressing forward with its hard blunt head. He hoped to Christ he wouldn't get sick suddenly and need to use the lavatory, his father would be annoyed, or make one of his embarrassing jokes.

Judd's father called himself Judd Senior sometimes, at other times he called himself just Kovacs, which was his last name. He was a flush-faced good-looking man, hair receding from his forehead but he wore a mustache, full, drooping, coppery-brown; unlike the other men he sometimes wore a necktie when they went into town, or a string tie that gave him a western look. He was forty-three years old and he told the joke on himself that he had never expected to live past thirty let alone forty: but here he was, and what the hell. He and Judd were staying temporarily at Vern's until he got them on their feet again. He'd had a string of bad breaks going back for years, the final blow was his car giving out, a '78 Plymouth, and all the decent-paying work he could get right now was part-time construction work on a crew with Vern Decker and Charley Ryan. He liked to tell people that Judd Junior was the primary thing in his life. Judd Junior was his main reason for living. Otherwise what was the point? The boy's mother had left them and betrayed them both. But now it was his responsibility to make things right again. And it wasn't easy, in fact it was fucking hard, a steady uphill climb.

Just for fun Judd took up his father's glass and swallowed a big mouthful of beer, almost gagging to get it down. His father was telling a story and laughing hard; he scarcely noticed. Most of the evening the men had been talking about people Judd didn't know, things he wasn't interested in, he was bored, sleepy, slightly sick, he couldn't even watch television because the bartender wouldn't let him sit at the bar. Once in a while Vern Decker would wink at him and say, "How's it going?" but the other men ignored him and in any case Vern didn't mean anything by it. Judd heard himself say suddenly that there was somebody right across the street, a girl, it looked like, did they see her? She'd been out there a long time, acting strange. Why he brought this information up out of nowhere he didn't know. So the men craned their necks around and looked. It surprised Judd that they were so immediately interested. Was she a hooker? Not dressed like that. Was she a kid? Panhandling? A runaway? The girl had come out to stand by the curb beneath a street-lamp, hands on her hips, hair blowsy and shaggy, one foot lightly tapping. Ryan said she looked good to him. Vern said she might be kind of young. Judd's father said she must be waiting for somebody and Judd couldn't resist saying no she wasn't: she'd been out there an hour just standing around, acting strange. He'd been watching her, he said. She didn't know what the hell she was doing.

So Judd's father heaved himself up out of the booth and smoothed down his hair and said, "Okay fellas, I'll check her out."

Judd watched in disbelief as his father left the café and crossed the street with brisk purposeful strides and came right up to the girl and began talking to her. He hadn't meant for anything like this to happen! He wondered if his old man was drunker than he appeared. It puzzled him too that Decker and Al and Ryan were so interested in what was happening across the street, craning their necks, watching, speculating: would she come back with him . . . ? They laughed and thumped the table in triumph when it appeared she would. Judd's father was carrying her duffel bag slung over his shoulder.

At first the girl refused to tell them her name. "That's for me to know and you to find out," she said in a nasal singsong voice, as if she were already slightly drunk. And where was she from? "That's for me to know and you to find out." She squeezed into the booth between Judd Junior and Judd Senior, taking up a good deal of room for her size, giving off a stink, Judd thought, of nervousness and excitement. She might have been eighteen years old—she was older, close up, than she'd seemed. Judd didn't think she was pretty at all. He thought in fact she was ugly. Her skin was flushed and coarse, her eyes close-set, damp, gray, something mean and smirking about her mouth, which was damp too, and fleshy. She had a broad face and prominent cheekbones but her nose was small and looked pushed in: Judd could see tiny blackheads in the flesh. Why was she so wriggly and excited, Judd wondered. She'd taken up the men's banter as if they were all old friends. She was hungry, she admitted, but she didn't care what they ordered for her. God she *was* hungry, she said, laughing, squirming. Al pushed a plate of cold French fries in her direction and she began eating them with her fingers, almost daintily at first. She drank thirstily from Judd's father's beer glass. Then the waitress came over and they ordered for her—beer, a hot roast beef sandwich with gravy, French fries, cole slaw, the works. She hadn't eaten, she admitted, in a while. She'd been on a bus.

Eventually it came out that her name was Agnes.

"Agnes—that's a pretty name," Judd's father said. "That's an unusual name."

"Oh hell it's *not*," Agnes said, making a swipe at him with the flat of her hand, as if he'd said something too intimate. When the roast beef sandwich came she ate quickly, leaning toward the plate, though she kept up a steady flirty conversation with the men, interrupted by explosions of laughter. She'd taken off her jacket because it was hot in the booth, everybody jammed together, and Judd smelled her underarms, her unwashed hair. The hair was a fair brown shade streaked with blond but badly matted as if she hadn't combed it in days. She was wearing a black V-neck sweater in a thin synthetic fabric that fitted her tight across the breasts and shoulders and showed the lumpy outline of her brassiere. Her blue jeans were tight too, and faded almost colorless. She loved the men's attention, them staring at her, asking questions, teasing, but she wouldn't tell them her last name or where she was headed. "That's for me to know and you to find out," she said, wiping her mouth with a paper napkin.

She'd only glanced at Judd when she slid into the booth and never bothered with him afterward.

He couldn't see that she was pretty, he wondered why his father seemed so interested in her. She wasn't nearly so pretty as his mother. She had a pimply forehead, a rough-looking skin, there was something piggish about her, and jumpy, and hot. She gave off heat, you could smell it. The men told her there was a party she was invited to out in the country and she kept saying in her singsong reedy voice, "The hell you say," giving a swipe of her hand, giggling and squirming in her seat. Under the table she kicked Judd a half-dozen times without seeming to notice. Her cheeks were flushed, her eyes so happy Judd didn't like to see. Was she crazy? he wondered. Or simpleminded? Retarded? She kept saying, "The hell you say," and blushing deeper. She told them she had business of her own in town, a place she was expected at, she surely wasn't going to any party out in the country she hadn't heard about till five minutes ago. Judd's father leaned toward her smiling and his mustache glistened with moisture. His eyes were a little sleepy-lidded, his smile slightly crooked. He called her Agnes. Agnes this, Agnes that. He belched and excused himself in a comical way. He asked her did she believe in the division of labor and the division of property; the revolt of class slaves; the rise of the people. Did she know she was of the people, he asked, good solid country people, the salt of the earth. Was she Protestant? he asked. She laughed wildly and told him he was crazy. Then she said she'd been baptized Methodist but had fallen away in recent years. "That means you're Protestant," Judd's father said, "and you're among friends."

They were discussing whether Agnes should ride out to Decker's with Al or Ryan, or with Decker in his car. Al and Ryan had their motorcycles parked outside. Agnes squirmed with pleasure. Though she seemed in-

sulted too. "Ride on some goddamn old dangerous motorcycle?" she said, rolling her eyes, appealing suddenly
to Judd. "I'm riding in a car like any normal person."

So it seemed to be decided, Judd hadn't noticed
just when. He felt sick and sleepy and worried, he hated
the way the men stared at Agnes and he hated how slow
and stupid she was, how hopeful her gray eyes shone, he
told himself he wasn't going to care, he wasn't going to
give the slightest damn, whatever happened to her.

When Judd's mother left them for the first time they were
living in a trailer park in Port Huron. She'd promised him
she would be coming back to get him if she could, she'd
telephone, she said, every night, but weeks went by, a
month, and Judd's father said she'd lied to them both but
it didn't surprise him. When the telephone rang Judd's
father shut the door so that Judd couldn't overhear.

He got in trouble at school for fighting, worse yet,
for "issuing death threats" as the parents of one of his
classmates called it. He said he'd stick a blade in some
kid's guts and the little fucker pretended to take him seriously. And there was Judd trying to keep from laughing
in their faces. And there was Judd staring at himself in a
water-specked mirror in the boys' lavatory, that fox-faced
runty kid, red-eyed, a sore on his upper lip, a silly grin.
Is that me? Who the hell is that? But he didn't really care,
he knew how things would keep on without him, drift on
their own way.

His father made arrangements in secret and one
day they drove south to Bethany Falls, where his mother
seemed to be waiting. She acted almost as if she hadn't

| | | | |

been gone for half a year so Judd fell in with the pretense. They lived in another trailer park not very different from the one in Port Huron except now he had to take a bus to school and the ride was forty-five minutes, he was in fifth grade, he had the idea he'd been in fifth grade at this school before, a long time ago in another lifetime maybe: his mother believed, she said, in former lifetimes, it was this lifetime, she said, laughing, she was having trouble with.

At this time Judd's father was a security guard for a local service that hired out guards to watch over warehouses, car lots, fresh produce markets, and the like, he even had a khaki-colored uniform and a cap, *Hercules Protection Services Inc.* stitched on his jacket. But he quit after a few months when he couldn't get licensed to carry a pistol. His pride was injured but mainly it was practical: he didn't want to be unarmed if a dangerous situation arose. "A man has only one life," he said. He was on unemployment for six weeks, which made living in the little trailer difficult, then he got another job in the machine shop of a nonunionized factory that manufactured small parts for General Motors. When automobile sales were stable the men had work, when sales dipped they were laid off, it was a rhythm no one could predict in advance and it left the men apprehensive and suspicious. Afternoons when Judd got off the school bus he would sit on the edge of a deep clay drainage ditch near the trailer waiting until he thought it might be all right for him to go home. He had memorized the wildflowers and thistles in the ditch, the old rotted tires, broken bottles, parts of furniture, toys. If his father was home he would have been drinking beer all day. If only his mother was home the situation might go either way: it might be unpleasant, it might be all right. There were times when his mother acted as if she were surprised to see him, as if he were coming home at the wrong time, meaning to frighten her. Then he'd have to endure being hugged, hard. Trying not to smell her breath. *Mus-ca-tel*, he thought. *Mus-ca-tel*. He'd tasted it himself more than once, it was sweet, syrupy, very different from the beer and ale his father drank.

Judd's mother's name was Irene (pronounced "Irene-y"). She was a bright-faced pretty woman with faint lines between her eyes from frowning. She had cloudy frizzy dark hair like Judd's and long thin arms, the wrists especially thin, all bones. A flash of teeth and gums when she laughed. Even if she hadn't felt strong enough to get dressed that day she liked to fix Judd a peanut butter and jelly sandwich after school and watch him eat. It seemed to make her happy. Sometimes Judd could smell vomit in the tiny bathroom though she had been careful to flush it all away. He cranked open the window slats to let the odor out so that his father wouldn't know when he came home.

When Judd's mother came out looking for him, the wind blowing her hair, her lipsticked mouth bright in her face, Judd's friends said it was hard to believe she was anybody's mother. She didn't look like a mother, they said. "No," said Judd, embarrassed, not knowing what he meant. "She isn't." She told him she suffered premonitions of disaster, seeing him lying on the ground with a bleeding head, lying on the edge of the highway, at the bottom of the drainage ditch. She'd come calling for him, frightened, excited, rousing up half the trailer park. To spite her he hid from her back in the woods. He told himself he hated her.

After she went away for the second time he knew he had been hating her beforehand to save himself grief.

Judd's father couldn't believe that his wife had filed for divorce this time—"filed for divorce"—it sounded like something in the newspaper. The first thing he did was get drunk, the second was to quit his job. He got drunk three nights in a row and when he came home stumbling and talking to himself, Judd pressed his forearms over his ears so that he wouldn't hear. Some nights Judd's father was so lonely he slept with him, lying atop the covers, only partly undressed, snoring and making weeping noises in his sleep. When he caught Judd dialing one of the telephone numbers Judd's mother had left behind he snatched the receiver out of Judd's hand and slapped him hard. It wasn't a time for disloyalty between father and son, he said. His eyes shone with tears that wouldn't spill and his voice trembled as Judd had never heard it before.

Judd's father had known about the muscatel, the secret drinking. It was hardly a secret when half the trailer park knew. They quarreled mainly because she lied to him, she couldn't be trusted. If he gave her money he couldn't trust her to spend it on groceries. People who drink by themselves are sick, he told Judd, you have to learn to pity them but not be taken in by their lies. On weekends he himself might drink two cases of ale—one case on Saturday, one on Sunday—but he never showed the slightest effect and he could get up on time for work

Monday morning. All his friends were like him, they could hold their alcohol, only very rarely did they get drunk and that was for special occasions. It's the difference, Judd's father told him, between alcoholic susceptibility and alcoholic immunity.

When Judd's mother left she packed her things carefully, took her time, she was nervous but she knew Judd's father wouldn't be home till past six o'clock and it was still early afternoon. She gave Judd three addresses because she didn't know exactly where she was going. And some telephone numbers too. When she got settled, she said, she'd be sending for him to come live with her. "Are you going to get married again?" Judd asked. He wasn't angry, in fact his voice came out bored. His mother didn't seem to hear the question though finally she said, "No. I wouldn't do that. No. Never again."

Weeks went by, months, Judd's father never spoke of her though Judd heard him on the telephone sometimes, speaking in a slow sarcastic voice or asking questions, short, laughing, angry, sarcastic, "Oh yes, *when—?*" "What—?" "Who—?" "*What* did you say?—didn't catch that." When he had to meet with her lawyer, or with his own, he came back subdued and tired-looking but Judd knew enough to keep out of his way; these were the most dangerous times. He was having credit card trouble too. And trouble with the Plymouth. "What is imminent is a complete change in our lives," he said frequently, smiling at Judd, his fingers picking at his mustache. "But I have to think how to maneuver." When he applied for his old job back at the factory and they turned him down he conceded it was for the best. He was finished with Bethany

| | | | |

Falls and with the trailer living, he said. From now on it would be just the two of them, Judd Junior and Judd Senior.

The night they brought Agnes out to the farm Judd slept in the hay barn where he sometimes slept in the summer or when things were noisy at the house. He knew they'd be partying a long time—they were going to telephone some other friends, they'd bought several cases of beer—and he didn't want to be in anybody's way. There was a mattress for him in one of the upstairs rooms of the house but he preferred the barn, he had a craving for certain smells, subtle mysterious smells, dust, old half-rotted hay, old cow manure, it made colors sift through his mind, goldenrod, sunshine, in the hayloft he had made a place for himself with a horse blanket, a pillow, he liked the smell of the old horse blanket too, and the leathery smell of the straps, it was a secret place of his where he could hide away during the day too if he had reasons for hiding. He didn't listen to noises from the house. Laughter, loud voices. He'd heard them before. If Agnes was lucky there would be a few women at the party for a while, girl-friends of the other men, if she wasn't lucky there wouldn't be any other women at all, but in any case the other women would be going home when the party was over and Agnes wasn't going anywhere at all.

But he wasn't going to think about her.

He wasn't going to think about his father, either. Or his mother and his mother's fiancé.

There was a promise to himself that in the barn he didn't have to think any of his regular thoughts. He might be off on his own, a thousand miles away, in the morning he wouldn't see Vern Decker's house or any landscape he knew. He could lie awake watching moonlight through cracks in the rough planks of the walls and thinking about nothing at all except how happy he was to be alone, how there were accidents in life (his father selling the trailer, his father meeting up with Vern, this barn behind Vern's house, and so forth) as wispy and delicate as a cobweb you could break without meaning to but you could avoid breaking too if you were careful. He never knew when he fell asleep, except his thinking seemed to blur at the edges. Ideas of things changed to pictures but the pictures came sideways, at a slant. Sometimes they were pictures of people he knew but most of the time they were strangers. Then he'd be asleep, he'd be gone, and in the morning he always woke early because of roosters crowing on a farm close by. He'd wake up stiff and dry-mouthed from breathing in the hay dust for so many hours but it was a good feeling to be awake so early, before any of the others, sometimes two or three hours before he could go in for breakfast. The point was, he could do anything he wanted: sneak out to the highway and hitch a ride north or south, flag down a Greyhound bus and see how far a dollar or two could take him. That was a promise he had made himself too, something that was waiting, but he didn't want to leave his father exactly, he didn't want to cause his father grief. He knew his father loved him because there wasn't anything else to love.

Little wife they started calling her after the first week or so, it was Judd's father's expression, teasing, mock seri-

| | | | |

ous, he'd sing a few loud lines of an old Johnny Cash song and mix in *Little wife, sweet little wife,* clowning around in the kitchen trying to get Agnes to dance with him. But if she fell in with him, raising her arms, smiling, a slow uncertain open-mouthed grin that showed her crooked front teeth, he'd back off and leave her standing there.

Judd didn't feel sorry for her because, near as he could tell, she wasn't ever surprised, or disappointed, or thrown off stride for long. She'd known to fit herself in with the rhythm of the household from the first.

Little wife, little wife. She'd bang around the house, upstairs and down, even in the cellar, as if she owned it. Humming the tune to Judd's father's drawling song.

Right away she lorded it over Judd. He saw that coming. He was only a kid, he was only twelve, but he'd have to help her out with things, washing up after meals especially, keeping the house picked up, and she didn't want him in her way or gaping at her. As if Judd would gape at her! She was nervous and giggly with so many men prizing her—not just Judd's father (who seemed to be her favorite) and Vern Decker but whoever else dropped by—and soon got bossy enough to nag Vern into getting the TV repaired. It had been on the fritz for months and nobody tried to watch it any more but Agnes insisted, Agnes put her foot down, as she said, and in twelve days it was working good as new and if she was left alone in the big old damn house—as she called it—at least she wasn't *lonely.* She kept the sound up loud whether she was in the room with the TV or not. Judd knew too that she talked back to the TV voices or was she maybe just talking to herself? rehearsing things she might say to all the men who were so crazy about her?

Much of the time she wore jeans but she took care to add a bright-colored blouse or sweater; she favored a shiny patent leather belt that cinched her waist in so tight Judd wondered how she could breathe. When her hair was washed it was fluffed and curly, she wore lipstick even during the day, sprayed herself with the strong lilac perfume Charley Ryan bought her at the Woolworth's in town. *Little wife, little wife.* She chattered when nobody was much listening but she didn't seem to mind. They'd given her her own room at the back of the house—a real bed with a mattress. Near as Judd cared to figure the men shared her, there was nothing secret or furtive about it after the first few days when Judd's father avoided looking directly at him or talking with him much, it was just the way things were going to be, Judd wasn't even sure how he felt or that he was called upon to feel anything. What business was it of his? What did he care? Agnes was quick to guess the moods the men were in—they could swing from being happy one minute to being angry the next—she was sensitive, Judd thought, even if she wasn't very bright—so it was mainly with Judd that she complained or tossed things around in the kitchen or shut doors hard. Sometimes it seemed she wanted him on her side, that they were both kids together, brother and sister maybe, other times she ordered him around, asked him what the hell he was gaping at, who he thought *he* was. Once she slitted her eyes at him as if she were practicing slitting them at somebody else. She said in a low breathy voice, "I got as much right

| | | | |

to be here as you. You don't own the place either, you and your hotshit daddy."

Sometimes it was Agnes and Judd's father, sometimes it was Agnes and Vern whispering in corners, exchanging secret looks, then again it might be Agnes and Al for a few days, or, after a wild ride on Charley Ryan's motorcycle one Sunday in early September, Agnes and Charley for a few days. He had finally managed to get Agnes drunk enough to climb behind him on the sheepskin-covered seat of the big black bike and clasp her arms around his waist and off they went, gone for much of the night. And when they returned nobody much noticed—Judd's father, for instance, was paired off with a woman of his own and anything that Agnes and fat-faced Charley Ryan did together wasn't significant.

Still, it gave Agnes a special nervous bloom for a while. Charley Ryan coming around, taking her to town on his cycle. Treating her good. It proved Agnes could get a man for herself, exclusively for herself, any time she wanted.

But she was jealous of women who came to parties at Vern's house. She accused them of looking down on her, not talking to her, laughing at her behind her back. She hated them, she said. Who did they think they were?— cunts like anybody else. So she'd sulk and hide away in her room with a bottle. And maybe none of the men would give a damn, or maybe one of them would kick the door open and haul her out. "Here's Agnes. Here's our pal!"

The mood of the party might be teasing and good-natured or it might not be so good-natured and the teasing got a little rough. Agnes shouted that she had her dignity and she intended to leave the next morning. She had business of her own, she said, and nobody had better try to stop her. Agnes with her hair in her eyes, her bright lipstick smeared, cords standing out in her neck. Then she'd start crying and Judd's father would be the one to calm her, patting her back, hugging her and winking at his buddies over her head. She was crazy about Judd Senior, that was obvious. "You know you're free to leave us any time you want, honey," he said, puckering his lips. "Don't you mind you'd be breaking all our hearts."

So she'd cry for half an hour more, then forgive them.

And in the morning Judd might catch a glimpse of her staggering into the bathroom at the rear of the house, just off the kitchen. He was never watching for her but it seemed he was always seeing her and then it was too late to look away. Agnes wearing that old lemon-colored "silk" shirt of his father's, a pair of white underpants or no underpants at all, the movement of her legs pale and fishlike in the shadows, all her movements vague, dim, swimming, as if she went where she went by instinct, her eyes closed. She didn't always close the bathroom door tight. He'd hear her inside, using the toilet. Or being sick—gagging and retching. Or crying. She did a good deal of crying now. And singing to herself on good mornings. Singing while she ran the faucet or the shower. Judd didn't know which of her noises he hated the most, he wasn't even sure he could distinguish between them.

| | | | |

For a while there was a joke in the household about Agnes having to use the john so much. Peeing every half hour, it seemed. Agnes said angrily that she couldn't help it. They teased her, they'd let it drop for a while then bring it up again, watching her get red, her eyes fill with tears. She didn't know what was wrong, she said, she just *had* to. And it burned, she said, every time she went. "Maybe I better go to a doctor," she said one day, but in such a vague flat voice it seemed she knew nobody was listening.

Agnes was in love with Judd's father so naturally she had questions to ask about Judd's mother but Judd knew enough not to get roped into answering them. What did Judd's mother look like; was she pretty; was she smart; did Judd favor her, or him? Judd just shrugged his shoulders and mumbled that he didn't know.

And it was true, he didn't. Or if it wasn't true it should have been.

She believed in reincarnation too, sort of. "Re-in-car-na-tion"—carefully pronounced. Souls dying in one place and being born somewhere else, ancient lives like in Egypt some people could remember and describe perfectly . . . like on TV one night there was a whole hour program devoted to the subject, wasn't there? And they wouldn't just lie about something so important.

She got in a funny quarrel with Judd Senior over what Judd Senior called the logistics of reincarnation. For instance, there are a hell of a lot more people living today than in the year 1000 B.C., right?—so where do the extra ones come from?

But Agnes didn't understand. "Extra ones . . . ?"

Judd Senior tried to explain but she couldn't follow. She was sitting at the kitchen table frowning and squinting. Her skin gave off a fruity warmth, her gray eyes, narrowed, looked shrewd and almost intelligent. Finally she said in a voice quavering with triumph, a slow gloating awakening to triumph, "Okay but *where did the first ones come from, of all?*" Judd's father just waved her away as if she were too stupid to deal with but Agnes thumped the table with both fists, hot and flushed, noisy as a child. "Okay Mr. Hotshot where did the first ones come from? Huh? You don't know, do you! *You don't know any goddam fucking more than I do!*"

She kept herself so secret about certain things, where she was from, for instance, who her people were, they couldn't help wondering, Judd Senior especially. He'd ask sly questions like was she the runaway wife of some crazy old millionaire? or the runaway mother of a half-dozen squawling brats? or an escapee from the women's detention up in Fredericktown . . . ? Which would get poor Agnes going, red-faced and laughing, or angry, or confused, giving Judd Senior a shove in the chest (though she learned to be careful since Judd Senior never allowed any female to poke him without he poked her right back). Eventually it came out that she was from a farm, or what was left of a farm, about fifty miles north of town. She couldn't get along with her family, she said. She'd had enough of them, she didn't want to talk about it.

Judd Senior kept asking, though. As Judd Junior knew, he didn't like secrets because secrets meant somebody was deceiving him. It was a kind of cheating too, Judd Senior explained, almost like you were being denied something that belonged to you. So he kept poking, asking his sly funny teasing questions, and one night in October Agnes got drunk and started telling them about her mother and her married sister who lived at home with her husband and kids, how they got in her way and tried to boss her around, ever since she'd dropped out of high school they were after her, it was Agnes this, Agnes that, if she had a boyfriend they raised hell because it wasn't the right kind of boyfriend and if she didn't have a boyfriend they talked about nobody wanting to marry her, and then her father got sick, he'd had to give up farming a long time ago because he couldn't make a living at it, then he worked where he could get work then he got sick, some kind of kidney disease they said wasn't cancer exactly but it sure as hell sounded like cancer to Agnes, then he died but it took him almost a year to die, he was a real nice man Agnes said, starting to cry, it was just how things happened to him that made him act the way he did, she could see that, she could understand that, but by the time he died everybody was afraid of him and hated him, Agnes thought she sort of hated him too, then after he died they were all still mad about something, she just couldn't take that kind of shit any longer, she had to get out and she wasn't ever going back. Now she was crying, sobbing, rocking back and forth on the sofa. The men were embarrassed and bored and it fell to Judd's father to pat her on the shoulder and tell her okay, that was enough, but she couldn't seem to stop, now that she got started she couldn't seem to stop, wanted to sit there crying and talking about her father, her married sister she hated, her grandmother who always had to know her business, saying she loved her, but the men drifted into another room and Judd wasn't going to get stuck with her so he turned the TV sound up loud so that, maybe, the TV would distract her, or make her feel better.

It was the next night that one of the men—Vern, or was it Charley Ryan—slapped her and bloodied her nose.

And nobody told him to stop.

And Judd Senior said she deserved it, talking so much, acting so smart-ass around the place as if she owned it.

And Agnes looked at the men and understood it was important not to cry right then, not to say anything, just to turn and go to the bathroom and fix up her face; and stay out of their way for the rest of the night.

II

The previous year, when Judd went to stay with his mother, the plan was that he could stay with her—with them—as long as he wanted. If things worked out. If they all got along. But Judd's father wasn't to know that that was the plan, exactly. He could be told later. So far as he knew Judd was going to stay with his mother a few weeks and that was all. Over the telephone, however, Judd's mother had said excitedly that she wanted him with her as long as he wanted to be with her, she missed him so, thought about him every hour, her precious baby, sweet foxy little Judd, she didn't want a new baby, she said, she wanted *him,* then she was crying, short breathless sobs that sounded almost like laughing, and Judd held the receiver away from his ear, his eyes shut tight: if one person gave in to crying the other had better not. That was some wisdom of Judd Senior's he'd overheard.

Judd's mother had left Bethany Falls in February and it wasn't until late November that Judd went to stay with her in a small-sized city named Cicero in the southernmost tip of the state. By then she was divorced from Judd's father and beginning a new life. She'd had a hard time, she said, but she wouldn't dwell upon it, now she was engaged to a man, a gentleman actually, named Flagler, whom Judd was to call Mr. Flagler: he was an insurance and real estate salesman, a very nice man, but sensitive, she warned, and ambivalent—"ambivalent" was his word—about the future. Judd didn't understand, what did ambivalent mean? His mother said vaguely that he could look it up in the dictionary. She hadn't actually looked it up herself but she believed she knew what it meant. The main thing was, she added, that small children made Mr. Flagler nervous because they reminded him of when his own were small.

Judd would have supposed that "small" meant children of two or three or four, not eleven, but he couldn't altogether be certain. It might apply to him as a warning.

He took the Greyhound bus to Cicero by himself, a five-hour ride. His father hardly spoke to him for days beforehand, then, seeing him off, he hugged him hard and said in a voice heavy with sarcasm, "Say hello to your mother's *boyfriend* for me, don't forget. Give your mother's *boyfriend* her husband's *congratulations and good wishes,*" but he was smiling too, one of his big broad mustache-curling smiles, so Judd smiled back and climbed onto the bus. He wasn't ever coming back again, that was *his* secret.

But the visit to Cicero didn't work out. Judd understood even before meeting his mother's fiancé that it was a mistake. They were living together in a large apartment complex called Cicero Acres that consisted of a number of two-story stucco buildings facing a central courtyard that held a swimming pool covered with a rotted tarpaulin. There were north, east, south, and west wings, and units ranging from "A" to "K." The sidewalks were gritty with ice and when Judd arrived in the late morning a crew of garbagemen, all black, was unloading garbage cans. They made so much noise crashing the cans against the dump truck, tossing them onto the ground, their shouts to one another were so loud and spirited, by the time Judd found his mother's apartment, number 11 in East Wing Unit "G," he had to ring the bell and knock for almost ten minutes because his mother was afraid to answer the door. She came to peek through the closed venetian blinds, finally, and let him in, hugging him in relief, kissing him wildly. She was terrified, she said, of those garbagemen— Wednesdays and Saturdays were their days—she was sorry she hadn't run to let him in right away. Even so, Judd could feel her trembling. She looked thinner than he remembered, the delicate bones on the backs of her hands stood out, and her hair was short, tightly curled, a lighter shade than he remembered. Her breath smelled just faintly sweet. Unpacking his bag she started to tell him about something that had happened a few weeks ago to a woman in a neighboring building, a woman living alone, her assailant was described only as a "black youth" and he hadn't yet been apprehended; then she thought better of it and changed the subject. He must be starving, she said brightly. All those hours on the bus.

Judd stayed with his mother for a little more than two weeks though he understood in the first day or two that he wasn't wanted: not really.

There was some pretense in the beginning that Flagler wasn't actually living in the apartment, just dropping by to meet Judd and to stay for dinner, watching TV in the evening with Judd and Judd's mother. He took them to see *Ghostbusters,* which had been playing at the Cicero mall for six months, then to a Howard Johnson's afterward; he even took Judd to a roller rink one Saturday afternoon and sat alone, smoking, his big body soft and relaxed-looking back in the shadows, his expression amiable, vague. Judd's mother had stayed back in the apartment so that Judd and Mr. Flagler could become better acquainted but when they were alone together they had nothing much to say. Judd considered giving the man his father's message, imitating the drawl and angry dip of his father's voice, but he hadn't that kind of nerve, in any case he didn't hate Flagler that much. Actually he didn't hate him at all. Flagler had a small dark mustache one quarter the size of Judd's father's, he had a puffy suety face, small sad evasive eyes, a weak mouth. Even when he smiled he looked aggrieved. His voice was surprisingly high for a man of his size and his words frequently trailed off into an embarrassed silence as if he'd lost the thread of what he was trying to say and it hardly seemed important enough to retrieve.

Still, Judd could hear his mother and Flagler talking alone together, their voices urgent and hurried. They weren't quarreling—he knew what quarrels sounded like—in fact Flagler never raised his voice all the time Judd stayed with them—but he knew they were talking about him. Flagler was being reasonable, Flagler was asking how long Judd meant to stay, what about Judd's father, etc., and probably Judd's mother was doing her best to answer, telling the truth as she saw it, or some kind of truth at least. Judd wasn't anxious or even especially curious about what they were saying because it wouldn't be a surprise to him. Most things, he thought, weren't going to be surprises to him any longer.

It was almost a year later that Judd started taking a school bus to a consolidated county school a few miles from Decker's house. He hadn't wanted to go back to school, any school, and his father hadn't wanted him to—Judd Senior was down on public education, conformist American brainwashing as he called it—but a county agent had come out to Decker's asking questions about Judd. How old was he, where had he been born, who were his parents, etc. Now that Judd's father paid some of Decker's monthly mortgage he was a bona fide resident of Fayette County and his school-age children if he had any were not only eligible to attend Fayette County public schools but obliged under federal law to do so.

By this time the men were getting fairly brutal with Agnes so Judd was grateful for school. He stayed away

| | | | |

from the house as long as he could and when he was home he kept to himself, working on his homework or reading. He'd stopped asking when they were going to leave Decker's house because the question seemed to upset his father, and he knew better than to ask what was wrong, what was happening with Agnes: why the men didn't seem to like her any more. Stupid cunt, they called her. It was a joky kind of thing most of the time. Stupid cow. Fat-ass. Fuck-face. But sometimes they hit her, pushed her around, knocked her against the wall, for the hell of it, maybe, or because she provoked them. She started crying or screamed at them and that made things worse. Even when nothing had happened for a day or two Judd could feel the charged atmosphere, an undercurrent of excitement in the house like the air before a thunderstorm.

He didn't know if he felt sorry for Agnes or if he was frightened for himself. He asked his father about it just once, when they were alone together, and his father stared at him and said, "Who wants to know?"

Poor dumb Agnes, poor little wife, that cunt with the pouting face, the swollen lip. Sometimes one or both of her eyes might be blackened, her nostrils encrusted with blood. They apologized afterward, the next day they'd all have hangovers and be sorry. The problem was that she provoked them. The kinds of meals she tried to get away with, the smart-ass things she said under her breath. She tried to play the men against one another and they didn't like that. She complained a lot and they didn't like that. Then she'd have a few beers too many and lose control and threaten to call the police and that would start it all again. A few days of peace and calm then another heavy session, Agnes screaming and slapping and scratching and kicking, and that meant real trouble: that meant one of the men might have to be held back by the others, and it always caused bad feelings among them afterward.

"The most devious thing about a woman," Judd's father told him, "is the trick of turning a man against his buddies. You watch for that, you hear?"

Agnes threatened to call the police so they told her to call the police. She threatened to leave so they told her to leave. But when Judd came home from school the next day nothing had changed, Agnes was still there, watching TV or messing around in the kitchen. Sometimes she seemed to want to talk, she asked him questions about school, if he was making friends, if he missed his mother, what his mother's new boyfriend was like, and Judd felt almost dizzy with wanting to get away; sometimes she'd give him a look of hatred and say nothing. A few days later there might be a party and he'd see her drunk and giggly, sprawled on somebody's lap—his father's, Vern Decker's, a stranger's—as if nothing had happened.

Maybe nothing had happened, Judd thought. If Agnes didn't think it had.

You guys gonna kill her? Judd wanted to ask.

If he knew to ask the question in just the right way, grinning with half his mouth like Judd Senior, screwing up one of his eyes like crazy Al—if he knew how to get the words out right—then he'd swallow hard and ask. *You guys gonna kill her? Okay but why? Don't you like her any more?*

But he didn't know how. His throat closed up at

the thought of asking, his lips were numb. And it wasn't any of his business, was it. He was just a kid, not even thirteen years old. Enrolled in the seventh grade at the Fayette County Consolidated School up the road.

One morning when the house was empty except for Agnes and Judd he peeked into her bedroom on his way out to catch the school bus. It was after eight o'clock but she was still asleep, she slept long and heavy and hard like a sick person. Lying on her back at a twisted angle across the bed, her head turned to the side, mouth open, a wet rasping gurgling snore. Her hair was stringy and greasy, her eyelids puffy. The blanket was pulled down to expose one of her breasts. Judd saw that she was thinner, her chest bones prominent, the skin pale and pimply except where it was discolored by bruises. Her nipple was raw-looking, rosy brown. The breast looked slack and queer just by itself. Was she sleeping? Judd wondered, uneasy, standing in the doorway. Or was she just pretending?

Judd's father said Agnes was always "putting on an act": even her shrieks and crying jags. His father said with a wave of his hand, Poor dumb cunt Agnes, don't pay no heed to *her,* she doesn't know her ass from her elbow.

She'd thought she was pregnant for a week or two but it was a false alarm.

She'd thought she had some secret thing going with one of Vern's pals from work, him and her talking on the telephone when nobody was around, making plans, plotting behind Vern's and Judd Senior's backs, but it all fizzled out: the guy wasn't that much of an asshole to fall for a pig like *her.*

Judd stood in the doorway, staring. He knew he should leave but he simply stood there. It was a surprise to him that Agnes's room was so small—about the size of the room they'd given him, upstairs. A stink of old un-washed bedclothes, lilac perfume, beer. The men's sweat and Agnes's own sweetish-stale smell. There was an odor too of menstrual blood, rank, rich, dark-smelling, Judd knew the mattress was stained because he'd overheard one of the men complaining and Agnes shooting back that it wasn't for Christ's sake *her* fault, as if it would be *her* fault, doing stuff like that when she only wanted to be left alone. . . . The blind on the window hung torn and crooked, yanked off its roll. Judd had the idea that some-body might come to look in, he'd see both Agnes and Judd, both of them at the same time. He felt his groin tighten with danger. If she opened her eyes, if she saw him, what then. Her cherry-red lipstick was nearly worn off but her mouth looked fleshy and damp. Her breathing was labored and irregular as if, each time, she had to think how to breathe; how to suck in air. Last night the men had been playing poker in the kitchen. Seven or eight men, Agnes hanging over their shoulders, caught up in the tension. Four clubs! Five spades! Queen! King! Ace of hearts! They told her she didn't know shit about poker but she insisted she had a lucky streak sometimes in any card game she tried especially gin rummy, why didn't they play a few hands of gin rummy and she'd show them, but the men weren't interested in gin rummy. Go watch TV, Agnes. Go stick your head in the toilet.

Why do you want to hurt me, says poor little wife, poor dumb cunt Agnes. Why do you want to hurt me

| | | | |

don't you love me Jesus look how I love *you*. Swigging ale like one of the men, lifting the bottle to her mouth. Blue jeans with a fly front open at the waist, tight red sweater, sleeveless, though the goddam house is freezing: none of the windows fits right. Is Judd spying? Is Judd listening? He's doing his math homework upstairs and doesn't give a damn about what goes on downstairs. For instance if Agnes loses her temper and starts throwing plates and silverware on the floor, screaming she's going to call the sheriff she's going to call her fucking brother-in-law to come get her, she's had enough of their shit.

But hey why do you want to hurt me? You know how I love you.

Love ya. Love ya.

Judd stood in the doorway, his own breathing queer and irregular. He hadn't slept many hours the night before and now he felt asleep on his feet. Once, a long time ago when Agnes had just moved in with them, he had opened the bathroom door by mistake and almost walked in on her and his father. They were both naked, fooling around, running water in the tub, hot and noisy and splashing, the air thick with steam. Judd's father had turned with an angry laugh—"Hey! Get the hell out!"—and Agnes had given a high foolish shriek, eyes wide, hiding her breasts with a towel. In disgust Judd had slammed the door on them and run away and hid in the barn and he hadn't thought of it since then, not that he knew. But he was still disgusted.

The sky was lightening, there were birds in the eaves, the crowing of roosters in the distance. Pale sunlight slanted through the cracked shade. It was a time of day he liked when he was outside and away from the house. He heard Agnes grating her teeth faintly, sighing in her sleep. One of her fists clenched. Her puffy eyelids twitching. The nipple on her breast looked like a tiny bud that had been injured and would never open.

He waited for her to wake and see him, he waited for the next thing to happen that would happen. But she didn't wake, she looked dopey, drugged. And he remembered the school bus suddenly. And he wondered if he had already missed it.

He had missed the school bus, yes, but it couldn't be helped.

He tossed his books down by Decker's mailbox and ran along the road for a while. No reason, just to run. His breath steamed, his heart was pounding. Nothing came by accident really. Nothing came by accident really: he believed that. But he wasn't going back to the house. He ran along the road, he followed a farmer's lane back into a field, running slow, trotting, his lungs beginning to ache in a way he liked, his eyes stinging from the cold. He had the whole morning, nobody knew where he was. He had the whole day. Through a stand of scrubby trees he could see a sheet of water, a frozen pond, then he saw a field of flowers, golden yellow, but how could there be flowers in the winter?—and when he got there he saw it was the remains of a soybean crop. The flowers were just leaves, dried and yellowed, dried to different shades of yellow and brown. But the field was pretty in the sun. The leaves were almost flowers. He picked one of the twisty little beans that hadn't been harvested and squeezed it between his fingernails, how hard, tiny beans inside like pebbles. He stood in the sun catching his breath, getting warm. Then he was almost too warm inside his clothes. He'd decided something without knowing what it was. He didn't have to think of it, it was done.

But he didn't go back to the house, he had the whole day. Farther along the lane he found a pile of debris neatly raked together, mainly tree limbs, broken branches, leaves, but a pane of glass too, cracked glass, about the size of a window. How could a windowpane get so far out here, Judd wondered. Who brought it out here, and why, and where was it from, where had it originally been used as a window? Judd stood staring for a long time. He might have been half asleep on his feet, he seemed to see the sun flashing hot on his hair, the back of his head. He was waiting for some notion to come to him, one of those quick flashing dreams that come just before sleep. But there was nothing. Just the broken glass, the way the soybean leaves had looked like flowers, like goldenrod, the way he was sweating inside his clothes and his lungs still slightly aching from the cold air. He was reaching but nothing came and it was all right, it didn't matter, it was done. It was decided and done.

Is Agnes sick? Judd asked.

She isn't *sick,* they said.

Her jaw was swollen, both her eyes blackened, one morning she was coughing up blood, too weak to get out of bed. She whined that her jaw was broken—she was scared—she couldn't hardly move her mouth—couldn't eat anything solid. Judd's father went in to sit on the edge of the bed and calm her down, smoking one cigarette after another, he was nervous and bored, getting fed up with the task. Hell sweetheart you'll be fine, he said, didn't nobody mean to hurt you and you know it but see it don't happen again. She whined would he call a doctor and he said sure. But a day went by, and another day, and Agnes didn't get out of bed, then it was a week and by that time she seemed to have forgotten. She'd stopped complaining and she'd stopped calling out for Judd Junior to come help, she began to sleep most of the time. Her skin tinged yellow, mucus in the corners of her eyes. The room stank of sweat and dried urine. She couldn't get out of bed to use the bathroom and nobody was around to help, it was just something she'd have to get over, they said, like the flu.

Judd asked his father who had beaten Agnes so bad this time, had he wanted to kill her, and Judd's father said vaguely that he didn't know exactly, he hadn't been in the house right then. "But shouldn't we get some help? Like a doctor?" Judd said. "She doesn't need help," Judd's father said. "Hell she's getting better on her own—it's just her attitude."

A while later he leaned into Judd's room, a can of beer in his hand, and said, "Look kid none of this is your worry, okay? Just concentrate on your schoolwork like you been doing." He smiled at Judd with the lower part of his mouth. The corners of his eyes puckered. "Keep your nose to yourself, you know?—we'll probably be moving out in a while, as soon as things get settled—I tell you I'm getting a new car the first of February?—so things are okay, hon, they're really *okay*."

| | | | |

Judd raised his eyes to his father's face. The room was so small, the mattress so close to the door, he could have reached out to touch his father's leg with his toes. He swallowed hard and didn't know what to say.

"How's it sound, kid? Nineteen-eighty Mercury owned by only one other person," Judd's father said. He was still smiling, stroking his mustache. "And we'll be moving out of here sometime soon, I promise you that."

Judd said faintly that it sounded great.

Past New Year's, and Agnes had been sick for almost two weeks, and they wouldn't let Judd go see her, but one day Vern explained to him what had happened, more or less.

It seems that this buddy of theirs, this guy, had come out from town to see her. Actually they'd already met—Agnes knew who he was—but she wouldn't cooperate. She was drunk and in a real bitch of a mood and she tried to give them a lot of shit, calling the sheriff, calling her brother-in-law, the same old shit, and next thing they knew she was running out the driveway barefoot in the snow, wanted to flag down a car or something, and they had to wrestle her down and carry her back to the house, it took three or four of them, Jesus she was strong, scratching and kicking and biting like a maniac, she *was* a maniac in fact, and that was how the trouble started.

Give a bitch like that a knife, Vern said, shaking his head, grinning, and she'd cut all their throats.

Judd wasn't going to peek into the room, he didn't want to see her. Through the door he could hear the TV voices—somebody had carried the set in so that she could watch all she wanted, they'd turned it on and left the volume high, but Judd didn't know if Agnes could watch TV any more, he'd heard the men joking that she had all she wanted now she sure as hell didn't need them.

The house was freezing, the house stank of food left lying around, dishes in the sink, underwear, towels, the bathroom that nobody ever cleaned now that Agnes was sick. Sinks scummy with dirt, dust balls on the floor. She was dying, Judd could smell her dying, it was the strongest smell of all. "How come the doctor never came?" Judd asked Vern and Vern shrugged his shoulders and never bothered to answer. He didn't ask his father because he was afraid of his father now.

So one morning he hid in the barn until the school bus passed, then hiked three or four miles out to the highway, to a Sunoco station where he knew there was an outdoor telephone booth. It was freezing cold and his breath steamed and his lungs ached from walking fast in a way that might almost scare him but he hadn't time to be scared. He could have made the call from the house— nobody was home—nobody except Agnes—but he didn't want to take the chance of any of them coming back.

He had two dimes ready in his jacket pocket. He had memorized the number of the county sheriff's office. He knew most of what he would tell them, the exact words even: a girl who was sick, a girl who was dying, a girl kept locked up by some men, then he'd give them Vern Decker's name and the location of the house, he'd repeat the information but he wouldn't give his name and he wouldn't say where he was calling from. Then he'd hang up. Quick

| | | | |

and easy, like that. Like that, and it would be done.

It would be done and what happened next would happen without him.

He was shivering and sweating too, damp inside his clothes; his breath came fast and shallow as if he'd been running. This is it, he thought. Okay, you little fucker, this is it. He could hear his voice saying the sheriff's telephone number, it wasn't a number he was likely to forget by now and if he did forget it he could dial information. He knew exactly what he would say when the call went through but he didn't yet know what he would do in the half minute and minute and hour following the call, after he'd hung up. That was the hard part he hadn't memorized. It was the part he would have to get through on his own. After he gave the information, repeated his slow careful words, hung up. He could picture himself slipping the receiver quickly back into its cradle like somebody in a movie worried that the telephone call could be traced if he was too slow. He could see that, and he could see the traffic out on the highway, cars, a truck, a bus, more cars, a big truck hauling cattle, the gritty snow humped against the road divider, the sun at its sharp morning angle in the sky, he could see the pavement cold and glistening stretching off in both directions but he couldn't see himself walking at the edge of the road, he couldn't see which side he would take, he'd have to wait for some notion to come to him when it was time, some strong nudge, which side of the road, which direction he'd take, whether he would be pulled one way or another, he'd have to wait.

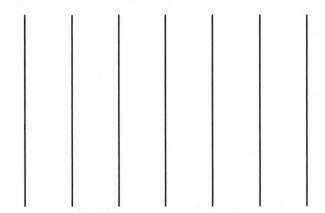

THE JESUIT

In those years she believed in God without wanting to examine the belief. She carried the idea of God inside her the way many people carry inside them the thought of their own eventual extinction—it was logical, perhaps even consoling, but it could not be confronted head-on. God was not a being, still less a personality, but a fierce hard light she could only bear in the corner of her eye.

She never prayed. Once or twice a day, usually while driving her car, she made a systematic effort to empty herself of herself, so that God might fill her. If nothing happened she felt saddened but not upset. Hers was to be a life, she knew, in which nothing would frequently happen.

| | | | |

She was separated from her husband after only two years of marriage but in fact she had known—they had both known—that the marriage was a mistake after two months. They had married so swiftly, they'd never had a formal engagement, and now, living apart, in different cities, it seemed to her at times that she was engaged. She "had" someone. She was spoken for. She lived alone but she was not precisely a single woman just as, in reverse logic, she had had a good deal of sexual experience yet was virginal again, younger than her age. She wrote long letters to her husband on the typewriter, read them in the morning, filed them away, embarrassed. Many years ago she'd heard an older friend of her parents say mysteriously, You can't force anyone to care deeply about you.

Though she was no longer Catholic, had stopped going to Mass at the age of fifteen, it happened that she was teaching in the night-school program of a small Jesuit college. Above the blackboard in every classroom of the old stone and stucco building was a brass crucifix that drew the eye sharply to it. The Jesuit dean who had hired her made it clear that she was under no obligation to lead her students in a formal prayer—the man was so exquisitely tactful he had not even inquired into the precise state of her religious beliefs—but she began each class with a brisk Hail Mary. It comforted her to cross herself and to observe most of her forty-three students crossing themselves as if she were facing a hall of mirrors. *Hail Mary full of grace. The Lord is with Thee. Blessed art Thou amongst women. And blessed is the fruit of Thy womb Jesus.* The scattering of non-Catholics in the class stood at attention, eyes lowered, and she understood that they too were grateful for the harmless little prayer, the agreeable fuss of sliding out of seats, standing, then sitting again. Clearing throats, coughing quietly. The prayer had nothing to do with God but there was, she thought, something wonderful about it.

"Aren't you clever!" her husband had said. "Aren't you the hypocrite!" he'd said. But in a light bantering voice, meaning no hurt.

Of the five or six teachers at the college with whom she was acquainted only one, a young Jesuit whose office was adjacent to hers, seemed to dislike her. In fact he hated her: he would stare at her with a loathing that seemed almost pure, it was so impersonal. At first she had nervously assumed that he was in an irritable mood, that something had just gone wrong, or that he didn't feel well—she was told he'd had a cancer operation a few years previously, a colostomy—but then it became gradually clear that he simply hated her. He had hated her, she thought, even before they were formally introduced.

He was tall, slope-shouldered, thin, with pale lashless eyes deep-set as if in bone, a long nose, wide dark nostrils, a mock-solemn manner. Thinning sandy hair, a scalp that shone through in glimmering patches. A space between his boyish front teeth. Black-polished shoes that creaked. Black umbrella tucked beneath his arm. Thirty years old, perhaps, thirty-one, -two: her own age approximately. The priest's costume gave him an air of slightly insolent authority, the clerical collar tight against his throat, he might walk past her without seeing her, he might pause outside her door to inquire, graciously, coldly, "How are you this evening, Mrs. Schneck?" Once he said, "You look tired, Mrs. Schneck, are our students exhausting you?"

Though he did not teach in the night-school program it seemed he was always in the building, in his office, on Tuesday and Thursday evenings when she taught her class. Sometimes he insisted upon accompanying her to her car in the parking lot—there had been several incidents lately of young women assaulted or threatened; a male faculty member was beaten and robbed. At such times his courtliness was impersonal, like his hatred. He did his duty, he couldn't be faulted, he was a Jesuit after all, quite clearly proud of himself. She could not have said to him suddenly, "Why do you hate me?—when we don't even know each other."

At one of their faculty meetings early in the year she noticed him staring at her. That youngish man with the long nose, the dark prominent nostrils. Eyes set deep in the bony ridge of his forehead. He was hunched slightly forward in his chair, a cigarette burning forgotten between his fingers. Staring, brooding. Contemplating something in her she could never have seen in herself.

He was from Massachusetts, he'd gone to Fordham, Harvard, had spent a year at Oxford. His field of specialization was eighteenth-century English literature and language, he'd already published a scholarly book on Pope's translation of the *Iliad,* he taught an extra course in Greek, he was said to be absolutely unsparing in his devotion to his subject and to those students who merited his attention. One of the younger breed of Jesuit, self-consciously conservative, even radical, having had quite enough, as

they said, of their elders' vague well-intentioned but finally promiscuous (and ineffectual) liberalism. . . . He
was sharp and lean as a knife-blade amidst the white-haired
senior Jesuits with their spreading bellies and red-creased
comfortable faces. Some students feared him and asked
to be transferred out of his classes. Others adored him,
took down his aphorisms, even his Greek and Latin asides,
in their notebooks.

He was fully recovered from the cancer operation,
it was said. But she saw the cancer shining in his eyes—a
pale luminous glow, a true passion.

Nine faculty members in the department of whom five
were Jesuits, four laymen. Of the laymen two were women,
one middle-aged, the other fairly young, both part-time
instructors teaching large sections of English Composi-
tion. It did not matter to them that their salaries were
very low, because a low salary is, after all, much better
than no salary at all. Also, the Jesuits themselves received
no salaries: they had pledged themselves to poverty. To
poverty, chastity, obedience. They were servants of the
Church and of God, it might be claimed that they had
refined themselves of the personal life entirely—the small
petty demeaning personal life—the grubby life of the
emotions, the body. Hopes, desires, ambition. They would
never marry and would never sire children but they were
to be addressed formally as Father.

The Society of Jesus was the most controversial of
all Catholic orders but the most celebrated, indeed the
most exclusive and glamorous. Through the centuries the
Pope had feared the Jesuits, and with good reason. The

Society had in fact been banned—so the tale went, the legend flourished—but somehow it had never died out and eventually it became the most powerful of all the orders; certainly it had always attracted superior men. And very politic, well-adjusted, agreeable men, usually.

When her husband moved out he said, "Now I know you'll be all right, with your job. With the Jesuits."

"Yes," she said, trying not to laugh in his face. "Thank you."

These days she was thinking of the Jesuit who hated her more often than she thought of her husband, who after all did not hate her. His seeing in *her,* or *in* her, something she was powerless to see in herself. The fastidious disdain, the loathing, jaw slightly raised, lips pursed, stiffened. What did it mean? Did it mean anything? If she believed in God she must have faith in meanings, signs. For God did not communicate directly but through signs. The Jesuit, the man of God. The soldier pledged to serve Christ.

Father, he was to be addressed, despite his youth.

Once when they met outside the library—she was walking with a student, he was in the company of several Jesuits—he made a point of not knowing her; passed by unsmiling, puzzled, at her tentative greeting. Another time she saw him walking with a well-dressed older woman who had slipped her arm snug through his. A tidy compact woman of late middle age with a carefully made-up face, a lacquered hairdo, white gloves, expensive wool suit, shoes. This time too the Jesuit snubbed her but he looked away, embarrassed, as she approached, and she knew better than to say a word, lift a hand in greeting. *Noli me tangere.* Touch me not. As Christ had commanded his mother. But the Jesuit's mother evidently touched him as she wished, held him snug and close.

Mirrors reflected a face she could not always believe, a face, she thought disdainfully, with a small banal truth to proclaim—pinched, narrow, delicate-boned, almost pretty, with large damp eyes prone to blinking. Grainy skin, lip-sticked mouth. She badly needed the lipstick, the con-scientious makeup, the furtive penciling of eyebrows. Otherwise she was a watercolor, easily smudged.

God, she knew, is a spirit that dwells within. Yet there is a spirit that dwells without too—the inarguable witness of others' eyes, strangers' eyes. No pity there. No mercy.

One December evening she heard herself say to the Jesuit who hated her, "Would you like to come to dinner sometime?" though she might have said, her voice dropping to a frightened whisper, "Would you like to come home with me? I live alone, I'm separated from my hus-band." They were descending a dimly lit flight of stairs, she saw his foot hesitate, grope for the next step, she felt his surprise, his shock, he might have been a dreamer panicked at stumbling in his sleep, but she was saying calmly, distinctly, "I'll also be asking Father Boyle and Father Chapelle, and maybe the Karls, you could all drive over together . . . Sunday at seven? . . . seven-thirty?"

Her invitation was so unexpected, her appeal so direct, the Jesuit had had to say yes.

But of course he did not come.

Sunday at three-thirty the telephone rang as she had half-known it would, and curtly, succinctly, he made

| | | | |

his excuse; and she put the receiver back faint with insult, humiliation. Shame. For she had known he would call. She had known. And yet she had exposed herself.

Her other guests arrived, the evening went well, she heard herself talking, laughing, as one must, she saw herself listening to the others and performing a hostess's comforting little tasks, harmless rituals. Why had he declined them, she wondered. They were, after all, harmless.

As soon as they left she dialed her husband. "Why do I do these things?" she said, sighing, making a joke of it. She meant the dinner party itself: of course she had told him nothing of the Jesuit who hated her. "Why do I try?" she asked, begging, not very subtly, for his commiseration. It was nearly midnight, her head spun. Her husband sounded sleepy but he said, "Look, we all have to try, don't we."

He cleared his throat. "We can't simply give up, can we."

"Yes," she said, pouring the last of a bottle of wine into her glass. "I mean no."

"Are you alone now?" her husband asked.

"Of course I'm alone," she said, laughing almost loudly.

"I thought I heard someone in the background," he said.

"Did you," she said.

They were silent for a while; then they began to reminisce about one or two memorable dinners they had given, evenings that had gone wrong, supremely and pathetically wrong, no one to blame, simply failed connections, people without a good deal in common apart from age and mutual attractiveness and ambition. They had been newly married then and newly domesticated, eager to establish a household. Odd, she thought, to have been so recently young.

"I do most of my eating out," her husband said. "Except for breakfast."

"Yes," she said. "I can understand that."

"It's a convenient arrangement," he said. "You order what you want in a restaurant, pay for it, that's that. If a meal doesn't work out you don't go back. If the atmosphere's off you don't go back."

"Yes," she said carefully. "I can understand that too."

After the dinner party the Jesuit who hated her avoided her for weeks. He was scrupulous, exact. She saw, however, that he now eyed her with a genuine repugnance, as if the purity of his hatred—its odd settledness, serenity—had been contaminated by her gesture.

She did not want to think that she was frightened of him.

She did not want to think that she was becoming obsessed with him.

Yet why did he hate her? Why could she not win him over? And why did she care so deeply, since she could not win him over?

She wanted to empty herself of herself, after all, in order to be filled with God.

But she thought obsessively of him. That sickly radiance in his face, the pale shining eyes. The certitude.

He hated her *because he knew her.* He had the power to see through her—her nervous little stratagems, her efforts to be friendly, even to be intelligent, professional. He saw too through her very indifference to him.

She thought of his graying sandy hair, thin at the crown of his head, gathered in wisps and curls at his neck. She wanted to touch the back of his neck. Just her fingertips. Lightly, experimentally. But she knew his skin would be burning to the touch. So icy cold it would burn.

When she drove home from the college, in the dark, she was besieged by a kaleidoscope of disjointed images, dreamlike flashes, her students' faces, the look of the classrooms, the rows of desks, the blackboard and her own chalked words with their spurious authority. The brass crucifix overhead. The face of the Jesuit who hated her.

She would have cried. But what purpose is there to tears, she reasoned, if no one is a witness.

Along the garish neon-lit boulevard, even in the freezing rain, prostitutes stationed themselves at regular intervals, standing close by the curb, gazing into oncoming headlights. There had been a brief scandal in the newspapers and for a while the women were gone, now they were back, many of them startlingly young, startlingly attractive. During her early weeks in the city she hadn't quite known who or what they were and one evening she had stopped to give one of them a ride—the girl hardly looked seventeen and she had supposed her a teenager hitchhiking home from school.

It made an amusing tale to relate to her husband over the telephone but he was not amused. He said, "Don't you know that part of the city is dangerous? Can't you drive home by another route?"

He said, "I'll try to get down there some weekend this month, we have to talk."

But nothing came of it.

She wore a dark, dark red woolen coat with a Persian lamb fur collar, a cast-off coat of her mother's that nonetheless exuded an odd sort of glamour. She changed her lipstick to dark red. Carefully rubbed a cream-colored makeup into the discolored crescents beneath her eyes. Brushed her hair until it crackled with static electricity.

Sometimes when she was alone in the apartment— but she was always alone in the apartment!—the telephone rang, late at night. And she knew before lifting the receiver that it would be a stranger. An anonymous voice. Falsetto. "Hello? Hello?" When she said faintly, "Hello? Who is this?" the voice would mimic hers, "Hello? Hello? Who is this? Hello?" She would hang up; the telephone would ring again immediately.

And ring and ring. Ring.

This too, she thought, must be a way of emptying myself.

She never prayed even now because God is not a being, a personality, to whom one might speak. If God were she would have said: Why is love so weak a membrane?—like Daedalus's waxen wings, too frail, too silly, even, for their heroic task.

She would have said: Tell me why he hates me, I can bear it.

| | | | |

The Jesuit who hated her was telling several colleagues—none of them fellow Jesuits—about an experience he'd had the other day. Administering the sacrament of extreme unction to a dying man. How the poor man could barely see, how he could barely open his mouth, how finally he had grasped and clawed at the priest's hands as if desperate to take the Eucharist from him. In relating the tale the Jesuit took care to keep his voice level, casual, his manner was unfailingly sophisticated, his expression deadpan, so that his listeners were made doubly uneasy—by the evocation of the dying man, and by the Jesuit's delivery that was, or perhaps was not, meant to inspire sardonic mirth.

Afterward the Jesuit said to her, "You seem to look a little pained, Mrs. Schneck, is something wrong, does this atmosphere displease you?" and she said, so quickly she realized the words must have been gathering, pushing at her, for many minutes, "I don't understand this instinct in men to say certain things, to test others, to disturb, shock—to see how much we can take."

He smiled. His pale lips lifted from his big boyish teeth in a sneering sort of smile, or a smiling sort of sneer. He said, "Now Mrs. Schneck what precisely do you mean, whom do you mean by 'us'?"

"Women," she said. "I think I mean women."

He ducked his head, laughing. A snorting, vigorous laugh. A profoundly gratifying laugh. She had observed him thus in the corridor from time to time, in the company of favored colleagues, giving them the sudden surprising gift of his rare laughter. She'd been stung by jealousy but now she saw that the laughter meant nothing, was in fact mirthless, mocking.

She said in a swift lowered voice, "Why do you hate me?"

He seemed not to hear. He recovered from his spasm of laughter and was now frankly gazing over her head, seeking escape. In his right hand he held a burning cigarette at shoulder height, ashes were scattered on his black coat like bits of dandruff. She said, "You shouldn't be smoking, it's wrong of you to smoke. Your health," she said. "Don't you have to be concerned with your health?" He looked at her with hatred, his narrow cheeks coloring, his lips again drawn away from his teeth. The pale luminosity of his stare was lightly threaded with red. Coldly, even formally, as if he were delivering a Greek aphorism, he said, "Your lipstick's smeared, Mrs. Schneck."

In the final weeks of the spring term she indulged herself in the most delicious of fantasies. She was almost an adolescent girl again, washed in fantasy.

She would learn the Jesuits' schedules for hearing confessions in the chapel. And she would go to confession, to him. Innocently she would kneel in the darkened booth and cross herself and whisper, "Bless me Father for I have sinned, it has been many, many years since my last confession." And the Jesuit who hated her would say, not knowing who she was, "How long has it been? And why have you fallen away from the Church?" And she would tell him. And she would tell him that she married a non-Catholic and that they, that is she, practiced birth control. That she had not gone to Mass and had not observed holy days of obligation, had not even thought of the Church, for years. That in fact she did not care about the Church because God is not contained in the Church or defined

| | | | |

by the Church. And the Jesuit who hated her would say, puzzled, perhaps unnerved, "Then why have you come to confession?" and she would say, "Because I think I have been the occasion for sin, because there is a man, a priest, a Jesuit, here at the college who hates me . . . whom I have offended without knowing how, or when, I think it must be a sin, it must be a mortal sin for him, crowding Christ out of his heart, to harbor such loathing for. . . ."

But nothing came of her fantasy, of course. Though it gave her a good deal of pleasure, as fantasies do.

And nothing came of his hatred.

It simply continued. Over the weeks, the months, the semester. Now and then there was a mysterious resurgence, he would rap at her opened office door, make an ironic little bow when she glanced up startled, he would ask with an air of icy mock gallantry, "And how are you this evening, Mrs. Schneck?"; but much of the time it was contained, subdued, no more than a tic or a mannerism of his, harmless perhaps if you wanted to see it that way. In May she informed the dean of the arts school that she would not be renewing her contract for the following year and when he asked why, hadn't she been happy teaching there she said, Yes, very happy, I've learned a great deal. She did not tell the dean that she and her husband were going to experiment with living together again, in another city, far away. She did not tell him about the Jesuit who hated her.

One of the final times she saw the Jesuit who hated her was on a Thursday evening in mid-April. Earlier that day the air had warmed with a fragrant premature balminess, since sunset the temperature had plummeted thirty degrees, now it was raining violently, hailstones were clattering across the roofs and pavement, and she had no umbrella, had not even worn a trench coat, and the Jesuit who hated her left his office and briskly locked the door and strode by her without glancing at her. She believed she heard him murmur, "Goodnight," even "Goodnight, Mrs. Schneck," but she couldn't be certain.

Since the evening she had invited him to dinner he had stopped offering to escort her to her car; he shrank even from falling into step beside her. She saw that there was nothing to be done. At the door he paused, unfurled his magnificent black umbrella, stepped out unhesitatingly into the night. She was left behind to make her way as she deserved (why hadn't she listened to the radio? why had she dressed so lightly, eager to believe it was really spring?), there was absolutely nothing to be done. For some minutes she stood at the door, watching the hailstones. Like bullets, they were, fascinating, quite beautiful really, blown by the wind in an unpredictable rippling against the pavement. She stared mesmerized, oddly dreamy, at peace. Emptied of her own wish, her own futile desire, emptied even of her hurt, she saw that there was no power in her to alter another's hatred, any more than she might alter another's love. It was that simple. It was that fierce hard light she could only bear in the corner of her eye but she could bear it, there. There was absolutely nothing to be done.

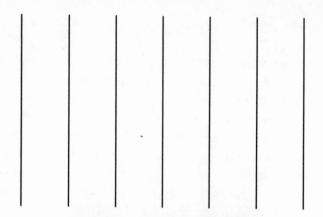

THE MOTHER

A long time ago when she was a girl she lay in secret with a photograph cut from a pulp-paper magazine smoothed carefully on the pillow beside her head, now she lies awake past midnight, past one o'clock in the morning, listening for her son to come home, waiting for the headlights to startle her skimming the ceiling and the noise of the tires in the gravel drive and the footsteps at the rear of the house that sound so shy and cautious. Then he will go to his room, he will close the door quietly behind him, she must imagine his warm flushed skin, the bruised look of the mouth, the quivering eyelashes, eyes lidded with se-crets, the smell of the girl on him that he won't wash off until morning, so many hours away. If she stares at him it must be in secret, he won't allow it otherwise, the soft down on his upper lip, the pale silky hair that is neither hers nor his father's, Why are you looking at me? Jeesuz!—but with a light nervous laugh, he isn't her baby any longer but a baby sleeps coiled up inside him, that deep clammy-still sleep of an infant whose breath you must check by leaning close, your ear turned to its mouth. The girls he sees don't wear lipstick so there won't be lipstick on his face, she can't allow herself to be angry.

Years ago she first turned a doorknob to discover it locked against her and she drew away frightened, ashamed, now she dreams of a hallway of doors locked against her, she calls out her son's name but no one answers, the voices are suddenly hushed, someone giggles softly, they were sitting atop a picnic table, her son and a girl she'd never seen before and whose name she did not know, she saw her son's arm slung about the girl's shoulders, she saw their heads nudging together, his blond hair gleaming bright as it did in a snapshot taken when he was nine years old. Do you think I don't know what you do with your girls, she whispered, do you think I can't guess. . . ?

So many mirrors in the house, upstairs and down. But none shows her true face.

At meals the son and the father get along companionably, the son and the father and the mother, there is the exchange of news, there is chatter, laughter, both men are good eaters which pleases the mother though even now, at his age, the son must sometimes be chided for eating too fast, and for dropping his head toward his plate.

| | | | |

Once she asked him why he was going out again so soon after he'd just come home, hadn't he been gone all day, at home for no more than forty minutes, why was he going out again, where was he going, she kept her voice light, calm, amused, in truth she *was* amused, it was so transparent, his lying. She saw how his eyes were hooded with secrets, how a pulse beat in his throat. She saw only that he wished to be gone since his life was elsewhere. She was pointing out that he'd been out late the night before, that it was raining, that he'd only just come home, it was all so childish, the game he played. A flush began in his face, that look of swallowed fury, shame, but she kept her voice light and unaccusing, she said, You're going to a girl's house, aren't you, please don't lie, isn't that where you're going, I'd like to know her name and I'd like to know if her parents are home and if they're not, I'd like to know if they know you're there, and though she was speaking calmly tears spilled from her eyes, her son backed away in shame, in embarrassment, in rage, as if he didn't trust himself closer to her.

Afterward every room in the house was a room he'd just slammed out of, the air was queer and sharp, as during an electrical storm, she saw her son's face growing smaller and smaller until the features were indistinct, she had to imagine the eyes, the set of the mouth, and cried out that he was so beautiful: so beautiful.

She would smooth the photograph out carefully on her pillow and lie down beside it, carefully, not daring to breathe.

Rain blown against the windows, spilling noisily out of the gutters. The most secret time.

THE MOTHER

At night the father sleeps heavily while she waits for the flash of the headlights, the sound of the tires in the drive, minutes sliding into minutes, hours into hours, the father's breath is usually hoarse, rasping, dry, and only when he swallows it, when she becomes aware of an arrhythmic patch of silence, does she hear him, or, rather, she suddenly hears the silence, his terrible absence, like a heart that has ceased to beat. But in the next instant there will come a startled little snort, swallowed too, strangulated, and then with an air of surprise the breathing begins again, hoarse, rasping, dry, rhythmic, this too the absence of sound, to which she never listens. Why do you lie to me, she is saying to her son, her fingers closing about his arm as they have a right to close, her nails digging gently into his skin, do you think I don't know what your life is now? the things you do? you and your girls? you alone? in your room? with the door locked against your mother?

His fingers drum on a tabletop, his eyes shift in their sockets, so beautiful, the flush in his cheeks, the soft tawny down of the upper lip, even his raised aggrieved voice as he tells her to let him alone, for Christ's sake please let him alone. And the long sinewy legs, the muscular thighs, arms, the very set of the head, neither hers nor his father's. Who can claim him? Who can possess him? Who dares? She shuts her eyes against the boy and girl, those frantic young lovers, only partly undressed as they couple, eager, impatient, shameless, she hears the boy's life torn from him in a cry of deliverance, a cry of triumph, while she lies sleepless beside a sleeping man, waiting for release, waiting for his footsteps, the soft sound of a door being locked against her.

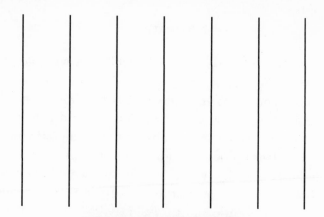

TESTIMONY

I'm quick to learn, I'm fast as an eel, I'm the good one sits at her desk with her fingers laced tight and the milkiest littlest crescent of eyeball showing. Humming under my breath. Maybe it's a prayer. Singing my boyfriend's songs that got the beat, the beat, the crazy beat you really need: Try me honey, do me right, I'm the Pure Thing, I'm the Holy Ghost. Singing, Baby you're gonna die 'cause Satan's got his eye . . . on you.

My boyfriend says I am pure as the dust of angels. We had a secret wedding, only one witness, she was prettier than me but not for long.

Get me that one, he said, it was a Saturday noon on the boardwalk, I knew it was the beginning of the experiment and felt the wind whipping right through my eyes. Y'see the one I mean? hey *go,* he said, squeezing where he knew to squeeze. No he never hurt so it lasted, the night before he'd given me this milky blue ring, see, a zodiac love charm, it could tame even the sharks in the ocean, it's a secret pledge. He never needed to point, I knew who he meant: skinny, cutoff jeans and a red halter top, transistor radio gripped between her knees, eyeing every boy that passed (except she didn't know any better than to be standing at the wrong end of the boardwalk): okay, I felt my spit go sour 'cause I was jealous, 'cause I could see she was prettier than me.

Eddy's Pizza and the arcade are at the other end of the boardwalk, here you don't get the action. A beer place, clams and hot dogs, saltwater taffy, that kind of shit, old people hunched on the benches staring like they never seen anything like you before, then when you walk past they're just staring at where you were or maybe at nothing.

Her hair was straw colored, wild and frizzed by the wind, up close I could see the little pimples by her mouth, her eyes were pinched, not trusting me at first, the color of dimes. Took the Greyhound from Camden that morning, she said, first she said her boyfriend was coming down from Stony Point to meet her, then she said it was some girlfriend, I was hearing a sweet heavy music in my head, going with the beat. You got anything to smoke, she said, and I told her I didn't but my cousin did. Hey is that your cousin, she said, and I said it sure was.

He took pictures of us, her and me together, first

sitting on the railing, then standing, walking around, you'd swear we were sisters, arms around each other's waist, even tickling a little, God is he cute, she was whispering, he ain't really your cousin is he, she said. There was a long dream I had before or after about the end of the wharf where he made us stand while he squatted with the camera, when the wind blows your thoughts away it's hard to remember, things fly away so fast, but there's the wharf anyway even if we aren't there, down in the water these foamy spitty things bobbing, dead fish, jellyfish, broken-off parts of things, your head's buzzing right and you can scare yourself seeing maybe a dead baby, a mess of eye-balls, fingers and toes, somebody's hair. God is he cute, the girl said, giggling, scared, wiping her runny nose on the back of her hand, I hated it how her hair whipped into my face and stung my eyes.

Also in the dream is something getting in my eyes and making them sting.

He had both his cameras, wore them around his neck on straps. They cost him a lot of money, he said. Which is why nobody'd better touch them.

Under the boardwalk we had a fast smoke. Told her, like he'd told me, his status: name Ruby Red, ex-acrobat, ex-wrestler, free-lance photojournalist. Never need to feel anything, he says, because it has all been felt be-fore, d'you read me? He asked the girl lots of questions, where's she from, how old's she (sixteen she said which was a lie, anyway she looked younger then), how come she's alone at the beach. I was picking up sand between my toes. Bending my toes tight like claws. Six-thirty I had to be home but that was hours away, I was feeling good, I was ready to fly, I *was* flying. Today will be the experiment, he said but I didn't ask why, I think I sort of knew.

He never hurt me bad, never so it lasted. There are rewards for being faithful. I was the only one he loved, he said, 'cause he didn't touch me or anyway it didn't show. Pure as the purest dust of angels. That white, white sand of beaches you only see in photographs. Get the right beat, he said, it'll carry you the full distance.

Six days and seven nights he had her there in his apartment, or seven days and six nights, it wasn't up to me to keep track. I wasn't there all the time. I was never there at night.

No need to feel anything 'cause it has all been felt before, he said. Only the camera is needed to record certain moments of certain days. Or the tape cassette.

I was the only one he respected, he said.

No, nobody ever hypnotized *me,* that's just shit.

Her? 'Cause he didn't respect her I guess. It was an experiment. Also she came from Camden. That's a long way—Camden. You could get lost in between, things happen on the buses. But Momma's place is just down the street from his, I can ride my bicycle back and forth any time.

Yeah I tell Momma I'm hanging out with some kids from school, I tell her Bobbie Jean (who was my best friend in eighth grade at St. Anthony of Padua before I transferred), Momma don't ask questions 'cause she don't want questions asked back.

Next morning I went upstairs at his place and

| | | | |

knocked at the door and he opened it when he saw it was me. His face was hot, his eyes were that hot red-brown color, just burning, like nobody else's ever are. She was in the kitchen and she was crying. One of the things he said was, Okay you can leave now, walk right out the door and get down those stairs, but she didn't budge, she was barefoot and she just stood there, crying and saying she didn't know where she was, she wouldn't know how to get home. Her nose was running and she didn't have a Kleenex so I gave her one. He hadn't started yet with the cigarettes or the other but he'd been hitting her a little 'cause her teeth were bloody. Something watery and red between her teeth.

She never looked at me. Then when she did, it was like a dream when somebody's eyes go right through you and you realize you aren't there.

She was crying, she kept saying, Where can I go? and he said, Back where you came from, and she said, No I don't want to, and he said, Okay, then don't try my patience again, Ruby Red ain't to be trifled with.

She wasn't awake all that much, toward the end. Inside the gag she screamed a lot, she cried a lot, at first, then she was mostly tired, her eyes were out of focus. Things started to get blurred.

I scrubbed out the bathtub twice: before he carried her in, and after he took her out. One other time I had to scrub out the toilet too because I was sick in there— threw up half in the toilet and half on the floor. But it's all sort of blurred now, this was back in August.

He was taking pictures all the time but I never saw

one of them. He used a lot of cassettes too that I did hear played back—he played them back for the two of us. There was music too, her transistor turned up high. Also the TV.

No I was never there overnight, Momma'd kill me if I stayed out late. Have to be back for supper, then back by ten, that's the rule of the household says Momma, other things she don't question.

I bought things for him at the Seven-Eleven and the Safeway. The drugstore. The hardware store. A half-dozen newspapers he wanted so I bought them, not every day but sometimes.

Don't hurt me, she was saying, and he said, No-body's going to hurt you, now the worst part's over. Her own attitude made it harder. She kept changing her mind. I mean at the beginning. There was a time he shouted at her to call the police, he held out the phone to her, but she wouldn't, I guess she was waiting for him to love her, she was waiting for things to get okay the way you natu-rally do. But I was the only one he loved 'cause I'm such a little girl. He can lift me in one arm if he wants to, there's a long sweet dream where he carries me that way, his own feet skimming the ground. 'Cause my hair's al-most white too, purest angel silk, he says. Nothing dirty ever passed between us like between him and *her*.

Don't hurt me, she was saying. Or maybe it was being sung over the radio. Sometimes when I think it's me in the midst of a dream it's really a voice over the radio, some sweet wild heavy beat behind it, or maybe I think it's a stranger's music and it's really inside my own head. Don't fight it, Ruby Red says. Don't resist.

| | | | |

There is a special God, he says, that the Sufis believe in. That He's creating us but we're also creating Him at the same time. Man creates God, God creates man, so we can see ourselves on both sides. It goes on and on, he says, dreamy, there's no logical place for it to end.

One night we went to the movies to see that one about the mermaid, I forget the title, something light and cute. Had a big box of buttered popcorn we shared, two big things of Coke. He sat her in the middle, him on the left holding her hand, and me on the right holding her other hand. We were high, we were set for some light entertainment. All the stuff he'd been giving her, she didn't know where she was, she sort of stared at the screen like a baby would. I put popcorn in her mouth but she ate it real slow and forgot to swallow. Then she spilled Coke in her lap and that scared her, she made a lot of noise and one of the ushers came over and shone his flashlight at us. She said in a loud voice that she wanted to go home. She started crying, looking at the usher through her fingers, she was saying some things you couldn't make sense of, then she stopped and just sat there crying, and Ruby Red told the usher it was okay: we'd take her home. Which we did.

She was wearing one of his shirts 'cause of the air conditioning, a silky blue with flowers or some sort of design in the fabric, she'd got it all wet down the front like a baby would.

That was the last time he trusted her out of the apartment.

They said he was thirty-five years old, I never had a thought of how *old* he was, I never had any personal thoughts about him at all. You wouldn't want to: there's the chance he would know.

His next life, he said, he'll be a wild horse out west, a wild red horse in the mountains. In New Mexico maybe. In this part of the world here, anywhere in the East, he said, even where you can see the Atlantic Ocean every day, the air isn't healthy to breathe. No part of the East Coast is healthy.

Ruby Red, his own name that he gave himself. Could lift me in one arm if he wanted. Could dance me all around the apartment.

The girl's nose started bleeding, he stuffed the nostrils tight with Kleenex. Next day blood was leaking from between her legs. He wanted her shaved 'cause in his opinion that kind of hair is disgusting but I couldn't do it right, my hands shook. A razor is so sharp.

He had her hands tied so she couldn't have touched me but it felt like she touched me. The back of my head. A towel tied tight around her mouth but I heard her say to me, Don't cut me, oh don't hurt me, help me, help me!—but when I looked around her eyes were closed and the lids were pearly blue like something on the beach that's been washed clean. What surprised me was, she got to be just skin and bones after a few days, tight-stretched grayish skin showing a lot of tiny bumps and pimples. Flat little breasts like a boy's. Like my own. The nipples ooz-ing blood. Ribs poking out. Collarbone. He was marking her *his*—cigarette burns, initials in her skin with a pocketknife, a special tattoo in code. She was going to be God, he said, when he was finished, when he got it all right. Secret words and wisdom. God looking down at Himself, or something. It's so long ago now it's sort of blurred.

The TV turned up high, Channel 7 all wobbly and zigzagged it hurts your eyes. The hard rock station in town that plays all night. The beat, the wild heavy beat. Do me honey I'll save your life. Do me, do me, I'll save your life.

It was at night she died, I wasn't there, like I said I was only there sometimes during the day. Even then we wouldn't always stay in the apartment—we'd go out, to the movies, down to the boardwalk. He had his cameras. His soul was naturally restless.

It was sort of disappointing, toward the end. She wasn't awake much, only just breathing funny, he tried to get her to swallow some milk but she couldn't, it ran right back out of her mouth. The inside of the tub was all filthy from her soiling herself, and the blood, it made me sick to clean it out but I had to. Also the floor. The cracks in the linoleum where the tub fits into the floor, and the toilet bowl, it took me a long time with the scrub brush and I never did get it clean. Later I looked in the mirror and my face was wet from crying but I didn't remember crying.

Is that cassette running out? I thought I heard some clicking.

Some things, I'll never tell.

Some things I'm beginning to forget.

Toward the end it didn't make much difference, anything he did. You couldn't hear her breathe it was so soft. Take the towel away and she wouldn't know it, wouldn't scream or even whisper, it was like she'd given up. Now you see who he really loves and it wasn't ever *you*, I wanted to tell her, but never did, there wasn't any point.

It's all sort of blurred now like a dream you try to remember but can't, then you decide to let it go and there's nothing but a funny feeling in your head.

Why didn't you tell anyone? they asked. Your mother, the police, somebody on the street. Why didn't you *tell*, they asked. I said I didn't know but really I wanted to laugh in their faces—they'd never understand.

Ruby Red, with those hot red-brown eyes that look right through you. Lifting me in his arm. Singing humming in my ear, maybe it's a prayer. Next lifetime, little girl, we'll spend together in the mountains, you got the love pledge to prove me right.

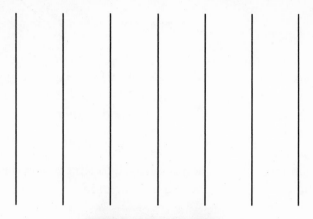

NUCLEAR HOLOCAUST

Jesus isn't angry because He brings us love but there's plenty angry in His place.

Your face shows how serious you're listening but I know better. It's just your salary. I don't begrudge it. I have got Jesus and Jesus has got me. I'm the one keeps setting her hair afire by accident. I keep falling asleep where I am and there's a candle lit or a burner on the stove. Then they shaved off my hair thinking it wouldn't grow back but it did. If my face wasn't pimply from this bad food I'd be pretty like before. I'm not angry but sometimes I forget and talk too loud.

Sometimes Jesus is explaining things to me and then I forget who I was when I started walking somewhere and where it was I believed I was going so when I get there I can't remember and then I'm angry. There's a smile comes over my face like a dirty joke I just heard the end of. I can fall asleep anywhere. On the bus, in the cafeteria, in the john. Sitting on the toilet. Also in the shower with the hot water running. I got scalded and they had to fix my skin, it took a long time. They take it from some place like your ass and put it somewhere else. Jesus was sorry for me but He didn't speak. In the hospital you're there one second and the next you're gone, they melt you away, there just isn't anything there. It happened in one instant when they put the needle in the back of my hand.

Just this morning I forgot where I was going and when I got there I didn't have anything in my hand to remind me. I noticed my shadow on the wall and had to laugh. Jesus says, A sinner hurries to get somewhere then when they get there it's the same shadow waiting for them. Once I saw a picture of a Japanese man whose shadow was baked into a wall when the atomic bomb went off. I studied that a long time. There's talk of a nuclear holocaust these days but I don't keep up. In that picture it was the man and his shadow both baked into the wall so the man himself was nowhere to be found. There's a satisfaction in this. Once I died and was floating on a big silver river under the stars. The element of the river was laughter, it wasn't grief. All those souls floating to Jesus. There was singing too, gentle and not loud. I joined my voice with the rest but it came out too loud and I was ashamed. Jesus was angry and sent me back here, so when I saw where I was I started crying. I was back here in sin. Now I'm always praying for things to get right again. You

| | | | |

look at me and you hear me talking, but in my heart I am praying for the return of all sinners to God.

Dear God, I say in my prayer, send the bomb to punish us at last in Your mercy and bless us in the same instant, for ever and ever. Amen.

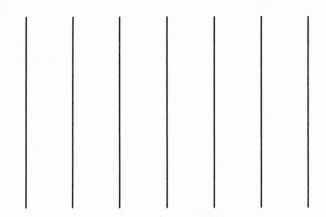

SURF CITY

His number finally came up, his good luck number, published in the *Surf City Gazette* and announced over the radio, he'd won $1,150 in the state lottery in which a retired grocer from Camden won $1,726,092 and somebody else, a woman schoolteacher from upstate, won $628,530. About time, he thought. Maybe even a few years behind schedule.

His name was Harvey Kubeck, he was thirty-one years old, had a two-year-old son and another baby on the way. Both pregnancies hadn't been planned but weren't exactly accidents either. Except for the weeks when he was laid off from work he made good money at Republic Steel: when they laid him off he got part-time work driving a truck for a local construction outfit, part-time work as a security guard at the shopping mall, short-term jobs with a tree service his wife's uncle owned, whatever came along. He'd never gone downtown to collect unemployment, no one in his family did. For a long time it had seemed to him that luck was running against him. It wasn't just the things you could put your finger on, talk about, it was how you felt about yourself, the air you had to breathe. In fact it seemed to him that his bad luck was like dirty water, stinking sewage water splashing around his head, his face, it sickened him to think he'd get it in his mouth and swallow it. Months and months of things going against you until finally it's years, you're thirty, then you're thirty-one, not a kid any longer.

He'd gone to parochial school so he knew the church's teaching on luck, it was supposed to be nothing but pagan superstition, it was supposed to be ignorant; good Catholics didn't put their faith in anything but God. But Harvey knew when his luck was bad and he was being cheated, it was just instinct to know. In any case he didn't believe in the church any longer, hadn't been able to swallow that shit since he was fifteen, sixteen years old, he'd been a wise guy then and had actually told one of the priests at the high school to go screw, his buddies remembered that to this day. The priests had expelled him for a month, his father'd had to plead with them to take him back. Now he tried not to think about religion at all. He'd be angry if he did so he tried not to think about it, stayed away from arguing with his family or his in-laws. He had a bad temper and the thing about a bad temper, his father always said, the dangerous thing, is that you lose it at the wrong time, you get the wrong people.

His wife, Marian, went to mass most Sundays, low mass at 10 A.M. said by an older priest who never took more than a half hour. Harvey made remarks, Harvey made jokes, why the hell did she bother when she didn't believe in most of that crap, and Marian said, flaring up at once, "A human being has got to believe in something, so keep your mouth to yourself." He thought it was funny, that's all. He just had to laugh, that's all, people believing crap being shoved at them year after year, it'd been going on for thousands of years in fact, he was only making the observation.

Still, he went along with the family, wanted to have his kids baptized, you never could tell about things like that—it was a way of betting, after all. He didn't, he told his buddies, want to fuck up things for his kids if the church was maybe right.

These past few months he'd been coiled tight as a spring, distracted, irritable, not really himself. He'd light a cigarette and put it down somewhere and forget it, then light another, coughing in a new harsh way that sounded angry, his little boy ducked away with his hands over his ears, which Harvey didn't like to see. Marian complained that he had a habit of working his mouth like he was arguing with someone, she wished he'd cut it out. It's really weird, she said, you should see yourself. He wasn't arguing with anybody, he knew that, but he did a lot of thinking, how it was time for his luck to change, he'd been laid off at the plant and re-hired and laid off again and again re-hired and these days you only knew from week to week how long you'd be working; it burnt his ass, he said, no overtime for anybody not even the guys with thirty years' seniority. There was a rumor also that the plant itself might close and relocate in Kentucky, or was it Tennessee, one of those shithead states; another rumor that the owners were stockpiling, keeping it all quiet, in case of a strike.

What's the point of a strike, Harvey went around saying in a voice heavy with sarcasm, why not firebomb the dump instead? It'd add up to the same thing.

It was hard for him to believe that he'd been there for almost six years now—he was still considered new, one of the younger men. He *was* new. Last time they laid him off with no clear promise of when he'd be called back, Marian said, "Honey just quit, tell them to go to hell," but he knew she didn't mean it, she'd worked before Paulie was born, waitressing mainly, salesclerking, she wasn't exactly eager to go back and now there was going to be another baby. Steel isn't the kind of job you walk away from, Harvey said. The pay scale was high. Also the benefits, the pension, all that, shit he'd have to be crazy to quit, he'd only wind up on unemployment and what then . . . ?

Much of the time he wore ear guards on the job, especially when he was welding, they had the strange effect of eliminating the little noises you never notice and emphasizing the big ones, the vibrations, that is, the feel of the noises. It was really weird: he actually found himself listening, trying to figure out what he heard. For a while he monkeyed around with his Walkman to fix it so that he could listen to good loud rock music from the Surf City station, the earphones under the ear guards, but it didn't work out, all the sounds came scrambled in together. After an hour his head buzzed and his jaws ached from clenching, he could get high, he thought, from wearing the ear guards themselves, then he'd go smoke a joint in the lavatory and everything would go floating, so weird there was no way to describe it.

Even at home he got into the habit of going around coiled tight, almost in a crouch, as if he were waiting for something to happen, some loud noise or surprise. His skin was hot and flushed, it was the blood beating inside, an artery throbbing in his forehead which was almost identical to an artery in his father's forehead he'd always hated since he was a young kid. His hair was a dark red clayey color bleaching out fair in the summer months, wavy, worn a little long, sideburns he kept trimmed. His shoulders and arms were muscular but there was a roll of fat around his waist Marian teased him about. He didn't know what his weight was, exactly, but he knew he couldn't be overweight, he wasn't the type.

He was good-looking as he'd ever been, Marian said, except for that habit of his, working his mouth like he was talking to himself or arguing with someone. Curling his lip at people when he really meant to smile. "You're getting to be some kind of asshole, sometimes," Marian said, pouting as if she'd been insulted. "Your mind's always off somewhere."

He'd take it light, wouldn't lose his temper, maybe make a joke or two like a TV comic with his timing down so perfect he doesn't even wait for laughs. But she just stared at him. Wouldn't smile, wouldn't give an inch. Pretending to be as dumb as one of her own asshole girlfriends who couldn't tell whether Harvey Kubeck was coming on to her or playing her for laughs.

When news came that he'd won $1,150 in the lottery Harvey didn't talk it up, went around acting as if he weren't

| | | | |

that surprised at winning, even that happy, at first, though he got happier when the shock wore off. He got a lot happier. The first night Marian looked at him and said, "How come you aren't more excited?—you didn't even call many people," and he shrugged, embarrassed, cigarette in his mouth; he said, " 'Cause I figured it was coming." He said, his face burning, "I figured it's been coming for a fucking long time."

Next morning and the mornings that followed, Harvey woke and before he even opened his eyes or wondered what time it was or what day of the week, did he have to work or not, he was thinking, This is more like it, Kubeck.

He said aloud, staring at his reflection in the bathroom mirror, the ruddy skin, the quizzical eyes, turning his head from side to side, slowly, pondering, admiring, "This is the way it was meant to be."

Basically, he thinks, he's a happy contented person. Things have always gone well for him: he got through school, got through the National Guard, married the woman he wanted, has a baby boy he loves—in fact he's crazy about Paulie, really eats him up, when he has the time to concentrate. He isn't a loser, he isn't one of those poor bastards (he knows plenty, in his own family even) who fuck up everything they try. Just the past two or three years when his luck has been running against him. Or is it four years, five?—the steel business in trouble and trying to blame the union. Something in the air he breathes, the way the sky looks when he happens to glance up, the way food tastes, nothing you can put your finger on but you know it's there, you know you're being cheated. He'd look at himself in a mirror in some lavatory somewhere, late Saturday night in Surf City, he'd been drinking whiskey and beer and none of it had done much good, out with his buddies, Marian was home or over at her mother's house with Paulie, he'd take a look at that face and think, Who the hell's *that*, I don't want nothin' to do with *that*.

But basically he's a happy person. His mother used to tell people what a sweet little boy he'd been, not crying much, making up games for himself, crap like that, Harvey doesn't remember any of it but he knows it's true. He knew when his luck was due to change even when he felt lousy with a morning hangover or when he was laid off again at the plant or when the telephone rang and he let Marian answer it because he felt too tired just then to answer it himself. (Who would it be? One of his in-laws maybe, or someone in his own family. Asking for a favor like all Harvey was was a strong arm, a back to carry out furniture or something. Or they'd be complaining. Wanting to commiserate with Marian, maybe. As if he wasn't right there in his own house trying not to listen. Sons of bitches, the fuckers, his blood beat hard and hot and heavy, he'd had enough of them all.) So when news came about the lottery he wasn't that surprised. Some of his family and in-laws came over to celebrate, they had a few beers, things to eat, his father took Polaroid pictures of Harvey holding up the check from the State of New Jersey Treasury, Harvey and Marian with their arms around each other, Harvey with little Paulie climbing in his lap, but it was like Harvey was really standing off to one side watching, thinking his own thoughts. So his luck had changed, well it was about time.

The sons of bitches.

Marian was expecting the baby in early November, now it was almost the end of the summer, the lottery money had come at the right time. The pregnancy hadn't been planned exactly but when Harvey got over his surprise he said he felt good about it, he felt right. Still, every few nights Marian would say, You aren't really happy about it, are you? and Harvey would say at once, What?—sure I'm happy. And Marian would say angrily, I know *you,* your mind's a thousand miles away. She'd rub her knuckles hard against his head until he stopped her. It's half your baby, isn't it, damn you, she'd say, and Harvey would say, kidding, Honey I can't vouch for *that,* and she'd get angrier, maybe try to slap him, they'd wrestle around for a while then go to bed, there he'd fit himself into her like a hand into a glove just tight enough, or maybe it was a shoehorn, a shoehorn and a satiny silky high-heeled shoe, she clutched at him and mashed her mouth against him as she usually did, it was clear sailing, Harvey thought, past a certain point, and then his mind floated clear, floated and floated, clear, a thousand no a million miles away.

The last time Harvey Kubeck had won anything it was $40 on the Sugar Ray Leonard–Thomas Hearns welter-weight match, four years ago, just a bet with a guy at work and nothing to brag about but he'd felt good for weeks; it was something to focus his thoughts on when he was low. Then the memory faded and he had to make an effort to remember what it was that had felt so good.

Sugar Ray Leonard giving lanky Thomas "Hit Man" Hearns the fight of his life, one great boxer humiliated by another.

The $40 hadn't lasted beyond the next day. What can you do with $40 after all? It's chickenfeed.

(Years ago when Harvey was sixteen he'd gotten the idea he wanted to box. First the amateurs, then the professional league, why the hell not, give it a try. He fooled around at the Y, took lessons, went to all the local matches, told people he'd be trying out for the Golden Gloves sometime, welterweight division, the girls were impressed and Harvey's cousins were impressed but nothing came of it. His mind was quick enough but his fists were slow—he knew what he wanted to do but couldn't do it. He was always stumbling over his own feet. He never learned defense—got excited when he was popped and went a little crazy then got popped again then he'd find himself sitting on the canvas not knowing what the hell had hit him, then he couldn't make himself get up again to take more, some instinct in his gut kept him down, weak. The boxing coach liked Harvey, teased him saying he'd be known as "Iron Man" Kubeck once he got the knack, but a lot of the knack had to do with getting up after you've been hit, and if you were hit by a punch you hadn't seen coming you didn't want to get up again and take more, just some goddamned instinct about it no matter how Harvey *wanted* to keep going. So that was that. He drifted away from the gym and nobody missed him or tried to get him to come back—he guessed he was better off anyway. Still he watched fights on television, admired top boxers like Leonard, Hagler, Durán, Christ he liked Roberto Durán—that hot spic!—the "Little Killer"

Durán was called—but Harvey always felt something secret and satisfied when the best of them got beaten. Like
Leonard outboxed by Durán in their first match, Durán
outboxed by Leonard in the second, stymied, humiliated,
hurt deep inside you could tell by the expression on his
face. Now you know what it's like, Harvey would think.
Now you fuckers know what it's like.)

   This time he intended to concentrate more on the
money he'd won, it surely wasn't chickenfeed. Maybe he'd
divide it up: some for Marian—some for his parents—
some for the loan company (Jesus, he still owed at least
half the list price on the Impala he'd bought three years
ago)—some for himself—and some for a night on the town
with his buddies. They'd drive up to Shore Acres Beach
and work their way down, back to Surf City, he'd treat
them all to oysters, pizza, corn on the cob, all the beer
and drinks they wanted, what the hell. But also he wanted
to surprise Marian and Paulie with a new color TV, nine-
teen inches, console model, and with the trade-in on the
old one that would still be how much?—$800 maybe, he'd
have to check. Which was a lot of money. And there'd be
the doctor and hospital bills for the new baby, and Marian was always complaining about the refrigerator, it's
wearing out, it isn't big enough, and the linoleum in the
kitchen looks like hell, and so on and so forth. It was
starting to make him sick, thinking of all these things. It
was starting to make him angry, that buzz in his head,
something beating in his forehead, maybe he should just
take the plunge and spend the money however he wanted.
But then Marian would be mad. She'd be seriously mad.
And he was frightened of her in one of those states, especially now that she was pregnant again and if she came

at him with her nails or fists, or kicking, kneeing, he couldn't even protect himself, the last time he'd tried, he'd slapped her twice, and Paulie had started bawling, and there was hell to pay for a solid week. She really made him eat shit, the woman knew how to do it. So he wanted to give her $500, let's say. And $500 for his parents. They could use it, they were maybe even expecting it, he didn't want to disappoint them. So that was $1,000 right there: leaving him $150 which was nothing. Which would hardly pay for a night on the town. And there was the loan company. And there was—what else?

Those sons of bitches, he thought suddenly, they'd given him one of the little crap prizes instead of $1 million or $700,000 or even $50,000. Or $10,000. And being given one of the little crap prizes meant—what?—*he'd never get one of the big prizes now.*

Some days he felt so queer, so numb, it wasn't even himself, it was the way he'd felt at the National Guard camp where you just wanted to get drunk or stoned or stay in the shower running the water hot until it was all over and you could go back to real life. Other days, though, he felt good: people were still congratulating him, acting as if they envied him. He shrugged his shoulders, looked away, muttered something about not being one of the big prize winners, but nobody seemed to care. The point was he'd won, hadn't he. That was the point.

He realized it was an asshole idea to divide the money up as he'd planned. So one Friday evening after work he went to Sears like it was Christmas Eve and bought a refrigerator for Marian, avocado green, self-defrosting, and an eight-ounce bottle of Chanel No. 5 for Marian, and a red tricycle for Paulie, and he made a sizable down payment on a nineteen-inch TV, a Westinghouse, top of the line the salesman said, with a carved mahogany cabinet. And Marian and Paulie were as happy as if it was Christmas. And Marian only said afterward, in bed, that she hoped he was going to save something, there'd be the hospital bills et cetera and they didn't have a whole lot in the bank, but she spoke almost shyly and didn't press the point when Harvey didn't respond. And when they went over to his parents' on Sunday Harvey took his dad off to the side and slipped him an envelope with a check for $350 in it. This is class, Harvey thought, keeping calm while his father thanked him, and then his mother; this is high style, Harvey thought, not showing off, just doing it as if it was something you did every Sunday just about.

And just as Marian assured him, the $350 meant as much to his parents as $500 would have meant. The idea was the gift. The sentiment behind it. They understood, didn't they, that Harvey had to be thinking of the new baby, that he owed on the car, etc., he wasn't a millionaire who could throw his money around. In fact Harvey's parents seemed pleased and surprised to get the check as if they hadn't been expecting anything from him at all.

"The point is, hon, you're generous to them," Marian said. "You're the best they have and they know it."

"Sure," Harvey said, cutting the discussion short. But he liked what Marian said and he knew it was true. He *was* generous. He wanted to be more generous yet, he wanted to show people how generous he really could be, suddenly he felt excited, a little dazed, it was like the sensation he had when he'd had a few beers somewhere then walked out into the cold, some winter night—left the smoky noisy barroom and walked outside with his jacket open, bareheaded, blinking with the surprise of the cold and the stillness, his breath beginning to steam. Eyes opening wide and clear. The way the cold air hits the lungs, slicing right in. The way it feels in the nostrils. Jesus Christ, Harvey thinks, blinking, wiping his mouth with the back of his hand, this is it, isn't it?—standing there smiling, dazed, squinting up at the stars.

He even sent a "floral display"—red and yellow roses, white carnations, mums of various colors, daisies—across town to his mother-in-law. Just for the hell of it. Just to give the old woman a thrill, and Marian a real surprise.

He was really himself now, he was really getting in stride.

Labor Day weekend, Harvey treated Marian and Paulie and Paulie's three-year-old cousin Ben (Harvey's older sister's kid) to a day at the beach: not Surf City which was getting tacky but Cohasset Bay where they could drive out to the old lighthouse. The lottery money was nearly gone, in fact it really was gone, but what the hell, it was a great day, the kids loved it, Marian said she felt like a kid again herself, lazing around all afternoon on a beach towel, listening to music, oiling herself, having a nap or two in the sun. She'd have preferred it that Harvey's sister came along but little Ben wasn't too much trouble, the boys were occupied in wading in the surf, chasing gulls, monkeying in the sand with their pails and shovels, the only problem for her was that the wind blew so hard,

you got tired walking into it or even standing up for long.
. . . Harvey thought the wind was a good thing, it kept
things healthy, the muggy air blown away. All afternoon
he kept looking at Paulie, and he kept looking at Marian,
he was feeling happy, sly, laughing to himself for no reason he knew, he *was* a generous man, people were probably talking about him. It was nothing for a millionaire to
give away money: the whole thing, the context, was different for a man basically without a lot of money but with
a generous spirit.

Marian had curly black hair, a skin that tanned
golden-dark, on the beach she wore white-rimmed plastic
sunglasses that made her look like some movie star, not
twenty-nine years old but twenty at the most, her belly
swollen just a little out, her breasts too looking swollen,
held tight in the tiny bikini top with the thin straps. She'd
shaved under her arms that morning and seemed to be
lifting her arms more than usual, yawning, stretching lux-
uriously, Harvey remembered how in high school he'd
stared secretly at the girls to see if they had hair under
their arms or if they'd shaved it off, and he and the other
boys would joke about it, also if a girl had begun to shave
her legs; and if a girl hadn't, and you could see the hairs,
you'd call out in a weird voice *Hair-ry legs!* and everybody would crack up while the girl wouldn't have a clue
what the joke was; or, if she did, she'd be too ashamed
to let on.

Marian noticed him looking at her, she didn't mind
being stared at when she looked good and she knew she
looked good today, she gave him a certain mock smile,
curling her lip in a way that was supposed to mimic him,

she wriggled her shoulders, her ass, he was squatting down doing something with Paulie and he got vague with what he was doing, just looking at her, it was almost as if she wasn't his wife yet, they weren't married yet, just out on the beach for an afternoon, rock music on the transistor, his buddies and their girlfriends somewhere close by, beer in the cooler but the ice was melting, the sun was getting too hot or maybe wasn't hot enough, the sky was getting mottled, it looked like rain maybe, the sky bruising up to rain, except the wind was so rough it might blow the rain away: and there was Marian looking at him, coming on to him, out here with all these people around, he knew what she was thinking and she knew he knew, he'd get hard just with staring at her, or not even staring at her but thinking about her, Marian sticking her tongue in his mouth like it was a joke or a trick, giggling and shoving at him, drunk or pretending to be drunk, all the guys thought she was just great, all the guys envied Harvey Kubeck and he said, Yeah you better believe it, Marian's hot.

He'd thought too, off and on before they were married, before things got straightened out between them and she was still going around with other guys, he'd thought something might happen, something terrible but necessary, one night he'd lose control and drive his car into a bridge railing or something, Marian screaming next to him, or worse yet he'd just kill her: strangle her: he thought about it a lot.

There was an older guy who'd doused his girl with gasoline and lit a match to her, then doused himself and did the same thing—and Harvey thought about doing that too with Marian, not all the time but sometimes, when they quarreled or she wasn't talking to him on the telephone or he heard about her going out with another guy, it wasn't a serious thought like the other, and nothing came of any of it, she saw things his way eventually, she understood they were meant for each other and that was that.

What stayed with him from the Cohasset Bay beach, what really got to him, was the sand sculptures Paulie and Ben and some other little kids made. He hadn't even been paying all that much attention, then Paulie led him over, and here was this fish, they said it was a dolphin, maybe five feet long, one foot high, the goddamnedest lifelike thing, with fins and gills and eyes and a mouth, and all around it they'd made little hard-packed things of sand from turning sand pails upside down, it just hit Harvey that this was a work of art, he got the camera and took some pictures, the kids clowning around but really proud, Paulie's daddy looming over them.

He said to Marian, who was impressed too, that it was a shame to leave the thing behind on the beach, nobody else'd appreciate it. Big kids would probably trample it down. "Well," Marian said, yawning a little, raising her arms to stretch, "Paulie's like you, hon, he's got a real imagination."

Next weekend, Saturday night, he treated his buddies like he'd been saying he would, though the lottery money was all gone and in fact he had to borrow a little back from his father, it was a secret between him and the old man and nobody else was going to know. Marian especially, who was acting worried about what she called the "future."

They got a late start, 9 P.M., supper at the Lobster Shanty then over to Gill's for a few beers, then down to the Windjammer where there was a punk rock band none of the guys liked, then they drove across the bay to Lenape Sound where there was a tavern run by some guy they knew, and as soon as Harvey stepped inside he felt at home, he felt great, it wasn't 'cause he'd been drinking all night, it was just a feeling you had, the right kind of atmosphere, even the noise the right level, some friendly place where things were lively too and your interest would be kept up. It was Stan and Jacky and Fritz and Pete. And Harvey. Who insisted upon treating. Round after round. They had whiskey, they had draft beer, they had tequilas. Marian said to telephone her around twelve, so she'd know he was okay, and when he was coming home, but he kept putting it off, then he couldn't find the telephone the bartender directed him to, then when he found it it was out of order or something, his two dimes just kept being returned. Fishing them out Harvey thought something was weird, then he thought, he realized, he wasn't angry at the telephone as he would have been most nights, some other night he might have tried to rip it from the wall, no he just felt it was all some kind of joke, he'd ride with the joke, he was feeling so good, riding so high, he wasn't about to let some fucking out-of-order telephone get him down. The point is, he thought, his 20 cents was returned—little things like that were part of his new good luck.

He weaved a little coming back into the bar but

he wasn't drunk, he didn't have any trouble finding his buddies though the place was crowded. There were Jacky and Pete in some kind of discussion with a big heavy guy in a T-shirt, *Harley-Davidson Sarasota Florida* on the back, nobody Harvey knew, he was maybe thirty-five years old, wearing his hair in a ponytail, going to fat, the shoulders, the small of the back, even the neck, weighed two hundred twenty pounds at least, a girl next to him maybe eighteen years old, hair like broom sage and wearing sunglasses in the bar, leaning against his big arm. Harvey came over ready to buy them all another round, ready to be introduced, the big guy's name was Terry and Jacky seemed to know him, but it turned out it wasn't any kind of friendly discussion, it was actually an argument, about somebody Terry knew that Jacky also knew, ran a gas station in Atlantic City, maybe, Harvey couldn't follow it except he knew right away that Terry was the kind of asshole he'd like to smash with his fists, you'd just like to see a wiseguy fucker like that laid out somewhere dead, wipe the grin off his face, put some respect in his eyes, the fear of the Lord as Harvey's father said.

The argument continued for a while, Terry was calling Jacky fuckface, and Harvey said to Terry go fuck yourself, and the bartender who was listening who seemed to be a friend of Fritz's or maybe a cousin, Harvey'd been introduced when they first came in but hadn't exactly heard, he came over and told them to keep it down please, he said to Terry maybe he'd better move on, there's lots of places on the strip and it was still early. So Terry and his girl left after a few minutes, Terry told them all to go to hell, go fuck themselves, bunch of assholes etc. but he kept on moving, the girl had to hurry after him in her high-heeled shoes and she looked scared.

So that happened, but again it was weird, Harvey didn't feel angry he felt instead like it was all part of his life now, him being out with his buddies, everybody having a good time, the way he'd planned it in his head almost from the first hour when the news came about the lottery, thinking of a place like this, maybe not in Lenape Sound 'cause he wasn't familiar with it like he was with Surf City, but a place like this, him and his buddies, Pete and Stan and Jacky and Fritz, then there was Gary who couldn't make it 'cause they were going out of town or something, he felt bad that Gary wasn't with them but just for a second or a half second, already the thought floated away and his good happy feeling returned, Jacky was making them all crack up with what he was saying about the guy with the ponytail, Harvey decided on another tequila and the bartender smiled at him, said, Harv this is on me, okay? and he felt that kick of something special, something just right, meant only for him, some kind of secret. Nah, he said, I can pay for it, but the bartender insisted, so he gave in, then they were all eating oysters, the second time that night, then Harvey was having trouble with the cigarette machine, laughing 'cause his coins weren't being returned this time, but a little pissed off too, starting to punch at the machine, a few kicks, one of his buddies pulled him away saying forget it: Harv could bum a cigarette from him any time he wanted.

They left that bar, drove a mile or two down the Bay Road to another place, big parking lot practically in the dunes, music inside, somebody else was driving Har-

| | | | |

vey's Impala now which irritated him a little but he didn't intend to get in a fight right now, he'd make his point later when they drove back to Surf City. This place, the atmosphere took getting used to, too many customers pushing around the bar, too many women maybe, couples trying to dance and getting bumped into, a lot of noise, but Harvey felt good after his first draft beer or two, his buddies were flying high just like him, lots of wise-guy stuff and laughing, almost choking with laughter, Fritz telling them how Harv had told Father Donahue to go screw, they'd heard it a hundred times already but it always cracked them up. Harvey thought he saw the big guy with the ponytail, he thought he saw him and the girl on the other side of the room, but then he lost them, forgot about them, he was bumming cigarettes which he'd light and drop on the floor, once he burnt his fingers with somebody's lighter, how the fuck it happened he couldn't figure out, those things were safety proof. Harvey was thinking he liked this bar as well as the other one, maybe better. He felt at peace. But well he felt excited too. It was hard to put your finger on—things going the way they were supposed to go. The way they were meant. Like the satisfaction of seeing a river or something running along, or even raindrops rolling down a windshield, it could fascinate you, it was hard to say why, Harvey saw the sky bunching up over the Surf City beach and the first raindrops pelting and the thunder sounding and there's that good clean fresh air, that almost surprising air, just before a storm, and he and the other kids ran like hell down the beach, yelling and laughing, trying to outrace the storm, the raindrops hitting like bullets, older people scrambling around putting away their beach crap, gathering up their kids, assholes acting like lightning was going to strike them the next minute.

He saw then that that guy with the ponytail *was* there in the bar, the girl with him, but they hadn't noticed Harvey and his friends. Actually they were on their way out, the girl had her sunglasses slid atop her head, pressing close against him with her arm through his, the guy gave a look around the room, a last look, but he still didn't see Harvey and his friends. The son of a bitch, Harvey thought. Who are you calling fuckface, fuckface? You're dead, Harvey thought, putting down his glass of draft beer.

The girl wasn't any eighteen either, probably Marian's age, heavy makeup on her face and black stuff on her eyes, her ass wriggling in some kind of a silky play suit, really short shorts, bare legs and those high-heeled shoes: a real slut.

Harvey poked his buddies and said, Look, and they looked, and he said, Want to get him? and they were sort of indecisive and Harvey said, Let's go, and they paid up at the bar, and followed the two out into the parking lot; it was good luck, Harvey thought, the bastard's motorcycle was parked way down at the end, way down, almost in the dunes. Harvey started in trotting, he wasn't even going to wait for his buddies, he felt so good, the whole night had been moving toward this, weeks and weeks, half his life, like a river running fast, his heart fast too, he knew enough not to call out any kind of warning, not even to bother calling the bastard a name, the trainer at the Y had said, Don't waste that rush you get, that good strong feeling, that's some kind of chemical or hormone, adrenaline, now you're going to need it and now you think maybe you're scared but remember you're *not,* you're just getting ready to fight. When it hits them there's lots of guys that panic or start talking too fast but don't you ever make that mistake, just ride with the feeling, okay?—just ride with it, let it carry you along, that good strong feeling, someday maybe it's going to save your life.

And when you're in the ring don't ever feel sorry for your opponent 'cause why the hell should you, he's your opponent and he's out for your ass.

So Harvey got first to the guy, just started swinging, the girl screamed, the guy shouted something and tried to block Harvey's fist but Harvey got him square in the face, left cheekbone, so hard his knuckles felt like they were broken but the hurt just faded away at once. Now the bastard was backing away, crouched, now Harvey could see the sick pleading look in his eyes, Harvey got him next in the gut, that big soft fat gut, a real belly blow that doubled him over, any referee that saw that the fucking fight would be over right now and Kubeck through for the season, but there wasn't any referee, just Harvey and the guy with the ponytail, trying to use his fists, trying even to use a knee, he swung clumsily at Harvey and Harvey just danced aside, knowing to do some quick peppery jabbing with his left, a hard uppercut with his right, shit it felt like his whole hand was broken now but he didn't give a damn, didn't have time to worry, the guy stumbled backward, fell to his knees, Harvey used his knee to get him in the face, there was blood streaming out of his nose and mouth, now Fritz and Pete were trying to pull Harvey away but he just shrugged them off, nobody was going to stop him, it was between him and his opponent and nobody was going to stop him; How d'you like it now, fuckface, Harvey said, okay you motherfucker, Harvey was saying, the air felt so good from the ocean, the wind so fresh and clean in his lungs, he was just getting higher and higher like his heart could burst with wanting to laugh, nobody was going to stop him now after so long.

The guy had fallen, even in the half-light from the parking lot Harvey could see he was bleeding pretty bad, the pavement and the sand were going dark by his head, then there were some headlights, then they heard a car door slam, Fritz said, Harv come *on,* but whoever it was wasn't coming any closer, they just weren't about to see what was going on by the dunes and Harvey knew ahead of time that that was how it was: he just knew. So he said, Here's one for the road, sucker, bringing his fist down hard on the back of the guy's neck like he was doing karate and wanted to break it. One of his buddies was keeping the girl quiet, the others were trying to stop him, he felt so weird, so certain of himself, he just kept punching, kicking, he kicked anywhere he could, the guy's head, the guy's fat belly, he was laughing saying, How's it feel now you son of a bitch, wiping his mouth with his forearm, How's it feel now you cocksucker, something jumped in his mind and he was thinking for a second he had on steel-toed shoes like at work but of course he hadn't, these were just his regular shoes, summer shoes, loafers Marian had made him get, they were oyster-white and pretty stylish, supposed to be Italian but not expensive like the real

| | | | |

kind, he'd bought them at the mall back in June before he ever guessed that his luck would be changing and his whole life would be turned around.

There was some confusion about getting back home, who was going to drive who, they'd come in two cars, Harvey's and Pete's, but finally he got home, it was 3:20 A.M. and there was Marian watching television, dressed for bed and barefoot, her face oily with cream. He could tell she was angry but she was frightened too which made him feel better toward her, he shrugged her off when she came over, asking right away about his hand though he was hiding it, asking if he'd been in a fight, he went past her into the kitchen and got a beer from the refrigerator, pulled off the ring and tossed it somewhere, Marian was pulling at his arm, saying he was drunk, saying he was cockeyed drunk and not to wake Paulie, her voice was low and flat and accusing but he could tell she was scared. He just shoved her out of the way and went into the bathroom.

He was in there awhile, five minutes, ten, he heard the telephone ringing but it was only his head, a good loud buzzing like Quaaludes but he couldn't remember having taken any that night, unless it was back at that place before the last place where the bartender gave him a drink on the house, hell of a nice guy, that was a place he intended to go back to, some cousin or somebody of Fritz's, but mainly he thought it must be just what he'd drunk and how good he felt from messing up that son of a bitch with the ponytail, Harley-Davidson T-shirt, big black bike, the works, and the girl gone crazy thinking her boyfriend was dead which anybody could see he wasn't:

not crawling around like he was and making noises like he was, puking into the sand, puke and blood, the son of a bitch.

When he came out of the bathroom Marian said in that low voice, "Barbara just called," meaning Pete's wife, and Harvey didn't bother replying, got his shoes off with a grunt, pulled his shirt off over his head without taking time to unbutton it, his fingers were getting too numb to work the buttons, he was suddenly very tired and ready for bed, and Marian pulled at his arm, Marian said, "She says there was some trouble tonight," but he just pushed her away, not hard, just out of his way. She said, "Was there?"

He was rubbing his face with the shirt. Waves of exhaustion like he'd been working overtime, two hours overtime, could hardly keep from keeling over, but there were waves of something else too, short quick stabbing waves, excitement, elation, the knowledge of something secret. He could smell Marian's hair and the stale powdery scent of her underarms. The special rayony smell of that shortie nightgown of hers with the lace top. Her mouth was close to his ear, her breath was hot and accusing, she said again, "Was there? Harvey? Was there?" and he said, "Was there what?" She was so close, he hadn't expected her so close, he reached around and grabbed hold of her ass, she gave him a slap, told him again not to wake Paulie, did he know what time it was, he could feel himself getting hard though he was almost too tired to keep his eyes open, stumbling to the bed and hauling Marian with him, she gave him a real slap on the side of the face so that his ear stung, he fell laughing onto the bed not giving a damn if the bedsprings broke, "C'mon shut up an' get to bed," he said, it really turned him on that Marian was always pushing him, seeing how far she could go with him, he wouldn't want some wife like his brother had or his brother-in-law or half the guys he knew, scared to death they were going to get it in the face, too scared even to cry, Marian *was* scared but she kept at him, her eyes showing white the way they did, "Look Harvey, was there trouble? I want to know," she asked, and he said, "No, there was not."

She said something he didn't catch, then she was drawing off her bathrobe, he had to watch her through his fingers because of the light that hurt his eyes, he liked that nightgown of hers that was a queer translucent aqua color, wide lacy straps like something a little girl might wear, lace bodice you could see through in the real light, he knew suddenly that the baby was going to be a girl and he knew that was right, that balanced things out, there would be Paulie and there would be Paulie's baby sister, that was the way it would work out, he'd bet a thousand dollars, his luck was going to hold.

The nightgown clung with static electricity to Marian's belly and buttocks, and seeing his face, his eyes, she turned slightly away, intimidated, maybe, or embarrassed. She could see things in his face, Harvey knew, he could never see himself.

In the dark he went for her, wordless. Marian resisted, then gave in, murmuring something he couldn't make out, she had to lift her hips, she had to help him get inside her, they were both breathing hard, then Harvey was pumping into her, his jaws clenched, his eyes shut tight, he hadn't known he was so hot, so urgent, his heartbeat so fast. Marian held his sides tight with her knees as she sometimes did, holding him back, trying to hold him back, so in his plunge he wouldn't squeeze her belly and breasts, wouldn't hurt her. She was whispering something, she closed her fingers in his hair but he paid no attention, he was panting, grunting, then suddenly it was over—that flame coursing through his groin and belly that always astonished him, it was so strong, so powerful, it was familiar but it always astonished him, knocked the breath out of him as if he'd been kicked. Then he was lying by himself in the damp sheets and Marian was in the bathroom, a narrow sliver of light, water running in the distance, or maybe it was the surf, the waves breaking, a waterfall, a cascade of water sparkling in the sun, suddenly he is sinking in a slow turn, weightless, wordless, a deep deep turning, now he hardly needs to breathe because it is all being done for him, he is turning slow into a dark pool of water secret beneath the crashing waterfall, this is his place, this is his secret, deep beyond dreaming, floating free, and here, here suddenly he is.

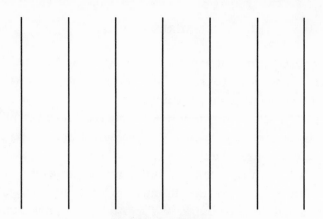

LITTLE
BLOOD-BUTTON

One of you's to blame but I don't know which, don't know either how deep a root it has. If the doctor's got to dig it out one of you bastards is gonna pay. Listen: got up this morning, looked in the mirror, there it was. Jesus! I said aloud. This thing growing on my lip, upper lip, right in the middle, little bud or pimple, hot black blood, scared me to touch it! From you kissing so hard. Kissing and pressing. Biting. Sucking. All that stuff—you know. Things you hadn't ought to be doing but when I said, Hey stop, you don't pay any heed just keep right on. So it started growing, after the lights were out probably. I don't know if I felt it or not. Just some bug maybe, a spider maybe, crawling around. Bedbug maybe. Yes it's been known to happen! So now there's this thing, swollen, hurting, so hot it burns the tip of my tongue if I touch it. Just feel!

Now I'm standing here looking in the mirror and can't even see *myself* 'cause it's so swollen and hurting, a hard little button of blood. Howcome it's black blood I wouldn't know—would you? One of you's got to answer for it. I'll call the sheriff. I'll call my father, don't matter if he's in Alaska or where. Maybe it's a blister, okay, a bug bite, yeah, but maybe it's a cyst, things they call cysts, that means cancer, somebody's gonna pay. Suppose the doctor says, That's gotta be yanked out by the roots! Twenty dollars to sit you in the fucking chair, another five to rinse out your mouth and spit it in the drain. Somebody's gonna foot the bill and it ain't me.

Momma said a long time ago, You're gonna die with your insides all scooped out dumped in a toilet bowl somewhere, Greyhound bus station I wouldn't wonder, *she* was the one to shrivel up like some old straw broom. No I don't give a shit. I don't. Who says cancer? It's just some black blood tasting of salt, c'mere and taste. If you got the wherewithal, hon, better use it; Momma used to say that too. Howcome I'm talking about her I don't give a goddam about *her*. Look: I ain't going nowhere, I said. Just got up. Just got my face washed and gargled out my mouth. Somebody stole my toothbrush or knocked it behind the toilet or I'd brush my goddam teeth too. What time? Never mind the time. That pile of movie magazines, daytime TV—push 'em on the floor. Take it easy hon I'm right *here*. Stick that fat tongue in deep. See I told you it was hot didn't I. This sweater's too tight to get over my head, the neck's stained, tight under the arms and stained too, skirt's got a raveled-out buttonhole I made with the scissors next to the regular buttonhole, putting on weight, goddam it's depressing, you got your own pot belly, hon: feel? Honey don't hurt! Honey I'm *here.* Yeah I'm hot, I'm wired up tight, all that kissing, biting, go on and suck right down to the roots, hon, suck this blood-button out clean. It's scaring me, I want it gone. Tastes of salt? Sugar? Hot brown sugar? Don't you get rough, hon, don't you worry, I fixed myself up fine, there ain't a single germ living, that's the God's honest truth, guaranteed. Sure there ain't. Says so on the label.

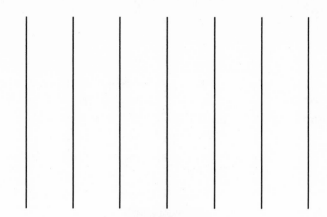

BABY

The second night my brother was home I told him, I told him straight out, not troubling to lower my voice, Well she's waiting for you in there isn't she, pretending to be asleep with the light out and it's only nine-thirty. I tried to keep my face from going heavy and sullen like it does. I said, You think I'm blind, the way she's been looking at you all day?—it just about makes me sick.

He's my half brother not my real brother, three years older than me though he has always acted younger, running off to the Merchant Marines when Ma was sick and losing weight so you could see the bones pushing through the skin, somewhere in the Red Sea (wherever that is: I never had time to look it up on a globe of the earth) when she died and yours truly had to make the arrangements and pay the bills and deal with the funeral parlor crooks who talk like butter wouldn't melt in their mouths. Already him and Etta's girl were probably carrying on behind my back but my brother looked at me all innocent and a little angry, and said he didn't know what the hell I was talking about.

I said again it just about made me sick, the girl was taking after Etta anyway, you couldn't stop that, but under Ma's roof it made me sick, you'd think some people would have shame.

He said again he didn't know what the hell I was talking about but I had better mind my own business, maybe.

I said right back not troubling to lower my voice that I *was* minding my own business, Etta trusted her girl with me after all and I'd be the one blamed, even if the daughter took after the mother (God forgive me for saying so but God knew it was gospel truth) and surely had tainted blood from the father's side (you could see it in that fat lip no matter how light her skin was, and her hair and eyes), and was already causing trouble in school.

How's she causing trouble at school? my brother asked, like he didn't believe me. She's too simple, they'd slap her down.

Oh no she is *not* simple, I said. That's just one of her tricks.

My brother got a beer from the refrigerator and started drinking it with no mind for his rudeness or the fact that I was still talking. I spoke calm as I always do on the subject of Etta's girl (in which yours truly has become an expert and could straighten out the principal and those psychiatrists or whatever they call them at the school but why should I go down there to be insulted?—I already wrote them a dozen letters), explaining that she only pretends to be simple around the house so she can get away with more tricks. Like she pretends to be smiling all the time and humming under her breath and taking an hour to do the dishes and then not drying half the plates right, or forgetting to scour the coffeepot or the oven, and crying when she wants to, her eyes filling up with tears like somebody on television. I told him Etta's girl had been asking when he was coming home for weeks, maybe for months, and the last few days she'd been acting so strange she didn't mind staying out of school to help with the cleaning, just forgot about school, when other times she's scared somebody will come to the door, or telephone asking where she is. I told him I had to laugh, him pretending he could fool *me*. I told him you'd think he would have some maturity at his age—going on forty wasn't it— no matter if the girl was halfway to being a slut and you could wait till Hell freezes over before Etta was going to admit who the father was.

He said he was going out, not to wait up for him— he had plans until pretty late.

I calculated he had been drinking since ten this morning, one beer and then another, taking it slow but drinking steady the way he learned from his father (who was my father too but belonged more to Etta and him, in my opinion), some of the beer here in the house though he knew I didn't approve, and the rest of it in one or another of his beer joints downtown. He was looking up his pals and making telephone calls and I just had to laugh, he got in such a rotten mood by the time he came home

| | | | |

for supper, one of his girlfriends moved away or wouldn't see him, that was written all over his face. He thinks he's good-looking because of his curly hair and mustache he keeps trim but from the side his chin just dribbles away, he has to stretch to close his lips over those big front teeth, ten times worse than mine. He thinks he's good-looking because probably one of his girlfriends (by which I mean some slut or whore he'd never bring to the house) flattered him to get some cash out of him: they know how to do it. And now Etta's girl, not fourteen years old, mooning over him and staring and stumbling like a baby cow when he's in the room—you can see how a man's head is turned.

I followed him out into the front hall and told him he'd better not make a lot of noise when he came back, and he didn't pay any attention, and outside I could hear him toss the beer can onto the sidewalk—that's the kind of pig they are, him and Etta both—not caring that it was right in front of the house probably and somebody (yours truly) would have to pick it up next day. This was going on to ten o'clock and near as I could figure out he didn't get home until early morning—five-thirty, maybe.

I thought, He won't dare, at first. He'll hold back as long as he can.

Which was maybe true, for all I know. He had twenty-one days at home counting the first day and the last.

Or maybe they started in right the next afternoon, when I was away at the doctor's office, first in the waiting room and then in one of his cubicles, all those hours.

Blame it on me for my trusting nature, listening to Etta's lies about when she'd send for her little girl, when she never paid half her share for Ma's funeral or anything else for that matter. (Is this your "little girl"? I asked Etta when I saw the child, but she never caught on to my sarcasm or maybe pretended not to hear. I had to laugh, seeing the size of her; and how much she guzzled when you weren't watching.)

First Etta begged, then Etta cried, she promised it wouldn only be for a few months, until she got settled. I never knew whether there was another man in the picture or not and wouldn't waste my breath asking: there aren't two sisters, half sisters or whatever, on the face of earth more different than Etta and me, praise God. She had the girl, who was eleven at the time, almost pretty except for her small close-set blinking eyes that looked at you scared, and her mouth that she was in the habit of keeping open (you could hear the poor thing breathe—it was actually panting), and some kind of pimply red skin rash on her arms and neck she couldn't stop scratching. And she had the little boy who was maybe eighteen months old but small for his age, high-spirited and laughing when there wasn't much reason to laugh. Sometimes the girl's daddy and the little boy's daddy was one and the same man (gone out to the State of Washington, going to send for Etta any day), sometimes you got the impression there were two men, two daddies, but I wouldn't lower myself to ask. Etta promised how she'd send money for the girl's room and board (as she called it) and for a few months there was $20 every other week or so, $45, $60 a month, then naturally it tapered off. The last postal money order came from Tampa, Florida, $45 and zero cents, no note enclosed. That was maybe a year ago.

At least the girl could work around the house and

do errands in the neighborhood, that was a blessing. Panting like a cow or a sheep or something, and sweating so you could smell it a room away, and talking to herself under her breath when she didn't think I was close by. . . . The neighbors said how good-hearted I was, they pointed out how Ma always claimed her youngest child (which was me) was the only one that ever loved her or showed respect, but anyway the girl could help out with the housecleaning, that was a blessing. Also, she never gave me any sass or ran away when she was being disciplined the way a brighter girl or boy that age would.

I didn't want to tell them that even so I'd have preferred the little boy, if Etta had given me a choice. (Of course she didn't.) He was noisy and made messes but he took to me right away, flailing his fat little hands around and laughing even when I scolded, like he didn't care what my opinion was, he had his own. One day Etta seen me looking at the baby and said with that nasty laugh of hers, He about ripped me in two, that one, took a night and a morning to get himself born, and the way she said it, and the fact she said it so straight out (we were right in the kitchen getting supper) made me sick to my stomach.

After Etta went away taking the baby and leaving the girl behind I sometimes heard the baby's crying, I thought, coming through the walls, or up the heating ducts from the cellar, but the girl never heard anything so I knew it was all in my head. Then later I forgot about him and told myself I'd better forget about Etta too.

There's one born every minute ain't there, my father used to say, pointing out some fool or idiot in the newspaper that got himself killed, say, for picking up a hitchhiker, or opening the door to a stranger at the wrong time of day.

All these things I explained to Baby when I judged him old enough to comprehend. No matter how ugly the truth is it's still the truth and must be honored, praise God.

How they managed to do their nasty tricks in secret, my brother and that thirteen-year-old slut (and her a niece to us both), I never knew, unless it was when I went Wednesdays and Saturdays to the market, or took to my bed with migraine. Or maybe they arranged to meet outside the house. Etta's girl could cut classes, and my brother could take her somewhere nobody would know about. . . . He was low-minded enough to give some thought to it, and her no better, in spite of pretending to be so simpleminded and sweet like she did.

Even before he shipped out at the end of December the girl was crying a lot and acting strange, but I had my pride about poking my nose where it wasn't wanted, and my dignity. Also, my brother's temper was getting worse and worse like it always does at the end of a visit home, and you'd better watch your lip around him, and feed him when he wants to eat, not too early and not too late; he got it all from our father, it runs in the blood. I wouldn't provoke him by asking questions, I wouldn't lower myself to such filth then or now.

One night he went on a drunken rampage, and me and the girl locked ourselves in the bathroom. He's going to kill us, he's going to kill us! Etta's girl was sobbing like crazy, hot and clumsy as a baby cow but trying to burrow against *me* as if I was her momma!—so I gave her a slap of my own and said loud enough for him to hear through the door, Anybody lays a hand on anybody else under this roof, the police already know who to arrest—and that's just the beginning of his troubles.

So my brother pounded on the door a while longer, and said I'd better unlock it, then he gave up and went away, and didn't come home until seven the next morning, sick-drunk and stinking of vomit. If Etta's girl was crying over *him* it serves her right.

Over the winter I saw how she was putting on weight in her belly, and the baby fat around her face became sort of hard and white and shiny, and she'd eat like a pig or maybe eat nothing at all for a day; so I knew the shame that was upon us and took her out of school. I was obliged to whip her a few times, it was my responsibility, but she cried and shrieked so hard my migraine started, and I didn't want to be too rough because something might happen to the baby inside her (who I did not call Baby at the time) and that would be a sin in God's judgment. It was bad enough to be born a bastard of an unclean union and draw ridicule and scorn upon us throughout the neighborhood.

What did you and him do that I never knew about, I asked Etta's girl, and she bawled and said they never did nothing, she wasn't a bad girl, you could ask Mrs. Cassity (who was in charge of the Special Education students at the school) if she was one of the bad girls or the good girls, Mrs. Cassity knew them all. Oh yes that's a likely story, I said laughing—I got so angry I was laughing lots of the time that winter and into the spring—*that's* a likely story, we can tell your mother that can't we.

But I gave up after a while because what was the use? Some people are born too wicked to feel shame.

Etta's girl stayed indoors but, still, around the neighborhood they started in asking, Who's the father? Who's going to own up to it?—looking me square in the face. But I never said a thing, I wouldn't give them the satisfaction. Then they started in asking me where we would place the baby. The Catholic adoption center was just a few blocks away on Grand River Boulevard but if you knew how to go about it there were plenty of couples desperate for babies of their own and they might pay, well, five hundred dollars . . . a thousand dollars. . . .

Yours truly never said a thing.

My plans were: buy myself a plain gold wedding band and see about renting another house across town where people would mind their own business.

By the middle of the summer Etta's girl had left off crying and just sat around the house, not watching television but only staring out the window into the street (did she think *he* was likely to come back?) or the rear yard. Where before she guzzled everything in the refrigerator if I turned my back for a minute, now she wouldn't hardly eat at all. Any kind of gravy made her sick to her stomach, and just the sight of fatty meat, and globules of fat floating in soup. I had a book I was reading on diet during pregnancy but Etta's girl just shrugged her shoulders. Finally I went out in 95-degree heat to buy a gallon of butternut-ripple ice cream one day to get her eating again. She said she'd be sick to her stomach but I handed her a spoon and that was it: once she got started she couldn't stop.

There were exercises she was supposed to do too, according to this book I had, but she was too lazy to budge. I told myself, Well, babies get born anyway, they always have.

It was queer how her stomach got—big and round and high, and hard-looking, not like an ordinary fat belly—while the rest of her was pinched and sallow. The baby fat disappeared from her face and her eyes were bruised-looking and old. Once I looked up at her in the kitchen—this was in early August, not long before Baby was born—and thought I wouldn't know who that girl *was,* if she was kin to me or not.

Already Baby was a strong presence in the house, you knew he was there, just waiting. He'd kick and I swear I could feel it across the room!—even before Etta's girl made one of her sharp whining noises like she was being stabbed.

Already you knew he was a *he.* There was never any question of that.

My timing was just right: we moved across town to Union Street, and a few days later Etta's girl went into labor (it lasted fifteen hours but they said that was normal enough) and Baby was born, seven pounds four ounces, no known defects, Caucasian male (as they called him).

It was like the baby book explained: you think they are ugly at first, and their skulls not right, and that flushed skin, and queer blackish hair and blind-looking eyes. . . .

Etta's girl laughed and said, *I* don't want it, later on she said (embarrassing me in front of the nurse), I don't know what it is, it isn't mine, I never had anything to do with it.

So I had to take charge immediately, or Baby would have died of neglect.

(Later I would think, or God would allow me to think, that Baby should have died right there in the hospital, he should have been born already dead, but of course I couldn't have such knowledge at that time.)

When Baby first came home I was frightened to hold him thinking he might slip through my arms, he could squirm and kick so, or he might stop breathing all of a sudden the way they say babies do. But of course nothing happened because he was too strong. He fixed his eyes on me right away and knew who I was.

Etta's girl pretended she was too sick to nurse so yours truly had to take charge as anybody would have predicted. At my age! . . . preparing baby formula, changing diapers (which did not seem so disgusting after the first week or so), giving Baby his bath and laying him down for his nap. In this new house (a duplex—I believe in upstairs and downstairs and having your own front and rear doors) Baby and I were situated upstairs and Etta's girl had a room off the kitchen that the landlord said was a dining room if you wanted one.

Baby's crib was white wicker, old-fashioned and sturdy, that I found in the old cellar when we moved. This was my own crib a long time ago, I told Baby, so it's right you should have it.

| | 287 | |

| | | | | |

Etta's girl lazed around the house too mean to nurse though you could see the milk staining through her clothes. She watched television now whenever she could get away with it and just laughed when I asked wasn't she going back to school?—she knew from the start how Baby had turned against her and pretended it was *her* doing.

Baby knows who his true mother is, I said, and Etta's girl just laughed, swinging past on her way to the bathroom.

Baby knows who hates him and who loves him, I said. Who his true parent is.

By this time Etta's girl had got so fat and sloppy you could feel the floorboards give a little beneath her bare feet. She had got so mean and lazy she whispered swearwords under her breath pretending I wasn't close by.

Once when I was telling her about Baby, and about how he knew more than he let on, she turned to me with an ugly grinning face and said, That baby don't know shit.

And when I went to slap her she dared raise her hand against me—both her hands against me, made into fists—like she was going to hit *me*. And Baby was a witness all along. So I knew I had let things go too far, I would have to notify the health authorities about Etta's girl and get her taken care of properly, as her condition required.

So Etta's girl left, and Baby and I were alone together as God decreed.

It was the right thing to do, having Etta's girl taken away, they told me at the county home not to feel bad about it, if I read the newspapers (which in fact I do if I have time) I'd know that more and more young mothers were doing injury to their babies. They were dependent, they told me, on people like myself stepping forward and speaking out.

One of the nurses told me a person like myself wouldn't believe what went on in that housing development on the west side, they were just animals there, if I knew what she meant. I said I did know. She said it made her sick sometimes to be called over into that neighborhood, it made her almost lose faith in the human race, but my niece was not of that category, of course.

Well, I said, wiping Baby's mouth with a tissue where he had drooled on himself, some people *are* animals after all.

That was our happiest time now I look back on it—three or four months when the house was empty of Etta's girl and Baby had not yet come into his powers.

He learned to crawl, and to walk, and to say things meant to be talking, all earlier than the doctor said to expect, which comforted me in the beginning because it meant that he would not grow up feebleminded like his mother. Even when he was asleep, though, he filled the house upstairs and down, there wasn't a room he wasn't in, I could feel him through the walls. No matter what I was doing—for instance scouring the oven one time—he could summon me to him if he wished without making a sound.

Baby knows who loves him, I would say. Baby knows who his true parent is.

And Baby stared at me understanding every word and smiling for of course he *did* know.

That's a husky baby, people said in the neighborhood, that's a good-looking baby, they would say, fixing their eyes on me and getting ready to ask (I had to laugh, I knew it was coming) where his daddy was. So I said, Well now his *daddy* is halfway around the world but he's good about sending money home, that was one good thing about him, and the way I talked you could tell they were puzzled but they didn't know to ask where his *mommy* was, which was none of their business anyway.

That's certainly a *boy* baby, a woman from across the street said, poking her nose into Baby's face, you wouldn't have any doubt he's a *boy,* she said, meaning to flatter, then smiling a big wide smile and asking what his name was—if I'd told her, she said, she must have forgotten.

Baby is what I call him for right now, I said. Baby is name enough for us both.

Yours truly was *not* rude—but kept the baby buggy moving.

Just when the Change started in I cannot say, although looking back there were signs all along.

Sometimes Baby would allow me to cuddle him, and rock him, and kiss him, and sometimes he would not—he'd fly into a rage and half choke with shrieking. *Like he did not want to be touched.*

Sometimes Baby would eat every spoonful of his food as I fed it to him (his favorite for many months being mashed apricots which I flavored with sweet cream and sugar) but sometimes he would not: he'd spit it out, maybe cough and vomit, and scream and kick and flail about as if someone had hurt him. (Which assuredly I did not—for I knew very well never to put hot food or a hot spoon in Baby's mouth, a common error it is said ignorant young mothers frequently commit.)

Sometimes, also, Baby would sleep peacefully when he was put to bed, but sometimes, what a commotion!—he'd shriek and clamber about in his crib, kicking and banging his head against the sides, I didn't dare lay a finger on him because he would only get worse, his face all wrinkled and purple and his breath irregular. What if he chokes to death in the blankets, I thought, what if he puts his head through the bars and strangles himself. . . . Next door the neighbors began to knock against the wall in protest and I was sick with shame, that strangers might know of our private business, and talk amongst themselves of Baby and his wildness.

You must learn to be good, I told Baby, half fainting because my heart beat so, you must obey your Mother, I told him, but he only stared at me cold and insolent like he had never seen me before.

There is nobody on this earth who loves you as your Mother loves you, I told Baby.

Baby laughed.

You could not doubt but that Baby *was* all boy, however, nothing weak or feebleminded about him. Thus I praised God as it became clear that his nature had skipped over my brother's and was close to being Baby's grandfather's if I remembered correctly. His hair had turned light brown and was very, very fine and curly. His eyes had turned the bluest blue.

Baby must have his way inside the house and out, and his Mother's legs, that have never been strong, cannot keep up. I laughed to myself saying that I had been fool enough to pay $7.50 for a big jar of cod-liver oil tablets sold to me at the door (by a high school girl a stranger to me) when Baby did not need extra help in growing . . . !

There were five hundred tablets in the jar, of which I gave one to Baby before his breakfast each morning, and by the time the jar was emptied the Change was well upon him—though I would not say that the cod-liver oil tablets were to blame.

By this time Baby had long since learned to dress himself and to go about his business as he wished, sometimes very quietly in the morning, so only the creaking of the floorboards alerted me that he was awake. At other times of course Baby romped about, and crashed into things, and chattered to himself as (it is said) small children will do at that age. I pressed my ear against the wall to hear more closely but his words were secret to me.

Baby, what are you saying, I whispered through the wall but of course there could be no reply.

How husky he was growing!—as all the neighbors commented, the mothers in particular who were perhaps jealous of Baby. For, by the age of three, Baby stood near to my shoulder (though I am not a tall person it must be remembered) and when we were seated, why, I believe we were of a height. Baby used his own spoon now—and his own knife and fork—and often ate with his head lowered to his plate as my brother did (though there could be no influence for Baby had never glimpsed my brother). It was not indifference to his Mother for I believe he loved me, but simply the way he was, thinking his own thoughts and forgetful of my presence.

There was much resistance to his bath now for Baby said he wished to bathe himself (feeling some shame perhaps at his nakedness—for Baby had rapidly matured); but I did not trust him to cleanse all his parts thoroughly. Thus we had frequent disagreements which flared up in quarrels leaving Baby blotched in the face and panting hard, and yours truly half fainting on the sofa, sick and dizzy with grief. (It is not the place to speak of my health but I am obliged to mention that my doctor expressed some concern for my blood pressure and an "erratic" heartbeat he detected with his instrument. Since moving to Union Street I have consulted a new doctor who knows me as "Mrs." and respects the ring on my finger and the fact that I am a Mother—although I am wise enough never to allow him to examine me down below, as, being a doctor, he would surely note some evidence that *I had not had Baby in any physical manner.*)

When I lay fainting on the sofa Baby would give evidence of remorse but (God forgive him) would not apologize. Doubtless he shed tears in secret—as I did—but his pride was such he could not be humbled.

Also, sometimes when I napped in the late afternoon (for my nerves were such I had begun to tire halfway through the day), Baby would appear silent by my bedside gazing down with no earthly expression on his face. Though my eyelids were closed I could see Baby clearly, as he was in real life yet altered with queer nicks and dents in his cheeks and a tawny glow to his eyes such as you find in the eyes of cats. Baby it is in your power to do great harm, I whispered to him (though my lips could not move), but I pray God you will show mercy to me . . . for I am your dear Mother who loves you above all the world.

Baby did not speak. His eyes were in shadow and his mouth was pinched inward like a fist.

As the months passed, however, the Change grew more and more upon him, and I fell into despair wondering what I must do.

He had begun to stay away long hours from the house despite my pleas; and where he once chattered and babbled happily under my roof, now he was silent days at a time. Why do you grieve your Mother, I asked him, but he turned aside as if the question were shameful one. When I tried to kiss him he went hard as stone or ice, shrinking from me in his soul.

Now it happened too that the mothers along Union Street rose up against Baby saying they no longer wanted him to play with their children. Has he injured any of them? I asked, my heart beating so hard I could scarcely breathe. He has not injured anyone yet, one of the women said unkindly. But he speaks to them, he gathers them around him to say such things they will not repeat to us, and when we approach they run away guilt-faced and laughing.

No, he is not a natural child, another told me, her face contorted with hatred. You must keep him away from our children!

Not a natural child! I exclaimed. How dare you say such things, when you know nothing of us! And in pride and scorn I turned from them to retreat to my house where Baby hid crouching at the window.

Not a natural child. The words lodged deep in me as a curse.

For Baby had altered to such a degree he was scarce recognizable at times; God was urging him from me whether I would consent or no. If I made to embrace him impulsively, as mothers do, even to stroke him with loving fingers, Baby shrank from me murmuring *Don't touch me! don't touch!* with scarce a movement of his lips. In hurt I cried that he was not a natural child but he laughed and paid no heed.

Not a natural child. But what would God have me to do, to make amends?

I wept that my half brother, the cause of so much sorrow, had abandoned me to his corrupt offspring, to live out my life in apprehension. For I could not control Baby. I could not control his thoughts or the wayward movements of his body. One night while bathing him suddenly I summoned all the strength in my frail body to push his head beneath the soapy water and hold it there . . . but of course Baby resisted as of late he resisted my every desire; and in the end, after much struggle, and kicking, and splashing, and shrieks, I relented and let Baby go: my bosom and skirts soaked, my face wet, pulses beating wild. I relented and let Baby go, to my shame, having not the physical strength nor, it may have been, the moral courage, to continue. For by now Baby had grown husky indeed, his muscles taut as steel seeking to prolong his life.

Afterward he lay gasping and whimpering on the floor, his mouth pursed still like a fish's and his eyes rolled back up in his head. I calmed him; sang softly to him an old lullaby sung to me, many years ago; told him his Mother loved him and would protect him, though his Father had abandoned him long ago. And Baby clutched at my skirts and sank into sleep in trust of me.

Often now I thought of my brother; and of Etta's girl (who is said to be happy amongst others of her kind in a Home in the country); and of my wicked sister herself (who has not contacted me for many years). I thought of them with some bitterness, yes and some rage hidden in my heart, that they have abandoned me to Baby, who watches me so strangely now, his eyes narrowed to slits, and his thoughts so secret and cunning. Now at the age of four he has grown to my height, and a little beyond; which is to say—for I measured myself against a doorframe—five feet one and a half inches. His hair is of no distinguishable color, and wild and springy; his skin smooth as a true baby's, yet coarsely flushed; his lips oddly full as if heavy with blood. Yet it is those eyes that frighten me, a cat's eyes intense with thought, peering into my very soul. *Yes? What? You? Who are you?*—Baby seems to mock.

I have not described Baby's voice because though he has a voice he rarely allows me to hear it save in shrieks or murmurs. As to *words*—never does he speak words, to me. (Yet I have seen him many times out in the alley, surrounded by children who listen avidly to his every word: and my heart is torn with affliction, for what does Baby say? what does he tell them, he will not tell his Mother?)

What would God have me do? I begged nightly. To make amends.

Thus it came about I took Baby into the country one wintry day, telling him it was time now for him to join with his true Mother, who missed him greatly, and was now summoning him to her.

And Father? he inquired in his low hoarse voice I could scarcely hear; a voice, I am sorry to say, quivering in mockery.

Yes: your Father as well, I stoutly replied.

Hastily I dressed him, at dawn, as for a long journey. Took him downtown to the Trailways bus depot where I bought tickets for a village I had located on the map (its precise name need not be recorded) some five or six miles from the Home in which Etta's girl is lodged. The tickets were round-trip for me, one-way for Baby, a melancholy fact he could know nothing of though during the morning's long ride he sat silent and stubborn beside me staring out the window, turned from me as though we were strangers. What is your boy's name? an elderly lady across the aisle inquired of me, rather cheekily I thought, though I answered her politely: His name is Baby, I said, he is not so old as he appears. Oh, said the lady staring, and is he a good boy? He is not always a good boy, I said frankly, hoping Baby would overhear (for he had turned resolutely away as if he knew me not) . . . no he is not always a *good* boy . . . his mother and father abandoned him long ago.

Oh, said the lady again, staring yet more rudely, I'm sorry to hear that.

Yes, I said. It is a sorry thing.

At our destination I took Baby firmly by the hand and walked him from the bus depot along a street that dipped to an area of warehouses, vacant lots, cracked and weedy sidewalks. Baby made no resistance. Though I had never set foot in this town before I felt not the slightest hesitation as God was now guiding my every step. At last we came to a deserted park, a playground with three meager swings and two teeter-totters and a drinking fountain damaged by vandals. *Here?* Baby seemed to cry out in his soul. *Here? Is it here?* Your true Mother is to come for you, sometime before dusk, I said. So you must not despair beforehand. You must not run away.

Baby's face was wet with tears but when I peered closely I could see the pupils of his eyes shrunk to pinpricks. *Don't touch!* Baby whispered; and indeed I did not.

So it was I was forced to leave Baby in the playground and to make my retreat. I too was crying in my heart but I did not slacken, not during the long journey back to my home on the bus, not till I unlocked the door to my house and stepped into the darkness. For it seemed he had preceded me! Baby, I called out blinking, are you here? Are you here, and hiding?

But Baby was not there, so far as I knew.

In the years following I have heard of certain hideous acts committed in the countryside, yes in the city too, no longer do I dare read the newspaper, for amongst its lies are tales of such peculiar mystery, I am led to believe Baby is the agent; yet I cannot know. And often in passing the playground beyond Union Street I see Baby sitting on one of the swings, idly turning, head bowed, or does he sleep, alone on the swing with no playmates near (for natural children avoid him), turning now from left to right, from right to left, slow and idle as the earth's turning on its axis, and his old secrecy about him, those cat eyes narrowed and aslant so that he can watch me pass by hurriedly. *Yes! You! It is you!*—thus his wicked heart calls out but I am not tempted to pause.

Not till I am safely in my house, the door locked against him, do I think of him with regret, and tears, and love; and I bite my lips murmuring, Baby if you have come so close to home. . . . But I have not weakened thus far: and God give me strength, that I do not.

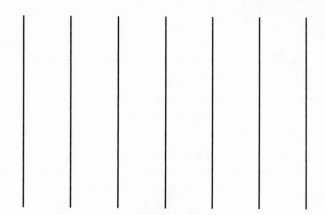

APRIL

Three days of rain, all that morning solid rain, then a gradual lightening until around two in the afternoon it cleared suddenly, the sun so bright and moist you had to squint going outside. I ran across the road to get Janet. She was there in the kitchen ironing, in her tight-fitting pink cotton slacks and bedroom slippers. The air smelled of damp laundry, the scorch of the iron, greasy cooking odors from the stove. They had a wood-burning stove still, not an electric stove, a messy stack of wood piled in the corner. I asked Janet did she want to—? and Janet was already saying, "God, *yes!* Yeah!" She set the heavy stained iron up on end on the ironing board without bothering to switch off the heat.

She checked herself in the mirror, an old mirror pried off a medicine cabinet they had fixed to the wall beside the icebox. She was chewing gum fast—I could smell the sweet Spearmint. Janet's hair was what's called dirty blond, thick and ribbed like a washboard falling halfway to her waist. She went through a curtained doorway into the other part of the house—I'd been visiting with Janet for seven years, had never been invited to step beyond the kitchen—and came back carrying her shoes and her soft black fake-leather jacket and her shoulder bag which was made of a soft woven fabric crisscrossed with fine red stripes. Janet meant to get out of the house without waking her mother but as she was putting on her shoes we heard the floorboards creaking, then there was Janet's mother pushing through the curtain, coming at her. "Where the hell are you going, you?" she said. She'd just put on her glasses, was still adjusting them on her nose, fixing the wire frames behind her ears. "Did you finish that ironing?" Though she could see Janet hadn't—there was a plaid cotton shirt hanging at the end of the ironing board, half ironed across the shoulders.

"No I didn't finish it," Janet said.

"Who's going to do it, then?"

"I'll do it later."

"When?"

"Later."

"You'll do it right now."

"Like hell I will," Janet said. Having me there made her funnier, more reckless. "I been cooped up in here all day—I'm going out."

"Where?"

"Over to Bonnie's to play cards."

Janet's mother looked at me as if she'd never seen me before. Her expression was savage but crafty. She worked the night shift at Kelsco's in town and slept when she could, much of the time, like now, in her daytime clothes, a stained housedress with buttons missing, old sweater, stockings rolled to her knees. She was a fierce fat woman with dents in her face like scars that weren't actually scars, bad eyes people said she'd gotten from the fumes at the factory, but Janet said, Hell that bitch had eyes in the back of her head, she could see around corners. Damn bitch could read your mind. Her gray greasy hair was pushed back behind her ears, fixed with rhinestone-studded bobby pins like the kind Janet sometimes wore to school. It didn't seem as if she'd been drinking but you couldn't always tell.

"Don't hand me that shit, you," she said. "Playing cards! Taking your purse, to play cards! *You're not stepping out that door.*" She made a grab at Janet, trying to snatch the purse out of her hands. But Janet was too quick. She lurched around the table, keeping the kitchen table between them. Somehow the ironing board was knocked over, the hot heavy iron went crashing to the floor, Janet's mother screamed she was a slut like her sisters, a liar, hitching rides to town and showing her ass on the street, she wasn't setting foot out that door, don't even try it. Janet said in a low voice, "Don't you *touch* me, I'll *kill* you," hair in her face and eyes wild but she was laughing too, casting me a sidelong look, trying to edge around to get out the door. The kitchen table was big and round, covered with oilcloth in a floral design worn smooth at the places where people usually sat for meals. Some-times on rainy days or winter days we'd sit around the table playing gin rummy or Chinese checkers, Janet and one or another of her older sisters and me, and Janet's mother would join us if she was in the mood. She liked games—liked to win. People in the neighborhood said she'd always been overweight but she'd been a good-looking girl and not that long ago either, but her face reminded me of something scrubbed too hard with steel wool, thin scratch marks showing. I hated the stink of her cigarettes and her eyes magnified inside her glasses, swimming up like weird round fish.

The dog came running in from the other room ex-cited, yipping, toenails clacking on the floorboards. I stayed out of his way. Janet's mother could move fast for a woman her size, those sausage legs straining against the stock-ings, fatty jowls quivering. Janet managed to keep the ta-ble between them, said she wasn't staying cooped up in this shithole another minute, you want the ironing done do it yourself you been sleeping all day, take that fucking iron Momma and shove it up your ass you're so hot for it. Janet was panting, furious, eyes teary-bright and the pupils dilated, like a cat's eyes. I could feel the heat com-ing from her. Touch me again Momma and I'll kill you! She was fourteen years old, my age, but big-boned, mus-cular, in town men stared at her on the street, whistled at her, boys called out things to her you weren't supposed to let on you heard. One time we took the Greyhound bus home from seeing the Sunday matinee and Janet was saving a seat for me but a navy guy, in his uniform, hung over her saying please could he sit there please pretty-please I been all the way to the Indian Ocean and back and Janet said no at first, she was saving the seat for her girlfriend, but he kept on smiling and kidding and finally she said okay and I ended up sitting by myself at the back of the bus, so disgusted with Janet I wouldn't talk to her for two or three days. She was sorry, she said. I asked what did they talk about, her and the sailor, and she said, Oh I don't know—the things people talk about. I was still angry with her, I must have said something, she flared up saying, You're just jealous. *You*—what do *you* know. Who the hell are *you*.

There was a pair of dull-looking shears on the drainboard by the sink and I saw Janet's mother go for them but Janet got there first. The shears went flying across the floor, skidded beneath the stove in all that dust and ashes. Janet made a break for the door—the two of us ran outside—Janet's mother followed in her stocking feet but couldn't go farther than the door, the back yard was all mud, yelling for us to get the hell out and don't come back, dirty bitches, sluts, everybody knew what we were and what we were up to, boy-crazy bitches just get the hell out and don't come back.

We ran doubled over laughing up the road, a half mile to the old Esso station where there was a crossroads and it was easier to hitch a ride. Puddles everywhere like slivers of glass, so bright our eyes stung. "Isn't she something!" Janet said. "Man, isn't she *weird*." Five minutes later a guy in a pickup truck comes by headed in the right direction, brakes to a stop on the road, shouts for us to get in. The truck looks like one that belongs to a friend of my father's but when we get closer the guy isn't anybody I know. "You girls want to go to town?" he asks. "Yeah," says Janet. "Okay, then get in," he says. Janet climbs in first, then me, the sun is high in the sky, reflecting off the dented hood, a beat to it, a pulse, such a wild feeling—you know you'll never get enough. The driver turns out to be nice, my father's age, lets us each take a cigarette from his pack of Camels and use his Ronson lighter. Janet makes that squirmy shivery movement of hers with her hips that means she's so happy she almost can't stand it. Pokes me in the ribs, whispers hot and breathy in my ear but loud enough for the driver to hear, "Well, kiddo—isn't this the life!"